Dedication

In memory of Ruby Evelyn Skidmore Fancett, my
beloved mother, who died of pancreatic cancer during
my work on this novel.

This is a work of fiction. Names, characters, places, and incidents either are the product of the author's imagination or are used fictitiously, and any resemblance to actual persons living or dead, business establishments, events, or locales, is entirely coincidental.

Saving the Marquise's Granddaughter

COPYRIGHT 2015 by Carrie Fancett Pagels

Contact Information: titleadmin@pelicanbookgroup.com

Scripture quotations, unless otherwise indicated are taken from the King James translation, public domain.

Cover Art by *Nicola Martinez*

White Rose Publishing, a division of Pelican Ventures, LLC www.pelicanbookgroup.com PO Box 1738 *Aztec, NM * 87410

White Rose Publishing Circle and Rosebud logo is a trademark of Pelican Ventures, LLC

Publishing History
First White Rose Edition, 2016
Paperback Edition ISBN 978-1-61116-554-8
Electronic Edition ISBN 978-1-61116-553-1
Published in the United States of America

Saving the Marquise's Granddaughter

Carrie Fancett Pagels

About Carrie Fancett Pagels

Carrie Fancett Pagels, Ph.D., was a psychologist for twenty-five years before becoming a Christian historical romance writer. An award-winning and bestselling author, she's previously published short stories and novellas as well as nonfiction material. Saving the Marquise's Granddaughter was inspired by genealogical research. She lives in the historic triangle of Virginia with her husband of twenty-seven years and their teen son, with an adult daughter nearby.

Prologue

Eastern France, 1742

Suzanne loosened the reins, and the sure-footed mare cantered out from under the thick tree boughs. Inhaling the piney freshness, she shadowed her brother into the clearing as they approached the ancient stone cottage.

They'd mastered the boundary of *Grand-mère's* estate, almost to the duchies of Germany.

Success. Laughter bubbled out of her as she tipped her head back to relish the unbound sunlight.

Guillame turned around and bestowed a satisfied smile. He had demanded they ride to the outermost region as practice.

In case we're ever found out. Her good humor fled. *May we never need to run because of Father's beliefs.*

Guillame reined in his stallion, but Fury shook his black head and lifted his white-tipped tail, demanding to be in charge.

Her own sweet mare obeyed instantly. *Odd that the horses should be so opposite of their masters' temperaments.*

Instead of the silver-haired woodsman's wife, a thin youth, holding an axe, emerged from the cottage. Eyes wide, mouth open, he turned and ran back inside before returning with another young man, this one more sturdy. His dark golden hair glistened as he stepped into the pool of light in the clearing.

Even from this distance, Suzanne could discern his fine, even features, wanting to get closer to see him better as he offered a beatific smile to her and Guillame. When they returned to Versailles she would sketch, then paint, his compelling image.

The door behind the young men opened again, and the woman joined them, wrapping an arm around each as though in protection. Were the youths Huguenots? Did the woman believe Suzanne and her brother were there to assist them out of France? *Non, we rehearse in case we ourselves are ever betrayed.*

"*Bonjour!*" Louisa raised a frail hand to her eyes.

"Bonjour, *Madame* Louisa. *C'est moi*—Guillame."

The elderly lady released the youths. The shorter one returned to the cottage.

Suzanne dismounted and led the horse to the water trough, mindful of Guy's admonition always to let him do the talking and to stay clear. Unable to hear his words, she went about watering her mare.

"Johan!" the woman's warning caused her to look up as the young man headed toward her.

Suzanne paused, chewing her lower lip. She must be very careful. Wasn't that what Guillame and Papa cautioned? *Say nothing.*

His face was even more perfect up close, and young. He couldn't be much older than she but was tall with broad shoulders. When she painted the cleft in his chin, she would shadow it carefully, for his was not too deep. But his eyes—she'd never be able to capture the light blue that changed to green like the ocean as he examined her face in return.

He touched her hair, lifting tendrils that had fallen loose from the queue. Heart beating faster, she stopped breathing as warm fingers grazed her temple. Smiling, he leaned in, his full lips so close she could kiss him if she dared such a thing. She pulled back as he held something between his fingers and then, cupping debris from her hair in his palm, outstretched it for her to examine. A husky laugh accompanied his word. "*Insekt*." His pronunciation startled her.

But that wasn't what made her cheeks burn. *Non!* She had been gaping at his appearance while he had been examining her for bugs and dirt as though she were a common farm animal. She, the Marquise's granddaughter. Even at this young age, admired at Versailles as a great "catch."

Johan bent and released his find back to the earth, then brushed his hands together, grinning—as though he'd just saved the world. Apparently satisfied, the young man walked away from her, responding to Louisa's second call.

Suzanne, the granddaughter of the family who owned these estates, abandoned now by this Johan, no gentleman at all; whose only greeting was a single German word.

Insect, indeed!

1

Versailles, 1745

Gossamer threads, woven by Etienne's words and affixed to Suzanne's heart, were all that kept her feet anchored to the parquetry floor. She tilted her head back, her neck stiff from sitting so still for the maids' ministrations. Tonight, *certainement*, in the ballroom of Louis XV, her future would be revealed.

Yet even as she imagined Etienne's proposal of marriage, her constant shadow-companion, dread, drew with inexorable strokes, a portrait of her family being carried off to prison. Such would happen to them if their secret Huguenot beliefs were discovered. Sweeping that image aside, Suzanne shook the hundreds of dark ringlets that tumbled from her upswept hair.

"Come to the mirror, Suzanne." Cracking open an aged leather jewelry case, her mother lifted Grand-mère's necklace before winding it around Suzanne's neck.

She shivered as the rows of cold pearls settled against her skin.

Maman's warm fingers fastened the heavy gold knot closure. "This necklace will be worn at your wedding."

Soon, with Etienne, Suzanne prayed. After their nuptials, she should be safe. But what of her parents and brother? Dread crept up and clutched the necklace, clung there, dangled like the large topaz in the center.

Maman decanted a beautiful bottle of rose-scented perfume.

Suzanne sighed.

Heavy perfume couldn't mask the unpleasant odor that recently clung to Maman with this maddening illness that would soon claim her.

Suzanne's gaze settled on the portrait, finally completed after two years. The sea-blue orbs of the German peasant she'd met stared back at her.

Guillame had threatened to show the painting to Etienne.

Etienne LeFort. How many balls had he attended? Surely, she was the only young woman in all the apartments of Versailles never allowed.

Her mother adjusted the sheer ivory fichu tucked into the tight stomacher. *Maman* padded to the gilded white armoire and returned with buckled shoes with high curved heels.

"*Merci.*" Suzanne squeezed into the tight pumps. She'd rather go barefoot under the full skirt.

Maman grasped her arm and led her to the main salon.

The front door swung in and banged against the wall.

Suzanne jumped and covered her heart with her hand.

"Maman, I'm back!" Guillame's boot heels clicked across the floor. "Sorry I'm late."

Glaring at her brother, she sucked in a slow breath, catching a whiff of soap and leather polish. "You, of all people should know better than to come barging in here like that. Like the guard would do if ever…" she hissed.

His too-handsome features pulled into a mask of contrition, and he clicked his heels and bowed toward her, in apology. *"Pardonnez-moi."* He crossed to kiss their mother's cheeks. "I heard Rochambeau's *aide-de-camp* arrived at the palace." Two spots of red dotted his high cheekbones.

Maman gripped his forearms. "We have been friends with Rochambeau many years, but you must remember, he once trained for the priesthood."

Lips tightening into a line, Guillame took their mother's hand in his.

She gazed up at him in maternal affection. "If you hear anything, come to me immediately. Understand?"

"Oui, Maman."

Suzanne, after her heart settled, despaired that they had to refrain from displaying any nuances that might betray her parents' religious beliefs. A word here, a word there—they all added up and could entangle them in a trap.

Guillame came to her side and took her hand in his, an apology still in his dark eyes. "Come on, Suzanne, I'll accompany you to the ballroom, and then I'll retrieve Jeanne."

Forcing a light tone, she shoved her former dark thoughts aside. "You know she only flirts with you so outrageously because you're so irresistible...and you're my brother."

Guillame's jaw muscle twitched. He lifted the focal piece of her necklace in his palm. "Grand-mère's."

The oval jewel was magnificent, like this night would be. Finally, after all this time apart, she and Etienne would be together at court.

Maman paused in front of the porcelain waterfall wall clock. "What's taking your papa so long?" Her silk brocade gown crinkled as she slowly moved to the divan in the main salon.

"The mirrors in the ballroom will reflect how much Etienne has changed," Guillame whispered in Suzanne's ear. "He's become as big a fool as his brother." He caught her hand before it struck him.

She glared at him. "The hall of mirrors will duplicate our love for all to see."

In the daytime, the ballroom's mirrors magnified light streaming from the wall of windows. The amplified sunlight illuminated the multitude of paintings in the vast room. But in the darkness, would candlelight do the same with their images, or had time changed their relationship forever?

"Wish Maman a good night, Suzanne, and then we're off."

She drew close, but her mother's eyes were closed. "Already asleep." She pressed a kiss to her forehead.

Guillame traversed the blue wool carpet to their mother and draped a light blanket across her. He tugged Suzanne toward the marble hallway floors and placed one finger over his lips as they exited the apartment.

~*~

The fresh night air carried hints of floral scents and the perfume of revelers en route to the dance.

Suzanne imagined herself in wedding finery, gliding to meet her intended. A gown of the finest satin, weighted with thousands of pearls sewn into floral patterns, would be topped by a coverlet of ivory damask, and studded with diamonds. The queen wouldn't be dressed in so fine a garment.

Guy rubbed his square chin and frowned. "I wish you'd rethink this infatuation with Etienne."

She'd be the mistress of a huge plantation in the Caribbean and live in a sun-soaked land surrounded by azure water. Etienne's horrid brother, Pierre, would reside at Versailles, and she and Etienne, half a world away. Shuddering, she banished all images of Pierre.

"You wish to ally with a powerful family, but they're not of our faith." Why did Guillame always have to interrupt her reveries?

The LeForts were of Grand-mère's faith and, like themselves, were *noblesse ancienne*—of the ancient aristocracy of France.

But the laughing boy she loved had grown distracted, even irritable, since beginning work with his brother.

The hum of partygoers increased the closer they got to the ballroom.

Depositing her in the archway of vines and flowers at the entrance, Guillame kissed her cheek. "I will go get Jeanne."

Not wanting to stand in the way, she spied a heavily draped corner to the right and slipped inside. She slid onto the taupe velvet bench and removed her shoes. With her feet already sore, she'd have trouble managing the night. But with Etienne's arms around her, she'd feel no pain.

Heavy drapes obscured all but a sliver's view of newcomers. Behind her, satin curtains rustled. She shouldn't listen but couldn't help overhearing the two men who conversed—one voice deep, the other higher and nasal.

"I've already taken care of the situation." The man's sonorous voice was familiar.

"The West Indies for him." The other gentleman sounded like Madame DeMint's son, Paul, a friend of Etienne's family. "But what will you do about *her*?"

"I know what to do." The first man emitted an earthy laugh.

Suzanne edged closer.

Madame DeMint, her godmother, was supposed to arrange—or at least encourage—the betrothal for her and Etienne. His family's sugar plantation was in the Indies.

"Her parents will never agree, already refused once." Well, that couldn't be about her, for her parents consented to the match. Papa wasn't happy, but he'd allow the union.

"They won't be given a choice."

Suzanne clenched her jaw in frustration, trying to discern if the gentleman was *Monsieur* DeMint. Returning to the bench, she sat and pulled the slippers over her silk stockings. Then she exited to the salon as spectacularly adorned guests glided past.

Framed in the entrance to the ballroom, Jeanne Trompier's blood-red gown clashed with her auburn hair and with Guillame's mustard-colored vest. Her friend's buxom figure was glued, like heavy toile wallpaper, to her brother.

Suzanne's head began to throb, but the curls prevented her from rubbing her temples without dislodging them.

Jeanne's clothing displayed that she was a woman.

Suzanne's bodice suggested otherwise. Now her silk dress seemed insufficient, a lady's gown on someone with the silhouette of a child. At least Maman had allowed a modest pouf of gauzy material secured on her hips, an illusion.

"Suzanne?" Etienne appeared at her side, bringing with him the scent of sandalwood and cloves. He kissed her hands, sending tingles to her fingertips. Etienne's satin waistcoat was beaded and trimmed to perfection. His dark eyes promised her everything as he promenaded around her, his eyes appraising her attire before he stopped in front of her. He took a step toward her. "Why are you alone in this corner? You cannot flee from me tonight, my darling." Suddenly, Etienne's hands settled warm and possessive on her hips.

She stiffened and pushed them away.

He laughed and held out his arm for her. "Did you notice?" He ran his fingertips along the seams of the inner garment, the tailoring exquisite, emphasizing his trim form.

She smiled but refused to comment on his physique. The blue and gold complemented her ensemble well.

"Was the vest made to match my gown?" Her heart leapt in anticipation, but Etienne's smile was enigmatic. Squelched, she looked down at the floor.

Abruptly, he turned her, clasping her waist with hard fingers. Her breath caught in her throat, and she searched his face to gauge his intent. Saying nothing, he led her into the ballroom.

She tried to absorb every detail of this golden treasure, the room transformed by night and candles into a glittering vision of its daytime glory.

Etienne's firm grip pulled her on as he wove through the crowd.

"Gaudy peacocks reflecting in the pond, *n'est pas*?" Etienne gestured to the row of dancers in the mirror.

Tension eased from her as they shared a smile of agreement. They continued past the many paintings, too quickly for her to get but a few details. Heavily carved with intricate woodland designs, the gilded frames of the pictures detracted from the aristocrats portrayed in them.

Ten paces ahead stood a cluster of young men, his new friends, ones her brother despised as milksops.

"Good evening, gentlemen." He pressed his hand against her back.

"Bon soir." All echoed the greeting. Amusement flickered on their smug faces.

Her throat closed. He didn't bother to introduce her.

She'd hoped for a hint at his intentions. Suzanne opened the beautiful fan from Grand-mère, hoping that as she hid behind the pierced wood treasure, its motion would chase away her tears.

Etienne hadn't even acknowledged that they were together.

One, a tall blond man, dragged his gaze up and down her figure as if assessing whether more was there than he could see. Swiping two flutes of champagne from a passing tray, he called out, *"Merci."* His Scottish burr mangled his pronunciation and she almost giggled.

She was tired of being considered inconsequential.

Etienne had always remained attentive until recently, when his self-preoccupation increased. Perhaps he didn't like his friends' gawking, for he practically dragged her away from them.

She scurried to keep up.

He stood with her for a moment, aloof.

She sensed her brother's gaze and searched him

out, finally alighting upon Jeanne, surrounded by a bevy of admirers, their hair powdered to perfection. Their heavy perfumes alone cost a fortune.

Etienne frowned and narrowed his eyes. "Your friend is indiscreet." His tone suggested disgust tempered by another emotion.

She blinked back the tears that threatened. So few friends remained at court. "My brother said he would talk with her this evening." She waved her fan before her face, grateful for the cool air it stirred.

"*Your* brother?" He pointed at Jeanne, who was kissing Etienne's older brother, Pierre, full on the mouth, his lace jabot dipping into her bodice.

Suzanne's body tensed as Pierre rose, cocked his head at her, and gave a lascivious wink.

The memory of Pierre's touch, once locked away, sprang forth. Suzanne shuddered. "What is he doing here? You said he'd be occupied the entire evening."

Etienne shrugged, but his narrowed eyes darted around the room. "Probably here on business. Or to ruin my good time."

Stomach in spasms, she turned away from the twosome. "I know I should try to get along with Pierre." *And to find a way to ignore the way he looks at me.*

"Just stay away from him." The irritation in his voice surprised her.

She swallowed. The noise of the partygoers seemed a cacophony in her ears. The desire to go home overwhelmed her. Turning, Suzanne caught Jeanne's triumphant smile at Etienne. What had Etienne confronted her friend about? Clearly, Jeanne thought she won some point with him.

Etienne rubbed his top lip with his thumb, a habit he had when he felt guilty.

She shivered. This evening wasn't going at all as she had planned. Overhead, the painted figures on the ceiling mocked her. *You'll never get him to marry you,* they taunted. She wanted to shut out all the overwhelming scents of the perfumes, the sight of so much exposed flesh, and the vulgar speech she overheard in passing.

"Let's get a drink." Edging them over to the large engraved bowl, her escort snatched two full silver cups.

Suzanne filled a plate for them with orange slices and cheese.

Etienne handed her a drink and plopped a strawberry into his mouth. "I'm hungry."

The vile scent of the punch suggested someone had poured spirits into it, but she desperately needed to quell the lump in her throat. She took one tentative sip. The liquid burned all the way down, and her eyes flew open wide.

Etienne raised an eyebrow.

"My apologies. I forget you don't partake." He patted her on her back.

Hurriedly, she consumed a few of Etienne's berries, hoping they would take away the foul sting. She swallowed the overripe fruit, disappointed in the strawberries' deceptive appearance.

Etienne squeezed her hand and led her around the edge of the ballroom, avoiding the mirrored wall. He swept her out onto the dance floor.

Suzanne refrained from gaping at the rows of diamonds gracing the long necks of several other women.

When the dance ended, Etienne leaned in. "How many vaults do you suppose were opened so that treasured gems might be displayed this evening?" His wistful tone reminded her that his mother's jewels might be passing by them, worn by whoever had purchased the collection.

She wanted to say she was sorry his father had almost ruined his family financially.

Etienne would have to ply a trade. He still had position, maintained his title, and had many friends at court, but the Marquis de LeFort needed his sons to be successful businessmen.

"Didn't your necklace belong to your grandmother?" Etienne's dark eyes roamed her face.

"Oui." Smelling lily of the valley, now in bloom at Grand-mère's estate, Suzanne turned her head, but couldn't locate the wearer of the scent.

Etienne kissed her fingertips, led her to the row of women, and then sought his place among the men.

The music began.

Grand-mère's necklace jostled against her as she and Etienne executed their portion of the dance together.

"*Belle*," he mouthed at her, and her cheeks warmed.

Through each new baroque dance, Suzanne gained confidence as she and her partner completed their steps. Minuet after minuet, they continued. The row of dancers swirled in colored silks, glistening jewelry, and high bewigged heads. Only moments seemed to have passed when, with surprise, she noted the candles being lowered.

"I hope they change the chandelier tapers to something casting more light," she called to Etienne as they passed each other in their steps.

He laughed. "Unlikely."

Suzanne wanted to wrap a finger around one of the black curls that framed her companion's perfect face. The most handsome young man at Versailles, Etienne belonged to her. And soon he would be her husband. All that remained lacking was his request for her hand. Her feet were on fire from the pinch of the slippers, but she mustn't leave now. *Not yet.*

Someone tapped Suzanne's shoulder and she turned.

Guillame. His face, paler than usual, with perspiration beading above his tight collar, caused her brother to appear as though he were being pursued.

Suzanne's stomach squeezed into the size of the oranges on the trees in the garden.

"Care to dance?" Guillame offered his arm and glared at Etienne as if daring him to deny them.

Etienne bowed toward Guillame and headed to a cluster of his friends.

Guillame took Suzanne's elbow and guided her onto the ballroom floor. The slower dance music held a hint of its rustic roots.

"Let's do one of our country dances, so I can speak with you, Suzanne." This wouldn't require that they change partners.

They moved to an open area of dance floor, enough space only for them to perform the steps.

"Stand on my boots," he commanded.

Peering down, she saw they were clean. But she'd anticipated they might not be. Their many forays into the countryside came to mind. Suzanne hesitated before he lifted her. One arm fit comfortably around her waist, and the other against her arm, their hands clasped.

The best épée swordsman at court, Guillame

exuded strength, and she relaxed into it. Soon his service to the king would be demanded. His own scent mixed with the lavender soap he used to bathe, but was still pleasant, unlike most of the men in the room.

Dark eyes clouded as he explored her face. "Do you need to go home now? I can see your feet pain you."

"You read me well." An uneasy sensation gripped her. Her brother perceived what Etienne hadn't.

"I've known you all your life. Of course I see your needs."

Did Etienne care for her as much as Guillame did? Maybe she was too sentimental, as *Maman* always said, wanting her husband to love and cherish her.

"Do you need to leave?"

"I'll be all right." She leaned her head against the soft wool of his jacket, shielding her face.

Overhead, the gilded ceiling, painted with legions of fantastic figures, seemed to writhe in the candlelight.

"This place disgusts me."

"Please, don't start talking about religion here—not tonight."

He pulled away from her. "Listen, I have received news that could be very bad. I'm leaving, but I'll be back to get you tonight."

Her back stiffened as he took hold of her waist and propelled her toward a more private area.

"What's happened?"

Guillame smiled at a blonde woman who whirled by them, lilac-scented perfume enveloping her. Not one to flirt, her brother was being very deliberate in his behavior.

"Rochambeau sent for me—perhaps to help guard the body of the king's dead courtesan."

Her stomach clenched. She'd heard the disgusting rumors that no sooner had the woman died than King Louis brought her sister to court, to replace his mistress.

"I'm surprised they haven't called me sooner to do my service."

She wasn't.

"With Grand-mère gone, we cannot further excuse my duty."

"But, what if something happens with us, if..." If they were found out, Guillame would take *Maman* and Suzanne to Aachen and then on to Amsterdam, where they kept money on hand. From there, they'd sail on to the colonies, where they would begin a new life.

They'd been to Amsterdam several times as a family, so that all would be familiar with the beautiful city. She swallowed and wished she could banish her anxiety. Dread began its way up her back, pinching her with spiky fingers.

"I cannot refuse his request." Guillame's proud voice pierced her heart.

"Nor this opportunity?" She hit her mark—pink returned to his high cheekbones.

Suzanne fought back the bile in her throat. This room seemed darker now, the candles lower, and the crowd ominous.

"There are other solutions for you than marrying Etienne. Suzanne, he has come under his brother's influence."

"He hasn't." Not yet, she hoped. "I love him, Grand-mère wished this marriage, and Maman and Papa have agreed."

Guillame's black hair fell across his face as he bent to kiss her cheek. "I'll be back. Look for me." He strode off, his bearing already that of a general.

Rubbing her arms from the chill she suddenly felt, she returned to Etienne, moving close enough to inhale his spicy fragrance.

As the orchestra struck up a lively tune, Etienne pulled her onto the dance floor and into position. "You're so petite; I can sweep you up off your feet in this minuet."

When their turn came to dance together, Etienne whirled her round instead of clasping hands. Her pinched toes thanked him as her feet floated above the dance floor. Crystal chandeliers adorned with hundreds of candles glittered overhead. Dizzy, she clung to Etienne. Time suspended as he held her in his arms above the floor. The onlookers applauded their altered version of the minuet steps but Suzanne's knees trembled beneath her pantaloons.

The music ended, and the musicians began to set their instruments aside.

Etienne still held her aloft.

"Release me, please," she whispered.

"Of course." He lowered her with great care.

She arched away so that she wouldn't be dragged against his body.

Etienne's ragged breath, hot against her forehead, begged her to come closer.

Dread whispered in her ear, *He's not the same—he doesn't know you or your family, not really.* One word from him and she and her family could all be killed.

Etienne kissed her cheeks then transported her across the parquet floor's fantastic, inlaid multicolored designs to a dark corner of the ballroom, near the wide wall of windows.

Multiple shadowed figures touched in intimate

ways. Such lewd behavior, and in a public place.

She backed away but bumped into Etienne, effectively stopping her. Suzanne blinked to clear her vision. Outside, in the garden, the greenery had turned to blackness, punctuated by pinpoints of candlelight. She longed for its freshness. "I should go home soon." How much longer until Guillame returned?

The duo in front of them might make love right there on the brocade chaise. The couples on the other side of the windows were too involved in their own trysts to notice, or perhaps they wished an audience.

Suzanne waved her fan near her chest and placed a tentative finger on the cool pearls.

Etienne laughed. "The ball lasts all night, *ma petite*, even if their passion doesn't."

That was all he had to say about this outrageous behavior? She had to get out of here, but he hadn't yet given her his promise.

Quelling the desire to confront him right there, she resigned to wait. She'd spent so little time with him in recent years, but she refused to believe this was his normal behavior. "Let's get fresh air." She would talk to him outside, under the cloudless sky.

His damp hand covered hers as he thrust the glass door open and led her out to the gardens.

A cool breeze blew away the fetid air and the sensation of filth.

"Come with me—by the wall." Etienne's hand closed over hers like the clasp on a lock.

A year ago, the image would have comforted her, but tonight her beloved friend seemed a stranger. The alteration likely resulted from the time he was spending with his brother. Once married, she'd keep him away from Pierre.

Etienne smiled at her with the same sweet, reassuring expression he'd always used to talk her into mischief when they were children. "It's more secluded back there."

A rest on the stone bench nearby enticed, but his hand imprisoned hers. While she wished to be further from the ballroom's crush, she didn't want to be isolated.

Candles, like fairy light, nestled everywhere in the garden. White tulips glowed above the ground. The orange blossoms enchanted with their luscious scent.

The loveliness lightened her steps as Etienne led her through the maze of gardens. When her aching feet protested and she resisted going any farther, Etienne stopped and wrapped her in his arms.

"Can you imagine it?" His breath tickled her ear. "Us—in the cathedral?"

Her heart missed a beat. The chill in the air revived her, but she couldn't speak. This could be the moment.

"Who would you invite?" A serious question, but his tone teased.

If he kept this up, she wouldn't be able to breathe. A shame that they'd have to invite Pierre.

"Etienne?" She licked her lips. Afraid to ask, she forced herself. "Did Madame DeMint speak with you of this?"

His arched eyebrows drew low. "Of what?"

Her mouth went dry. She shouldn't have said anything. Maman would say she affronted him with her boldness. Etienne must propose. Goodness, his cologne was so strong he may have bathed in it. "Nothing." Why did his meaning have to be so obscure?

His smile crept back, and she touched his mouth with her fingertip. His lips were so beautiful. She couldn't let him think her a complete prude. Perhaps tonight she should let him kiss her. Exhaustion began to muddle her mind. She closed her eyes. Should she wait until they were officially engaged, the announcement made?

Etienne's hungry mouth settled on hers. She tensed. His kiss, rough and insistent, frightened her. He clutched her so hard, she counted the buttons on his vest as a dozen of the offenders speared her chest. She wriggled, trying to loosen his hold. When his hand slid low on her back, nestling in the folds of her gown, she tried to pull away, but he forced her to still as he yanked her against him. He wasn't stopping, but was taking indecent liberties with her, as his brother had tried.

Suzanne had to jerk hard and slam her foot on his.

Startled, Etienne released her.

Her hands shook so hard, she couldn't raise one to slap him. She wiped her bruised mouth with the back of her hand. Smelled the rose perfume Maman had dabbed there.

Etienne stared over her shoulder.

Suzanne whirled around to spy her brother, her body singed by shame. Trying not to panic, she took a deep breath. This was her fault. Her brother had tried to warn her. Intensified by her rapid breathing, the sweet oranges' scent cloyed.

"We've known each other a long time, Etienne, or I'd challenge you for my sister's honor."

Her brother didn't blame her. Gratitude washed humiliation away.

"Suzanne?" His brow covered with perspiration,

Guillame panted as though he'd been running. "It's time to go." His command left no room for negotiation.

"I can accompany her home." Etienne's voice was smooth, but the edge razor sharp.

Guillame's lips twitched. "Unnecessary."

Relief mingled with regret to form a potent but deadly elixir, one she despaired of tasting.

Etienne's hands fisted.

"This way." Her brother hauled her along the candle-strewn path to the end of the *allée*.

She tried to keep up with him.

Guillame's boots crunched on the pebbled path. "He's a pig, like his brother. You're much too genteel for either of those swine."

Her brother led her to the hidden gate in the wall, holding back the greenery so they could get through. The heavy metal structure screeched as the ancient iron unhinged. He expelled her from the garden.

Beyond the thick perfume of the tuberoses, a horse neighed in the blackness.

Guillame hugged her before he gazed up at the full moon, its light revealing his grave countenance. "We've been betrayed. Someone has informed the king that we worship as Huguenots. Get home to Maman as quickly as you can."

2

Palatinate duchy, Eastern Germany

Johan Rousch adjusted his heavy leather hunting bag over his shoulder before trudging on. He took only what his family needed, but more on this day since he was to travel. Soon he could fish in the river, which he much preferred.

Exhaling loudly, he gazed at the crumbling ancient castle ahead in the clearing, his ancestral home, bestowed by the Holy Roman Empire and long abandoned. Sometimes, he allowed himself to imagine the dark-haired girl there, a young lady now, Suzanne. He pictured the castle new and bright and the two of them together, happy. How grateful he was that his family retained rights of ownership to the woods. No one could run him out of here. He hefted the bag to his other shoulder, glad that he was strong, healthy. Emerging from the tree line, Johan headed across the fields toward home.

As he neared, Mama waved her scarf at him from the front door. "Dinnertime!"

After taking care of his bag's contents, Johan washed at the well, pouring the cold liquid over his hands and wiping them dry. He strode to the house and entered the kitchen.

Mutter handed him a pork-laden platter and he brought it to the table. She followed him, carrying a wooden bowl piled high with rolls, which she set before his father, who beamed up at her.

Johan lifted one leg over the trestle bench to sit adjacent to his father.

"Son, are you ready to go to Aachen Cathedral again?"

He paused for a moment before he brought his other long leg over and sat. *The holy shrine for Catholics—yet his family was Lutheran.* But with his great-uncle a priest there and with Aachen a meeting point for Protestants heading to the American colonies, the ancient cathedral stood as a welcoming beacon. *"Ja, Vater,* why?"

His older brother, Nicholas, mumbled something.

The two of them almost hadn't returned from their last foray. Then again, they weren't supposed to have journeyed on from the shrine to their great-aunt's home in eastern France.

"We'll speak of it later. Bow your heads." Papa blessed the meal.

Mama passed a bowl of turnips to Johan. "You'll go on horseback with a pack, as we discussed."

He'd never gone alone. His brother had been furious when the French soldiers almost caught them.

"This is important." His mother patted his hand. "I need to send word to Father Vincent now that the roads are sound."

"We know we can trust you." His father beamed approval.

Knowing his father relied on him filled Johan with warmth.

Nicholas scowled as Papa handed Johan a mended halter.

Taking the halter, Johan ran his hands over the sturdy leather. *"Danke*—you fixed it well."

Papa cut his meat into small pieces. "Tomorrow you go to our kinsman."

"Johan, your great-uncle is an old man." Mama's own hair had begun to show streaks of gray. "Aunt Louisa and I are his only family left. She hasn't been able to send anything in a great while."

Aunt Louisa—he longed to check on her. To see if the French girl still came riding to her cottage in the woods.

Nicholas shoveled a forkful of mashed turnips into his mouth and glared at him, as if he could read his mind.

Every day Johan prayed for the peasant girl. Sometimes he prayed that she was a Protestant, like himself. Other times, he prayed, for her sake, that she wasn't.

~*~

"Suzanne!" Maman's voice called out from shadows adjacent their building. "Come."

Heart hammering, she went to her mother and embraced her. "Maman, what do we do?"

"Chin up. Act normal." Maman took her hand and pulled her onto the walkway, handing her a small travel bag.

Six metal cage baskets flamed adjacent to the drive as they strode alongside. Firelight illuminated the gold markings of her godmother's own brougham.

A burly man jumped down from the carriage and Suzanne gasped as he hoisted both Maman and her bag up inside the coach and then Suzanne.

Her mother opened her mouth, as though she meant to protest something, but said nothing as the doors were closed on them. "Madame DeMint takes too great a chance, letting us use this coach," Suzanne whispered to her mother as she settled onto the dark leather seat. She prayed the King's guard wouldn't harm her dear godmother.

A muscle jumped in Maman's cheek. "The DeMint carriage will ensure our safe exit from Versailles—as we get past the guards."

Suzanne tried to settle back, but the cushioned bench was so deep that her trembling legs dangled. She set her bag beneath her feet so they could rest atop her few possessions.

The carriage creaked, the wheels crunching steadily over the cobblestones, its lanterns casting eerie shadows on either side. Her heartbeat pounded in her ears in time with the horses' hoof beats. A short distance ahead, she saw the closed gates, with several guards posted.

"Cover your face." Her mother handed Suzanne a loo mask and raised one to her own eyes. "Act like you drank too much of that punch you told me about."

"You expect me to act intoxicated?" How nonsensical. Suzanne was more likely to have a seizure, she shook so hard. And she was so furious with Maman and Papa. She wanted to run from the carriage and scream that her parents' Protestant beliefs were a mistake.

"Here, lean against me." Maman's command and her firm hand stilled her, brought her against the fragile frame, once so strong.

A guard yawned and then peered in. His prominent nose was red, likely from drinking on duty. He affected a slight smile at her. She could run, jump down, and go to Etienne. She'd beg him to protect her, to keep her there. *Oh, Lord, I don't want to die.*

"First ball—too much excitement, I fear." Her mother's laugh tinkled. Maman was a far better actress than Suzanne had realized.

The soldier grunted in amusement. This was their great protection at Versailles? Suzanne grasped the loo mask with both hands, the one hand shaking so hard she had to calm it with the other.

"*Bon chance!*" He tipped his hat toward them before calling up to their driver, "Not too many people leaving yet, so take care on the roads."

"We will." The coachman called down in a gruff voice. "*Bon nuit,* or rather I should say *bon matin?*"

Pale pink light would soon rise in the east and jeopardize their journey.

"Should be quite safe between here and Paris. The king's men will be guarding the roads."

Her mother's benevolent smile wavered.

The carriage lurched forward, and with it, Suzanne's heart. She turned around. Rows of *torchères* lit the palace entrance, which disappeared into the night. She could jump out, run back, and beg Etienne's favor as her oldest friend to marry her. Why hadn't she told him at the ball? He could take mistresses—no, she couldn't bear that. She was losing her mind—this couldn't be real. Whatever came to pass, she couldn't leave her mother. Guillame would come to them. He'd put things right.

"Your father was arrested and imprisoned by King Louis. They'll no doubt execute him in the morning." Her mother's hollow voice sounded much like a recitation of their menu for dinner. Maman must be experiencing the same shock now settling over her.

Suzanne's empty stomach squeezed into a knot.

Executed. Not Papa. Such a good man, a devout Protestant, the best father. Her mother's glazed eyes gave her the appearance of a madwoman, but Suzanne's entire world seemed to have gone insane. Maman slumped back against the cushion as a strange deadly calm settled over Suzanne. This wasn't real. It couldn't be true. This was a nightmare from which she would awake on the morrow.

Maman ran her tongue over her dry lips. "Even now, they must be looking for us."

To throw them in prison as well. To kill us. Her hands were like icicles and Suzanne began to tremble all over.

"This cancer claims me, my dear." Her mother threw a hand toward Suzanne, as though apologizing.

She grasped it, the dry skin loose on her mother's flesh. What would she do if her mother died? She sucked in a breath. "Maman, what can I do for you?"

"Make sure they get me home, to Grand-mère's, to the country."

They? "Who, Maman?"

Her dark eyes, full of despair, searched Suzanne's face. "I thought I had our escape, a new life, figured out—what to do—but now I'm not so sure." Her bony fingers kneaded her silk handkerchief, over and over, until it appeared she would work a hole into the delicate material. "I sent word to Anne DeMint for help. I cannot go on to Aachen, much less the colonies, and now Guy is with Rochambeau."

Her godmother could sponsor her; Suzanne was young enough she could be protected despite her family's beliefs. Some Huguenots had been spared execution when a devout Catholic fostered them. Was that why Rochambeau had sent for Guillame? But her brother was too old for such an arrangement.

Suzanne stared out the window into the darkness, watching the miles slip by. Having chewed her lower lip until the skin tore, she finally asked her mother, "Guillame said he'd come to us as soon as he can. What is his plan?"

A gentle snore was the only response she received. Tears pooled in Suzanne's eyes. She couldn't feel this pain—its intensity would overwhelm her. Fingering the smooth rosary beads at her neck, she prayed. This had to work. She closed her eyes and repeated her special prayers, the rhythm soothing the pain—the unremitting grief she'd experienced since her beloved Grand-mère had died and Maman had taken ill. Her head began to nod.

The coach hit a rut, rousing Suzanne, her thumb still looped through Grand-mère's rosary. *Oh, Lord, this nightmare is real.* They should be near Paris by now or even past the great city. Her mouth dry, she retrieved a mint from the bag, the sugar coarse yet pleasant on her tongue.

Maman squeezed her hand, and a thrill shot through her. She was still with her. Suzanne handed her a *pastille*.

Both watched as they drew closer to the great city, one they would never see again. Too dark to make out the church spires and tall buildings, though. The road grew more crowded and the driver had to move over to wait for passing coaches in several areas where the road narrowed.

Through the carriage window, many torches shone—some bobbing over throngs of men on foot and dressed in peasant garb. Their gaunt faces announced them as the poor from the countryside around Paris. At least in *Grand-mère's* district, much farther east, most people were well fed.

She shifted in her seat, uncomfortable with so great a number of people surrounding them. "*Maman*, would Madame DeMint care for you, if you need to stay?" Her mouth was as dry as parchment. Where were the oranges she smelled? She needed one of those or a drink.

"I need to get home. I wish to be buried there." Maman's face was set.

Torchlight identified a column of French soldiers.

Suzanne tried to catch her breath. No, they couldn't be looking for her and Maman, for they surrounded a long caravan of large carriages. One was a funeral hearse, with a gilded crest illuminated by one of its side lamps.

Heart pounding, she slid to the edge of her seat. The erect bearing of the rider, and the glow of light on his mustard vest, revealed her brother.

Their driver moved off the road to let the crowd past, rocking her mother against her. *Dear Lord, don't let them harm us. Protect us.*

Men, lining the sides of the road, called out. "That's it."

Nausea welled up in her. Their carriage swayed as the frenzied mob swarmed around.

"Haul her out of there." They surged toward the funeral procession. Would they attack them, too?

Suzanne held her breath. Dizzy, she fell against her mother, who moaned. "Maman! What should we do?"

"It will all be over soon, Suzanne." Her mother's almost weightless hand patted her shoulder through the cape and rubbed her back. "Close your eyes."

She wished her mother's words were true. Dread took hold of her and shook her shoulders. She sat up on the edge of the seat and peered out.

"We know what to do with the body of the King's harlot." Curses and terrible oaths continued as the rabble shouted their plans for Louis XV's deceased mistress. The woman's own sister had already taken the dead lady's place at court. Perhaps the people in the countryside couldn't stomach such debauchery.

What did they intend to do to the woman's corpse?

Their carriage lurched forward, and the frightened beasts snorted as they pulled on past the crowds, into the fields surrounding the spectacle. Soft soil spit up at the windows.

Soldiers on horseback struck down at the rioters, who swarmed like ants on honey.

A shot rang out, and Suzanne's shoulders jerked. She leaned across her mother and pressed her hands and face against the cold glass window. Splotches marred the pristine mane of Guillame's horse as her brother struggled to remain upright. A dark stain spread across his chest, illuminated by the torch before it fell from his hand.

"No!" Her mouth wide, Suzanne gasped for air. *Lord, don't let him die!*

The mob pulled Guillame down off his mount. Every fiber of Suzanne's being longed for her to launch herself from the carriage and go to her brother. But she could not. She began to sob.

Tears trailed down her mother's face. "I don't wish for my entire family to join me where I'm going. Pray God spares your brother."

They bowed their heads, held hands and prayed together as the brougham rolled on.

~*~

With daybreak came the realization that her mother's soul might soon leave the earth. Pink tendrils of dawn's first light battled to bring joy to the emptiness in Suzanne's heart. What she saw along the roadway broke her heart. She bit back the desire to share her observations with her mother. Bedraggled peasants, children whose faces bespoke poverty and deprivation, and mothers whose blank expressions announced their despair, lined the roadway.

"Don't think too badly of me when I am gone." Maman leaned against the window, her feverish head fogging the glass.

"Why?" She must be delirious to think such a thing. *Oh, Lord, please don't take her.*

"I feel I've made a terrible mistake." Her mother coughed and then gasped for air.

"About what, Maman?" *Dear Lord, forgive me for not telling her about Guillame.*

"I wanted to go home but I didn't intend for you to come with me." Maman's guilty expression revealed her plan. "Your father and I finally agreed that if he was taken then you'd be safer to remain with your godmother instead of going to the colonies—especially if Guillame couldn't immediately accompany you."

Heat spread across Suzanne's cold cheeks. All their plans for naught. *Guillame must survive. I cannot bear to be without them all.*

"I knew you'd want to come, as we'd planned, but I thought remaining with your godmother might be best."

Part of her wished to stay with Madame DeMint,

but she couldn't abandon her mother. Remaining at her godmother's country estate appealed. With all its comforts, she could await being returned to Versailles at a later, and possibly safer, date. The idea of her mother unable to get to her childhood home, denied the right to die there in peace, disturbed her. What if her mother insisted Suzanne stay at the DeMints' chateau while she, dying, tried to go on alone. How could Maman manage?

"I cannot stay there." Suzanne clasped her mother's hands. Every muscle in her body ached. She tightened her gown in her fist as hard as she could. She must quell the idea of being totally alone that tore her to shreds inside.

Maman stroked Suzanne's hair, as she had when she was a child. "Papa and I disagreed about some things."

Suzanne had overheard a loud argument when they'd returned to Versailles. "Oui."

The tree line thickened as they rode farther away from the city. Bright new spring buds covered many formerly naked trees while those with fine, dark needles formed a backdrop of consistency in the changing forest.

"I know you loved your grandmother, so much."

Suzanne nodded.

"Wanted to be like her." Maman gave her a quick squeeze.

Staring out the window at the countryside, Suzanne struggled to find words to explain, to apologize, for the differences between herself and her mother. Nothing came as the carriage continued.

"Your secret was always safe with me, you know."

Suzanne's breath caught in her throat, but she

fixed her eyes on the woods beyond. Her hand wrapped around the rosary beads and caressed the smooth stones. Saying nothing, she noticed her mother's breathing had become more labored.

"I love you, Maman." Turning to her, she threw herself into her mother's arms, holding fast. Refusing to leave her mother behind, she determined to see her on to Grand-mère's estate.

Her mother patted her back.

"Suzanne, wake me when we get to the crossroads. The other carriage should be waiting." Maman planted a kiss on Suzanne's forehead.

"Yes, Maman." Sliding over against the end of the bench, she made room for her mother to lie down.

Her mother curled up on the seat, her head on Suzanne's lap. Despite the light streaming in through the windows, Suzanne slept—dreams of betrayal, disease, and death tormented her.

~*~

Following his nose to the wonderful odors coming from the kitchen for breakfast, Johan found his mother seated alone by the fireplace. Warm brown eyes searched his face before she pressed an envelope into his hands.

"No one, not one soul other than Father Vincent, reads this." Her dark eyebrows rose high in warning, her lips pursed. Behind her, bacon sizzled over the fire, its tempting aroma making Johan's mouth water.

"What if..." He stopped himself, knowing his mother didn't like his lists of questions. But he needed them answered. Wanted to be sure he did exactly as he was told.

Mother shook a finger at him. "No what-ifs!"

Johan folded his hands around her pointing finger and squeezed it, then pushed her hand down gently.

She laughed. "Oh, Johan, I can never be too serious with you. But listen, you cannot let anyone else read this. Doing so could mean danger for the people Father Vincent helps."

Quick, hard steps coming down from upstairs announced Nicholas's arrival. His footsteps stopped in the alcove outside of the kitchen right behind where Johan stood.

His neck tightened. Johan leaned over and kissed the top of his mother's head. This time he would help bring gifts and messages to Father Vincent. "I won't give this letter away, Mama, I promise."

She laughed. "Not like the gloves I made for you or the food I sent to school with you."

Sweat broke out at his hairline. He waited for his brother to mock his tender heart and Nicholas didn't disappoint him. "Not like me, Mama."

His mother shook her head. Nicholas was stingy with everything except his criticisms.

"I promise."

Mutter smiled up at him. "When did you get so tall, son?"

He lifted her and gave her a hug. "When you weren't looking—I went to the barn and rolled in the manure every night, and I would grow a little each time, like the vegetables in the fields." He set her down carefully on the brick floor.

"Too bad you didn't bother to bathe before you came back in our room those nights." Nicholas waved a hand in front of his nose.

Johan chuckled. "I'm sorry if the odor upset you,

brother."

Glancing from one to the other, their mother sighed. "I won't send you two together anywhere, anymore."

While Johan had met the most beautiful girl he'd ever seen, his last trip into France with Nicholas almost left their mother and father childless. But French Huguenots' lives were at stake and he and his brother were the only options Father Vincent had to assist the travelers on their secret journeys to Aachen in Germany. And they did love spending time with their great aunt, whose fervent faith inspired him. If their mother knew they had separated to confuse their French pursuers…

Papa pushed through the front door, one hand swinging a basket of wood for the fire. "Just in time for prayer." He set down the wood. "Come, let us give this request to our Lord."

They formed a circle and grasped hands. His mother's cool, limp hand contrasted with that of his father's warm, viselike grip. Johan glanced across at his brother, who already had his head bowed.

"God bless my son on this journey and protect him. May all that the Lord has intended be done, all gifts given, all blessings received. Give our son divine revelation and assurance that this task is from You and for him. Bring him home safely to us, with all that You have entrusted to him, great and small."

As Papa prayed, a strange and uncomfortable chill rose up through Johan's body. When he peeked over and saw his brother's eyes clamped shut, Nicholas's head bowed low, alarm gripped his neck and held him. That his brother would pray like that, for him—Johan couldn't put words to the fear he felt. But he was going

only to Aachen, not into France. There would be no soldiers at the cathedral.

~*~

"The crossroads! Wake up, we're near." Suzanne grasped her mother's arm.

Warmth still radiated from her body, but Maman's chest barely rose and fell.

Suzanne pressed one finger to her mother's mouth. Would those tender lips ever kiss her good night again? Pressing her palm hard against the middle of her mother's back, she felt the slow movement of her mother's shallow breaths. Relief coursed through her. Maman hadn't left her yet.

Shifting in her seat, she glanced out the window. No other coaches or horses appeared at this juncture. The fields were the glorious light green of spring and their promise of new beginnings offended her. Her world was ending. She squeezed her eyes shut.

The coach rolled on, over the muddy road. No one was at the intersection. Perhaps the next carriage waited at the DeMints' or the attack in Paris may have prevented the next coach's arrival and the driver had chosen to continue on.

Fatigue beckoned her to sleep, but she wouldn't accompany that traitor or give up the time left with her precious mother. Suzanne held her mother's hand. Sunlight illuminated Maman's face, beautiful in this rest before death. The cancer inside her couldn't take the loveliness of her countenance away.

Something thumped the carriage, waking her. Thick woods surrounded them. How much longer would the coachman drive? She exhaled a shaky breath. She forced her eyes to remain open.

Small hovels dotted the roadside—homes of the unfortunates who didn't have a master, or a mistress, as kind and generous as Grand-mère.

She recognized the road and the terrain. The DeMint home should be ahead. In a short time, they were rolling up the hill to the circular drive in front of the country chateau. She perched up high on the seat, rubbing the stiffness from her lower back. The vehicle stopped and the doors to the carriage were thrown open.

"Mademoiselle? Madame?" The man's voice was gruff. The coachman had huge eyes like Guy's, but his were hard as steel.

She peered behind him, at the house—no movement. Was no one at the gray stone chateau to greet them?

"Monsieur DeMint didn't tell me your mother was ill." The driver's words were accusatory as he rubbed his chin.

The only Monsieur DeMint was the widowed Anne's son, whom Papa and Guillame despised. The hair on her arms rose.

"Maman has nothing you can acquire. Please bring her in. Madame DeMint mustn't have heard the carriage pull up." Suzanne hoped she was right about their hostess. She inhaled the moist country air, a relief from the sickly smell inside the brougham.

The man stood taller. "Madame isn't here. She's at Versailles."

Suzanne stared past him at the house, forbiddingly empty. "Is anyone here?" Surely, there must be some staff.

The coachman raised his broad hands, as though

in surrender. "He didn't tell me. I don't want any trouble." He muttered something under his breath.

"Monsieur, what do you know? We were to have met someone else at the crossroads to take Maman" — she hesitated, unsure what she should say — "on from there. Please, what were you told?"

"Monsieur DeMint paid me well to get you here as quickly as I could, but keep you safe." His eyes narrowed as he examined her. "How old are you?"

Suzanne stood tall. "I can take care of my mother if I have some help."

The man shook his shaggy head. "Mademoiselle, I can get you and your mother into the chateau, and bring your things, but I fear..."

Trembling, she couldn't help but agree with him. "*Moi, aussi,* I fear for my mother and myself." Suzanne bit her lip, fearing she had said too much. "But we should be safe here once Madame arrives."

He cursed softly. "I do only this job for him. I'm not his regular man." The driver twisted his soft hat in his red hands. "Mademoiselle, I don't believe Madame DeMint knows of her son's plans for you."

"What plans?" She heard the tremor in her voice. The country air chilled her.

"Madame Richelieu!" A wiry man ran from the stables, wiping his hands against each other. "What brings you here? Madame DeMint is not yet home."

Suzanne heard her own sigh. She was so tired, wished her head lay atop her pillow at home, but that comfort was forever gone.

The stableman ran a hand through his thick hair. "Our housekeeper has the servants' quarters in order, but I am afraid that is the chateau's only section opened this season."

"Could she prepare a room for Maman?"

"Mrs. Boudreau went to visit her son and daughter-in-law in the village, but you could use her room and the maids' chambers. The housekeeper had those ready in preparation for their arrival from Versailles next week."

"Next week?" Suzanne croaked, raising a shaking hand to her throat.

"Oui, but come, let us get your mother settled."

The coachman passed their bags to the DeMints' servant, who carried them on toward the house.

The driver touched her arm. "Do you know Monsieur LeFort well?"

Suzanne hadn't realized she'd been holding her breath until she exhaled in relief. Etienne LeFort— Madame must have made the arrangements so that she and Etienne could be married. Still, visions of his behavior toward her in the gardens at Versailles made her stiffen. "Oui, I know him well…"

The driver's face reflected shock then disbelief. "Truly?" Astonished relief mixed with concern on his countenance. "Monsieur DeMint will be here soon to bring you back to Versailles."

"But what of Maman? She was supposed to go on to my grandmother's, the marquise's, estate." Now their estate, but not for long, now that their father was exposed as a Huguenot. And although her aunt stood to inherit the title and land, *Tante* Isabelle hadn't ever returned from New France.

He frowned. "I know nothing of that arrangement, only that you'll be brought to Monsieur LeFort."

Etienne and she would be married; things could be set aright. Suzanne would figure out a way to help Maman. A gorgeous black mare trotted past, a stable boy sitting high on her tall back. He removed his cap and bowed toward Suzanne. Timothy, the stableman's son, had grown since she'd last seen him. She followed as the driver carried her mother through the house's huge oak front doors. Suzanne squeezed her unconscious mother's limp hand.

The coachman stopped, looked down, and narrowed his eyes.

Suzanne was taken aback by his hard perusal. "Not much more than a girl, and you seem to be such a good daughter."

"Merci."

"You should think twice before going to LeFort. You must have other choices."

A warning sounded in Suzanne's mind, so similar was this speech to Guillame's comment in the garden at Versailles. And like her brother, the driver seemed genuinely concerned.

"Mademoiselle, why sell yourself to the devil?"

3

The driver opened his mouth as if to say more, but stomped up the stairs after the stableman. The rude coachman. Returning empty-handed, he tramped back down the stairs, giving a curt shake of his head to her as he hurried out.

Pact with the devil? Whatever had their driver meant?

The stableman frowned at the back of the departing man as Suzanne joined him in the third-floor room. Hot, stuffy air oppressed on this level.

"Is there anything else I can do for you, Mademoiselle Richelieu?"

Make her mother well. Fly her, like a bird, to Aachen. "Water, please?"

"At your service, mademoiselle." He closed the door as he left, shutting them in their tomb.

Suzanne surveyed the sparse room. With the house not yet open for the season, only this area was free from coverings. Needing fresh air, she thrust the creaky window open then wiped the grime from her hands. The DeMints' home lay unused this winter, from the looks of the fine dust covering the latch and the books on the side table. If Madame truly was expecting them, she'd have paid one of the villagers to clean.

Lilac trees in shades of lavender, purple, and white encircled the stone pavilion behind the house. Tulips, hyacinths, and jonquils dotted the yard, with clusters around the iron benches beneath the window. Now bare, the grape vines covering the center trellis would not yield their fruit until later.

As the breeze entered the room, Maman stirred. "Something is wrong here."

"Our friend remains at Versailles." Wouldn't be here for a week.

"Did you hear what the coachman said?" Her mother's eyes remained closed.

"About what?" Suzanne sat next to her mother. Her stomach seemed filled with a ten-stone weight.

"He said *him...*" Maman lifted her chest as she asked the words. "Not *her.*"

A knock on the door interrupted. "*Voila!* The water."

"Merci, monsieur. Here, Maman, sit up a little and drink."

When she couldn't raise her mother on her own, the servant assisted her.

Her mother quickly emptied the half-full glass.

An hour later, freshly washed and changed into different clothes, Suzanne tucked pillows under the maid's bedcovers. She carefully opened the adjoining door to her mother's room.

Stifling heat on this warm spring day persisted as the sun rose higher, but the breeze flowing through the window dispelled some of the room's stale air.

Before her mother went to sleep earlier, she'd made accusations about those she felt had betrayed them. None of these ideas made sense. Such talk commonly occurred among those who were dying from her mother's malady, though.

Please let Maman tell me what I need to hear.

"Suzanne?"

She exhaled; Maman was awake. Wide boards creaked underfoot as she went to her. "Yes?" With care, Suzanne rearranged the linen covers under her mother's chin.

"Paul DeMint." Maman tried to raise her head.

Suzanne supported her mother's head and fluffed the pillow to make her more comfortable. "Madame's son?" Guillame once referred to Paul and Pierre as "a pair of greedy vultures come upon a fresh carcass."

Maman closed her eyes. "Bad...leave here..." Maman's words were hard; her skin a paler version of Guillame's yellow vest.

Suzanne shuddered. Had her brother survived his injuries?

"Go to Aachen." Eyes glazed, Maman strained upward, on her elbows but collapsed.

"I want to be with you." But the boys' clothing she'd donned, out of an urgency to do so, announced her preparations to flee.

"Non." Maman arched up, forcing the word out.

Her neck tensed. Paul DeMint journeyed here. She sensed it.

"Go alone?" *Impossible.*

She was an excellent rider, but could she get to the next safe house unaccompanied? And if need be, go on the rest of the way by herself? Almost as dangerous as staying at Grand-mère's estate.

"Now." Maman's hands trembled as she grasped Suzanne's.

Hot tears washed her face. Why was she being punished for her parents' choices? They could have accepted the Roman Catholic faith.

"Promise...me." Each of Maman's words came with tremendous effort.

Brushing away tears, Suzanne laid the back of her hand on her mother's hot cheek. *Please don't let her suffer terribly.*

"Cathedral...then colonies." Her mother struggled to breathe.

Suzanne propped another pillow behind her, and then pressed a glass of water to her lips.

Bleary eyes bored into hers. "Pierre."

Why did her mother mention him?

Maman took one more sip. "He asked..."

Wiping her wet face with the bed sheet, Suzanne leaned over and kissed her mother's forehead.

"For you..."

A chill coursed through her body and she wished to rise and slam shut the window to the outside world. This couldn't be.

"Would Pierre take me to Etienne?" Suzanne twisted the bedclothes in her hands, bunching them into knots.

"Papa..." Her mother's gasps matched Suzanne's quick breaths. "Said no."

"To Etienne?" Suzanne pressed her head against her mother's hand, now hanging over the side of the bed.

"Pierre."

Wallpaper strewn with vines and roses might better have briars and thorns intertwined on the creamy background.

"Very angry..."

Suzanne's skin prickled all over. *Dear God, please don't let that be what it sounds like—that Pierre asked Papa for my hand before that horrible day at Grand-mère's.*

The thought raced down the hallway of her mind—marriage to Etienne wouldn't have been an open door out of this nightmare. The men behind the curtain in the ballroom—Paul DeMint and Pierre LeFort. The man they discussed bound for the West Indies must be Etienne. In her mind, she closed the LeFort door, barred the exit, chained it and shoved a chair beneath the doorknob. For beyond that door lay degradation, humiliation, and defilement of the basest sort if, indeed, Pierre stood there.

Maman gasped for air, her throat gurgling. The court physician warned them this could happen at the end, but Suzanne never thought death would come this quickly.

She grabbed her own water glass and drank her fill. The next safe house was well away from the DeMints'. She had burned the names and villages of helpful Huguenots into her memory. The next stop from here would be hours of steady riding.

Chest arching, her mouth open, Maman struggled to breathe. Suzanne couldn't bear to watch and to hear the death rattle. *Please, God, don't let her suffer any longer. I cannot bear to leave her like this.* Tears streamed down her face and she let them fall as a strange peace overcame her.

Then blessedly, unnaturally, Maman ceased her exhalations. *Gone.*

Suzanne bent over her mother, listening and feeling no breath caress her cheek. After kissing her mother's forehead and choking back sobs, she did as her mother ordered, pausing only to give one quick glance back. Maman and Papa were together in heaven. She was alone. An orphan.

Her heart hammered as she wiped her face dry with the back of her hand. Only one deviation would delay her. She'd stop at Grand-mère's estate and ask for someone to retrieve Maman's body and transport her there for burial. This small courtesy was the least she could do.

If Paul arrived soon and found she'd left, what would he do? Send someone after her? She wouldn't compromise the stableman and his son. She would only tell them she wished to go for a ride. Alone.

She grabbed everything necessary for the journey's next portion, and then ran down the back stairs, grabbing more items in the kitchen. She dashed to the stables and stopped at the stall of a black mare. "You're beautiful." Suzanne offered a piece of dried apple she held in her flat, outstretched hand. "I'll call you Bella. Maman would have approved of you."

She gritted her teeth, as if that would stifle her grief. She must think straight if she were to succeed. *Gloves.* She needed to protect her hands from the reins.

"A lift up?" The stable boy appeared, laced his fingers together and lifted her into the saddle. "I see you're a boy again, mademoiselle. Have you been fencing lately, too?"

"Shush, you mustn't say anything. You don't see me."

"Oui."

As far as fencing, she couldn't have gotten Guillame's name past her throat if she'd tried to explain that he'd been too preoccupied of late to parry with her.

"Don't forget your riding gloves." He handed her up the pair from the previous summer. Someone had lovingly rubbed in oil to keep the leather supple.

Peering down at the boy, and seeing his blush, she realized who'd done this for her. "Gaston, I need a favor. A big request."

The boy nodded slowly, waited, his hands clasped. Suzanne settled herself on the mare. "If anyone asks, I'm sleeping and don't want to be disturbed, and my mother, also."

"Only Monsieur DeMint is expected, mademoiselle. Do you wish me to tell him?"

Suzanne swallowed hard. "*Oui*. Say only that, nothing else. Tell your papa the same."

Horses' hooves, then wheels, clattered into the courtyard.

Suzanne nudged her mount outside and positioned them behind the stables. Her heart beat hard against the tight boy's undergarment. The gold DeMint seal gleamed in the sun. Sure of who'd be inside, she resisted the urge to gallop away from the property. She and the mare waited in the stable's shadow.

"Monsieur DeMint! Welcome. Let me help." The stableman's forced cheerfulness was evident to Suzanne. Did Madame's son recognize the falseness in the tone?

"Did the women arrive, Gaston?" Paul's voice was hoarse, ragged. He sounded drunk, or recovering from the effects of too much alcohol.

"Madame Richelieu and her daughter?" She knew the stableman didn't consider her a woman.

"Of course. Isn't that what I said?"

"Oui, monsieur, both are resting on the servants' floor."

Madame's son launched into a fit of obscenities. "Get that housekeeper here to make a proper room up for her downstairs."

"Oui, monsieur, so sorry, I'll take care of the chamber right away."

Suzanne knew he had no intention of locating Mrs. Boudreau.

"Gaston! Come help Monsieur DeMint to his room."

"I don't need any help. Just bring my satchel up to my room later. There better be food for when I wake up, too. Didn't sleep at all..." Another round of profanity ensued as Paul explained that they, too, had been interrupted by the riot outside Paris. "Don't rouse me until dinner is ready tonight."

"Oui, monsieur."

"My friend is coming—Monsieur LeFort. He started on horseback and should have been here before me."

Oh, Lord, no, Pierre. But was Maman wrong?

"He hasn't arrived."

"Not surprised. Probably stopped in Paris to find one last young girl to spoil. He pays well for that privilege. Imagine he'll become richer yet once Mademoiselle Richelieu becomes his bride. At least if she remains as childlike as she appears now."

Her stomach plummeted toward the ground beneath the mare. The perverse man he spoke of was Etienne's older brother. Hot with shame, she rejected the feeling—Pierre should be ashamed, not she.

But Pierre LeFort wasn't yet here. With that blessing in mind, she exhaled loudly in relief, her horse shifting beneath her. She patted the mare's neck. Pierre's delay gave her at least a few hours to get a head start. As soon as the heavy doors to the chateau closed, she ducked her head and directed Bella onto the trail through the woods, leading to a good country road. Energized, she noticed every detail as they rode.

The new green buds on the trees, tiny white

flowers peeking up from the undergrowth, birds flying, gathering for their nests. Fresh green growth, moist dirt, and humus were the best perfume she had ever inhaled. They smelled like promise and freedom and hope. A light breeze caressed her cheek, as though her mother was giving her a last kiss goodbye, blessing her.

Grand-mère's rosary nestled against her chest, swaying as she rode. *Non, c'est impossible*—but it was possible—she'd removed her marquise grandmother's beautiful topaz when she'd washed. And left if behind. While costly, the necklace was of far less value than Maman.

~*~

Aachen Cathedral, western Germany

The tower of the Palatine chapel beckoned to souls seeking sanctuary and to the weary, like Johan. Flanked by tall buildings on either side, the chapel courtyard overflowed with flowering trees. Sunny blue skies, dotted with puffy white clouds, cheered him. Brick paths, bordered by fresh spring grass and tulips, led to the high arched entrance of the Palatine chapel, the concave area above the doors filled with stained glass geometric designs. The workmanship was unbelievable, so perfect was its execution. The domed top of the chapel, dark with triangular sections, was most unusual. What must it be like to build such a magnificent homage to God?

Something about the cathedral stirred the core of Johan's being. His father said the Rouschs were descendants of the man, the king, who'd built this

German cathedral. Johan didn't want to see his bones, though. Keeping Charlemagne's bones as part of a shrine, struck him as wrong. He'd not say anything to his uncle about that, though.

Johan searched the perimeter for a barn for his horse and finally spotted the low white building far out to the back, the green field behind it filled with horses. He approached a short priest, whose white hair floated in wisps around his dried-apple face.

Stomach growling, Johan regretted eating all of his food so early on in the journey. What he would give for a hot, steaming bowl of Mutter's onion soup with a little loaf of crusty rye bread slathered with butter.

"How can I help you, my son?" The voice was as crackly as the man's face.

"I'm here to see Father Vincent. I've brought gifts from well-wishers in the Palatinate."

The man crooked a gnarled finger at him. "You're his nephew, aren't you?"

"Ja." His stomach rumbled loudly.

The priest laughed. "Come, I'll bring you to him and get you food and drink." He motioned for a younger priest in a rough brown robe. "Take care of this animal, will you?"

The other man nodded and led the horse off.

"Danke..." Johan called after him.

"You may call me Father Marcus." His wizened face uncrinkled when he smiled so broadly. "And what should I call you?"

"Johan."

Soon he was seated at the priest's table, a loaf of crusty French bread accompanied by soft cheese spread over it. He prayed. *Dear God, take care of all Your lambs and Your goats and us people, feed us, protect us, and give us safety today and travel mercies to those making their way to this sanctuary. And, Lord, make me able to do anything You would have me do, for Your glory. Amen.*

When finished, Father Marcus led Johan to the cathedral.

"You'll find Father Vincent through there in the confessional." The priest pointed forward and Johan retrieved the letter from his pocket.

Citrus oil scented the air as Johan entered the building adjacent the sanctuary. He tried to walk softly, but his heavy boots made that impossible. No one was in the area reserved for the choir, though he could have sworn he'd heard singing. The saints' images smiled down at him in the large empty building. Arched windows in this Gothic section extended high overhead.

How insignificant he felt in the midst of this beauty. But God wouldn't call him inferior, Scripture told him this. Tipping his head back, Johan gazed up at the center of the octagon, at the fabulous mosaics. The beautiful statue of the Lady of Aachen seemed to smile at him as did the Christ child in her arms. Candles flickered in the Barbarossa chandelier. "*Mein Gott*, You are so good. May I always do Your will."

From somewhere nearby a door clicked open.

Johan turned in the direction of the sound — the confessionals.

Someone shuffled across the mosaic floor, the edge of a cassock visible behind one of the ancient pillars. Candles flickered overhead and in the walls' recesses.

Sunlight broke through the side windowpanes and illuminated his great uncle's face in a golden glow.

"Nicholas?"

"No, Uncle, it's me — Johan. Mutter sent me."

"Johan." He grasped Johan's hands. "Thank God. I have something I need you to do for me."

~*~

Backside in agony, hands burning, and face chapped from the wind, Suzanne rode her newest mount, a chestnut gelding, through the countryside toward Grand-mère's holdings. Suzanne couldn't ride further today—she must rest. *If the King's guard or Pierre searches for me, would they also look at the countryside manor?*

As she emerged from the tree line, the estate lay before her, the chateau's white stone shining a beacon in the bright sunlight. How incongruous that after all that had happened, the house remained the same. She'd expected the mansion to be in ruins.

A white-haired man, Monsieur Kull, cut tall flowers and placed them tenderly in a basket, as if Grand-mère were still alive and he was bringing them to the house for her pleasure.

Suzanne half expected her grandmother to come out to greet her. Perhaps this was all a horrible dream and she'd wake any moment. She dismounted.

The gardener held out his arms. "The King's Guard was here, mademoiselle, but they left this morning. We told them we hadn't seen you. We spoke the truth." Monsieur Kull glanced nervously around the property before taking her arm and guiding her toward the chateau. "They searched the grounds. Strange, they were but a few men and didn't possess military bearing—very sloppy."

"Monsieur Kull, I need to rest before I go on."

"Oui, let's feed you and then get you to your

room."

"Merci."

"And I'll have someone take care of your horse."

After partaking of fruit and sliced ham, and tending to her personal needs, they'd climbed to the darkened third floor, where none of the doors to the rooms were open. The high mahogany bed hailed from the Caribbean—where she'd believed Etienne would take her.

"Madame Vachon and I will hide you here. We know about your papa."

She ducked her chin.

"I'll leave this door ajar in case you call out for me."

"Merci." Suzanne lay in the soft bed, under the down-filled comforter, inhaling the scent of dried flowers.

Sleep evaded her. She opened her eyes as a sunbeam glinted gold off the hilt of a sword hanging on the opposite wall. A Spanish sword taken from the Netherlands when they were under Spanish rule. Grand-père's. Slowly she slid out from beneath the comforter, not disturbing the bedding. Lowering herself beside the intricately carved bed, she got on her hands and knees and crawled beneath it. Old Spanish gold and silver pieces of eight, saved by her great-grandfather, lay hidden in a leather pouch, tucked inside a wooden box Grand-mère had given her. She stretched through the dust, secured the container, and dragged it toward her.

Releasing the pouch, she tucked the gift inside her pants. Lying still for a moment, she thought she heard horses' hooves beneath her window. In the darkness, she remained stretched out, waiting.

A crash sounded two stories below, as the heavy front door was thrown open at the front of the chateau, banging into the walls. She flinched, her heartbeat ratcheting up.

"Where is the rider? Who came in on that fine gelding?" A man shouted this question. It sounded as though several other men stamped their feet.

"*Messieurs?*" Cook's plaintive question echoed up. "That horse belongs to the gardener's nephew."

They didn't respond.

Either that or she couldn't hear them. Suzanne froze as heavy footfalls pounded upstairs to the second level. One after the other, every door on the long hallway was thrown open.

She cringed with each echo. Clutching her beads, hands shaking, she began to pray. *Dear Lord, be merciful. Save me.*

"Come on!" Steps clamored to the third level.

She shivered, awaiting her own door's mistreatment. It banged against the wall, crashing something to the floor, which shattered. Her floor creaked with stealthy footsteps.

"Looks like a girl's room. Check carefully."

Thank goodness, she hadn't disrobed, nor slept. The thick covering on the bed wouldn't reveal that the sheets had been disturbed. Candlelight flickered on the toes of two pairs of boots, visible beneath the bed frame.

"Nothing, no one up here."

"I'm tired of this nonsense. I want my pay and to go."

"Monsieur LeFort can sort this out himself. We're done with this now. I say we return to Paris." The soldier coughed. "Enough time wasted in this musty old place."

"Oui, she's his problem from here."

Trembling, and taking short breaths through her itchy nose, Suzanne was sure she'd sneeze again. As they slammed the front door to the chateau, she sneezed loudly.

4

Dinner with Madame Vachon and Monsieur Kull the night before brought order to Suzanne's mind, as did the full night's rest.

The poor gardener slept right outside her door, should anyone come.

Bathed, her hair clean and pulled back, and donning a fresh set of young men's clothing set everything aright, at least for the morning. Suzanne set out across the field to the barn to see Fury, Guillame's black stallion.

"Good morning, mademoiselle!" The stableman called out, the jaunty red scarf around his neck bobbing. "Your brother's horse is ready whenever you are. I go to enjoy Madame Vachon's excellent breakfast now." He bowed slightly, and then headed for the back entrance of the chateau.

How she'd love to take Fury all the way to the colonies with her. *Impossible.*

Hooves tramped the dirt.

Suzanne stepped behind the edge of the barn and peeked out.

A dappled-gray gelding trotted up the road to the estate, his rider seated straight and high in the polished saddle, a gilded *L* glistening prominently near the pommel.

She gasped. *Etienne's favorite horse, a gift from his*

parents for his last birthday. But the rider was too broad, sat too low in the saddle, to be her beau.

Pierre LeFort rode the gift horse. So, he'd taken Etienne's gelding, too, as he did everything else.

Suzanne shuddered. She ran to the back of the stable to Fury's stall, and willed her heart to stop hammering in her chest. She bent and took a slow breath. *Think.* After ensuring her hair all remained covered by her cap, she grabbed a pitchfork and began to muck out the stall, the black stallion nuzzling her pockets, searching for food. Suzanne Richelieu would never have cleaned a stable.

Snuffling, stamping of hooves, and tails flicking sounded through the barn.

From the corner of her eye, she sensed Pierre by the stall. "You there—come help me!"

Feigning being startled, she hurled a forkful of manure in his direction. Suzanne choked back a laugh.

Pierre jumped about, wiping at the horse dung that landed on his green brocade jacket and tan breeches. He waved his hat in the air as though to rid it of the filth. "How dare you, you insolent fool!"

"Pardon, I didn't know you were there." Her peasant boy's accent sounded believable to her ears and she hoped to his, also. If only she would stop shaking.

"You imbecile, do you see any other stable boys within earshot?"

"Non, monsieur." She pulled the cap over her eyes and bent her head obsequiously as she went about helping her tormenter.

"I'm here to retrieve Suzanne Richelieu from this estate. She's my brother's fiancée and I will bring her back to him." His deceitful tone grated.

Suzanne stiffened. Her mind, clear after a good night's sleep, recognized the lie. "Monsieur?" she feigned ignorance.

"Mademoiselle Richelieu? Where is she?" Pierre shouted, entered the stall, and cuffed Suzanne to the ground.

Stunned and in pain, she still held her cap to her head. No one had ever struck her. Ever.

Fury snorted and sidestepped toward Pierre, nostrils flaring.

Pierre backed out of the stall as Fury lowered his head and moved between him and Suzanne.

How she wanted to stare into Pierre's face and read what she suspected was true—that this man betrayed her father, and thus, her now dead mother. And he would've done so with her brother had Rochambeau not called him. She needed Guy—him and his sharpest sword. For now, though, Fury performed an excellent job of keeping the monster at bay.

"Monsieur LeFort!" The stableman ran in through the back of the stables. "I'll have the groom take care of your horse, but there are soldiers here who wish to talk with you."

Oh, no, those two from yesterday—they'd come back. It sounded as if an entire regiment marched into the stable behind them. Did it include the two men from yesterday, and would they demand to see the phantom nephew?

She had to get out. *Now.*

"What happened to you, LeFort?" a cheerful voice called out.

"Looks like you took a tumble?" a different soldier taunted.

"And do you need help getting away from that stallion?"

Snickers, insults, and profane jeers continued until Suzanne took hold of Fury's reins.

Pierre exited, cursing under his breath.

These soldiers were different men than the day before. Their uniforms were impeccable; boots spotless, whereas Monsieur Kull indicated the others were slovenly.

"What are you doing here, anyway, LeFort? We've been looking for you."

"I could ask you the same question. What brings you so far from your camp?" These last two words were spoken like an epithet. Pierre was well known for being one of the few men to have successfully avoided service to his king.

Guillame, however, had been chomping at the bit to go for as long as she could remember.

"We, monsieur, were tasked to bring home the body of Madame Richelieu, for burial—something we had to strongly persuade your friend, Monsieur DeMint, to allow."

How she wished to see her mother interred, there next to Grand-mère and Grand-père. But she couldn't risk arrest. She mounted up and urged the horse into a trot, away from the stables. Suzanne gritted her teeth, awaiting a call from one of the soldiers or a shot overhead to warn her. *Nothing.* What would keep them so preoccupied with Pierre?

On she rode for what seemed like hours to her next destination. Chilled through by the damp forest air, Suzanne inhaled the blessed scent of wood smoke. She sighted the woodsman's cottage as she exited the forest into the clearing. Suzanne patted the stallion's neck.

Fury displayed his temperamental nature at every opportunity, and her arms and thighs ached from the constant effort she had to exert to control him.

Dread, her old companion, kept her mood in a dark place. Had Rochambeau betrayed their family, also? Had he sent Guy out to his death?

The arched doorway to the house swung out, a young man filling its frame, shaking his shaggy head of gold-brown hair. His dirt-colored clothing appeared shabbier than her own and much too small for his stomach and chest. But he had a presence.

"Welcome, stranger!" He was far too cheerful-looking to suit her foul mood this day.

Suzanne peered back at the big oaf, who seemed delighted with her arrival. The woodsman's relation had no idea who she was, yet he welcomed her with joy. She frowned. Why couldn't she be like that? Betrayal; that was why—its offspring devoured her trust in others. Her heart ached; she missed her family. Suzanne slid off the horse and choked back the urge to retch as she tied the stallion to a hitching rail.

"You all right?" The young man stepped toward her.

His huge hand radiated warmth down her back. She turned and bumped into his broad chest. Good heavens, he wasn't a Frenchman at all. He reminded her of those German warriors she'd studied about, who hid in the forests and attacked the Romans during the time of the Holy Roman Empire. She half-expected his countenance to be painted blue, but when he took a step backward and Suzanne looked up, his cheeks were ruddy, with a grin still affixed on his bearded face.

"Pardon!" That feminine voice wasn't what she planned to use.

The smile vanished and his golden eyebrows rose, eyes wide, his hands now raised as though in surrender. "You're a girl?" Gruff German words accused.

Suzanne chose to ignore his question and would have walked around him if her legs hadn't buckled. "Oh!"

Arms, even hotter than the hand that had stroked her back, captured her. "A long ride?" His halting French was tender. "So young, why alone here?" The young man lifted her and headed toward the cottage. He shifted her and she rolled forward, toward his chest. His face, though covered with a short beard, looked young.

Suzanne couldn't help but examine him, she was so close. His eyes were the same shape and color as the youth she'd painted. *Could it be?*

"One of the Huguenots?" A white-haired lady leaned against the doorway.

"I don't know, but you need to feed her." He lifted her to demonstrate. "Near to starving, so tiny she is." Back in his native tongue, his voice was more melodic.

Suzanne didn't want to let him know she understood his words. Stiffening at the insult, she recalled eating bread and cheese at each stop, other than at Grand-mère's, but not much else. And this overfed giant certainly didn't need to eat.

A dry hand, like an autumn leaf, pressed against Suzanne's cheek. Filmy eyes blinked, but the woman's face registered recognition. "The marquise's granddaughter?" she whispered in French, into Suzanne's ear.

"Oui," she whispered back. "But please, can you help me?"

The young man peered into her face, his sea-blue eyes curious. "What's that you say?"

"Dear God, the child has traveled safely here. I wished she would, even though I didn't think it safe." The elder woman's hands fluttered around her face. "I'm so glad your uncle got the message." She closed her eyes and prayed in a whisper. "You may call me Louisa," the elderly woman said to Suzanne. "And Johan has come from Aachen to help me." She set her cane aside and rubbed her hands together in agitation. "Johan, get some wood and come build the fire."

Suzanne sniffed. The place reeked of strong wood smoke. Anymore and she might be unable to breathe in the small cottage.

"Let's see. Clothes that fit but conceal. Something more German-looking. You are to be Johan's younger brother, if stopped. Dear Lord, why me? I'm an old lady. Why not me, though, Lord? Yes." The woodcutter's wife continued to mumble to herself even as she began opening a small trunk filled with clothing and set about gathering items necessary for the trip.

"The brown gelding Johan brought is rested. My cart horse could make the journey to Aachen. Father Vincent can send the sturdy mare back. My, we didn't have much notice, did we?" Louisa's white head trembled.

"No, I cannot leave my horse. My brother's horse. Not yet." Suzanne blinked back tears. "The stallion will be fine once he's rested. He's strong."

"Water and feed the horses, Johan. I'll get your suppers ready. Suzanne, go wash up by the well in back of the cottage. Here's a cloth, there's soap Johan left down there."

"Oui, merci." She followed Johan out. She'd never seen such a broad back. He looked capable of lifting an ox. She stifled a giggle.

Johan turned around and grinned at her. "Good to hear you laugh. Very musical. I like it."

He acted as if he knew her. And that gave her comfort. Was this the youth she'd painted?

~*~

What had happened to the girl—a young woman now? Johan hadn't recognized her when she rode up alone. He'd been expecting at least two, perhaps three family members, according to Uncle Vincent. But an emaciated boy riding alone? He'd been taken off guard. And then to discover the rider was the girl he'd dreamed of for so long. Only she hadn't seemed to have matured. At least, not physically.

Was it true that the Huguenots in France starved in the countryside? She seemed to be proof of that. Or had there been something more? Her narrow shoulders seemed weighted down by the cares of the world. And where was her brother?

When he'd met her before, she was vibrant, full of herself. That was one reason he'd teased her then. She was a young woman who seemed well aware of her charms. A blossoming flower. And he'd been the bee. Now the rose had succumbed to blight and struggled to overcome the disease.

Johan set about caring for the girl's horse, his mind running faster than a hare escaping a chase. What could he do? He could pray. And come alongside her and help her on her way. Bring her back into the sunshine, find nourishment for her body and soul, and help her find her way back to who she was supposed to become. *Not much.* He laughed at himself. But with God, all things were possible.

Once he'd finished caring for the magnificent animal, he washed and returned to the cottage.

Aunt Louisa ladled a savory meal into three bowls. "Sit down, Johan."

He scooted in next to the girl whose dark eyelashes fanned out against her ivory skin.

Louisa passed a bowl of rabbit stew to Suzanne. Her hands shook as she accepted it. "Merci."

"Here's yours, Johan."

Twice as many thick mounds of dumplings covered the meat and new spring vegetables in his large bowl. "Danke."

Aunt Louisa lowered her aged form into her chair. He wished he'd helped her into her seat, but he'd been too distracted by the newcomer.

"Please ask the blessing, nephew." Louisa bowed her head, as did Johan.

The presence of God stole over him, bringing comfort. He prayed in German and when he peeked, the girl's facial muscles twitched as though she was straining to understand him. "Amen." He lifted his head. "Johan, this young woman needs to get to Aachen Cathedral to Father Vincent as quickly as you can take her."

"How far behind, do you think? The soldiers?"

"If they follow, they could be here even tonight." She kept her head low over her food.

"Good thing my aunt has many grandchildren who like to visit." Though none as pretty as the girl who'd ridden up with her brother years earlier—he on the same magnificent horse. Something about that didn't make sense, but he was too tired from his own travels to think about it. "Your brother—where is he?"

Where there were to have been three or four, now only one sat.

Tears trickled down her cheeks. "I'm alone."

The savory broth turned bitter in his mouth. "Ja, I'll do it."

"If they catch us, they may kill us." Suzanne let that drop like dough into the stew.

He'd experienced such a chase before. And survived. Had God sent him ahead for this purpose—to carry this Huguenot girl to safety in the Palatinate?

~*~

Johan fixed his inquisitive gaze on her.

Suzanne's heart thumped. She awaited his response and refusal. His even features were undisturbed, his blue-green eyes covered with the reflection of firelight, small flames flickering in them. Why did she want to touch this stranger, to draw from his strength? Would he be afraid to take this risk?

Johan stared at the small stone hearth.

Burning wood crackled and hissed as she anticipated what careful words would partner his denial.

"God will see us to safety." His mouth formed the words. His lips were sweet looking, almost too soft for such a large man.

Suzanne snorted in the most unbecoming way. "You know this how?"

"He told me."

She hadn't realized her body had leaned in toward

his torso and she jerked away. Anticipating what? Those arms around her again. She shook the thoughts from her head. This young man heard voices. Would a lunatic accompany her? She should go on her own. Yet, Suzanne desired his companionship so much she could almost feel him riding at her side, his strong profile painted on the canvas of her imagination with dark, firm lines.

She brushed her hands together. She barely knew him. "Today I rode alone. Tonight I can continue with a fresh horse and provisions." Her words echoed in her ears—stupid and proud. Alone in strange woods at night.

"I remember you." Louisa's filmy eyes gazed over the bowl as she raised it to her mouth. "And your brother."

This was the farthest she and her brother had ventured in practice for escape. They'd ridden out on their horses, certifying that they knew the lay of the land, paths, streams, and the safe houses. Just in case they ever needed to leave Grand-mère's for Aachen and then on to Amsterdam from where they'd depart to the colonies.

Huguenots weren't tolerated, certainly not at court, but when her grandmother was alive, they'd benefitted from the auspices of her fervent Catholic faith.

"Did you ask if she's crazy?" Johan asked his aunt.

How impolite—to discuss her in his native language, as though she wasn't there. Yet his aunt spoke to her in French and Suzanne hadn't considered whether he understood or not.

"No." The elderly woman screwed up her face as though taking a bitter tonic. Clucking her tongue, she added, "I think Suzanne fears for *your* safety. A brave young lady. Are you afraid, nephew?"

"Without God's help, yes, but I will obey Him, for He directs our path."

Etienne's sensual smile hovered in her mind, imposed over Johan's friendly grin, even as he discussed her "insanity." Her beau faithfully attended services, believed in God. Why hadn't she trusted him and asked him to protect her? But she trusted this stranger. Everything seemed mixed up. She untied her queue of hair to ease the tension from the back of her head.

Johan bent toward her and swiped her cheek with his thumb, then displayed the gravy he'd removed.

Sudden shyness washed over her. Suzanne closed her eyes; afraid she might see *something* in his face that would make her more afraid. That horrible hungry look of Etienne's. But this peasant only scrutinized her face, his mouth set and eyes sad.

"Very tired—look at her, Aunt Louisa. Let her sleep. We go at morning's first light. Something tells my soul the soldiers can bring us no harm."

Louisa nodded, her rheumy eyes bright. "I pray that is so. Pull the benches together when we're cleaned up and we'll put the cushions on. She can sleep there."

Johan lifted the heavy benches and settled them together before the hearth.

Louisa handed him bedding and he arranged the quilts and pillow.

"Merci."

Fire from the grate flickered in his eyes. She sucked in her breath. Maybe this *was* wrong. But that thought was washed away as sleep overtook her.

As dawn broke, Johan's elderly aunt awoke them. And after taking care of her needs, Suzanne returned to the house where a baguette of bread and hot *café au lait* awaited them.

Johan barely met her eyes as he wolfed down his breakfast and then went to ready the horses.

Louisa handed Suzanne a bag of food. "Take this with you."

Johan returned to the cottage, unsmiling, sweat beading his brow.

His aunt turned to him. "Nephew, I'm an old woman."

"You'll always be my beautiful and sweet aunt." He bent to kiss her.

She patted his cheeks. "I'll never see you again in this life."

"Auntie…" He tilted his head at her. "Don't say that."

Shaking her snowy head, she smiled and closed her eyes before pressing her hands against Johan's brow. "May God bless you and keep His hand upon you and protect you and guide you."

Then she turned to Suzanne and blessed her, also.

A chill raced down Suzanne's spine as the frail woman's whispered words took root.

When she finished, Johan took both of Louisa's hands in his and kissed them. "Mama will kill me if she finds out I was here."

The elderly woman stared up at Suzanne's new companion. "Johan, don't regret your choices. I haven't. Never forget that doing God's work is reward enough. We'll all answer to God in the end—not to our earthly parents."

Earthly parents? Suzanne no longer had them. But

her heavenly Father? And dare she look to this young man to protect her? If only her grandmother yet lived. But she didn't.

5

Far western border of France

The sun hung above the evergreens, their freshness wafting down to envelope the two riders.

Suzanne glimpsed blue jackets through a gap in the pines. Startled, she reined her horse to a stop. This was the fifth time they'd diverted their path because of obstacles.

A trio of soldiers on the main road laughed and took turns juggling green plums. Their coats were ragged, unlike those of the soldiers who'd taken Pierre.

Johan shook his head at her and raised a finger to his lips.

She shrugged at him in question. Although they'd avoided the highway for most of their journey, they needed access to it to get to Aachen. She exhaled, holding Fury's reins tight as he tried to pull forward. Clenching her jaw, she yanked as hard as she could on the reins without causing the beast to rear up.

The voices of the three soldiers carried through the trees.

"Kill him if he doesn't say," the thinnest man insisted.

The brawniest of the trio unsheathed his sword, a glint of light piercing their cover. "This beauty slew a nun. Right in her sleep."

The two others cackled, an unholy sound in this sanctuary of woods.

We're within a stone's throw of murderers.

Johan's wide shoulders were hunched over, his eyes closed, his golden head bowed as in prayer. She felt for her beads, comforted when her fingers wrapped them tight.

One of the men grunted as his heavy feet thudded to the ground. Bridles jingled as they were undone. They intended to remain there. Her breath stuttered.

Breeze, high in the treetops, wafted the piney incense of fresh new growth, and the whisper of needles.

Johan motioned for her to back up her horse. She complied. Then he gestured her in a different direction, away from the criminals. And how would they get to Aachen now?

Several hard hours of riding later, they stopped by a bubbling stream near a small boggy clearing.

Suzanne inhaled the acrid air of the dense woods shielding them. With the sun now in the west, she knew they headed south, not northeast as originally planned.

"Where are we going?"

"All routes to Aachen hold danger." A muscle in his jaw twitched. "We cannot travel there." Johan dismounted and secured his horse, his hair loose and covering his face.

"But I need to go there." She gritted her teeth. If her legs and thighs weren't so stiff, she'd have gotten off the horse by herself.

Instead, when Johan took her reins in one hand and then lifted her down, she gratefully allowed herself to sink into his arms.

"Merci." Leaning against him, legs trembling from the long ride, she clutched his shoulders, her face pressed against the sturdy fabric that covered his broad chest. Warmth flowed through her.

"Get out the food from Louisa." He released her and moved to examine tracks near low green foliage in an opening favored by the sun's rays.

Does he think I'm his servant? She bit back the retort that he should get the food himself. Suzanne frowned at his back and retrieved their midday meal, her stomach growling.

"We should stand and get our legs back." Johan stretched.

She shook her head and offered him bread. But she held onto the loaf.

Johan had to tug. He raised one eyebrow at her as he broke off a chunk and then held it aloft. "You don't wish to share?"

She wasn't used to being ordered around but if she said so, this peasant may ask more questions than she should answer. Instead she scowled at him.

Johan tilted his head and laughed.

She couldn't help laughing, too.

This man could well save her life and she begrudged his directives? He probably kept them terse because of his lack of French language skills.

He set out a blanket on the ground and motioned for her to sit. After settling themselves, they leaned against two trees and ate in silence. Stealing glances at him, she found her companion giving her his slow, crooked grin. He irritated her the way Guillame had. *Not quite the same.*

Did her brother live? A trip to Aachen may be futile, regardless.

Johan crossed to the horses, patted down the mare, and examined her legs. "Pretty good, for a cart horse.

Not so fast, but steady and sure-footed."

Suzanne thought she understood him.

"On the road she'll do even better." He stroked the horse's back.

During their travel time, Suzanne remembered more German phrases as he used them. While Johan seemed to understand some French, he didn't speak many words. He'd repeat if she teased him and gave him the proper pronunciation. His voice was so melodious; she could listen to him forever. But in a few days, they'd be separated. The thought made her sad.

"What activities do you like?"

"Fencing." The word exited her mouth before she realized it. Only nobility fenced. She cringed at her mistake, wishing she could take the word back.

He struggled to repeat the word. "I don't understand."

Good thing. She relaxed. "I can…" Master of the pianoforte, and an artist, she doubted Johan valued these abilities. She could embroider and sew a pretty stitch but had never constructed a garment. "Stitch."

He plunked down onto the ground. "Do you cook?"

"*Une peu.* A little." She'd observed Cook on a number of occasions.

"Good. Mama could use help."

His mother? "You're taking me to your home?" Her heart beat harder, but whether it was from sitting so close, or from his news, she wasn't sure.

"Ja, it's best." He tapped his chest.

"Do you have brothers or sisters?" *I hope his mother has plenty of children to help. I don't want to be a burden…*

Color drained from his ruddy cheeks. "A brother."

"That's all?"

"Ja. One." His voice was strained.

What wasn't he telling her?

"And your brother—what happened?"

"I hope I still have a brother." A tear slipped down her cheek.

Both remained silent as they rested.

Water gurgled in the brook nearby. "Does it flow all the way to the Rhine?"

"Probably."

Answering its invitation, Suzanne pushed up her sleeves, the idea of washing up irresistible.

Joining her, Johan stood by the flowing spring, his arms and face raised toward the sky.

Above she discerned only thick clouds, most dark gray around the edges–clouds associated with storms. "The weather doesn't favor us."

Johan shook his head, wavy hair bobbing. "Ah, sun is there, still, behind clouds. I talk to my Father. Like sun, he's there even on a cloudy day."

"Are you praying?"

"Ja, shield us. Where to turn."

"Didn't you just come from Aachen? Don't you know where we're going?" She bit her lip.

He stared at her, his mouth set. Piercing—how those light eyes could do that to her she didn't know. She trembled, a little afraid of Johan's stern look. If he wanted, she was sure he could be quite fierce.

Johan shifted uneasily. "I take you to my home."

"Why?" she blurted out. "Where?"

Seeming to consider his words, Johan rubbed his beard. "Safer, south."

Additional travel meant more time alone with him. They rode on in silence. One more hour in this infernal stiff saddle and she wouldn't be able to walk for a week. Here she was following a strange German man to his home. She knew almost nothing about him, and communicating with him remained a trial.

What if she was wrong and the French soldiers at Grand-mère's had been there to help her? Adjusting herself on the saddle, she imagined that Rochambeau had sent them at Guillame's request. She pictured the soldiers there to safely return her to court. Madame DeMint would take her into her care while she and Etienne made preparations to marry. In the cathedral. She'd go to their apartment and get...

Visions of soldiers ransacking her home and Pierre disrupting the wedding dashed her daydream to bits. She pressed her eyes shut against the image. "Do you think someone who believes in God has the right faith, Johan?"

He laughed. "Even Satan believes there's a God."

Etienne believed in God. And so did she. But she'd not followed Him in the same manner as her Huguenot parents had. She didn't want to dwell on this topic.

Johan pointed to the farm ahead. "This place marks the Palatinate duchy's Western edge."

"We're out of France?"

"Yes, let's ask them for water. And about swapping your horse." They dismounted and led the horses behind them.

Hanging her head, Suzanne followed. If she pushed Fury any further, he might become lame.

A young man, almost as imposing in size as Johan, emerged from the barn. He stopped, covering his eyes from the sun's rays. Taking her hand, Johan pulled her toward the farmer. "Hello! We're traveling through. Thirsty. Might we have some water?"

As they stepped through the hard-packed dirt

between the small house and the barn, Suzanne caught the stranger's eyes first upon Guy's horse and then upon her.

He tilted his head. "Why do you dress like a boy?"

Johan opened his mouth, and a puzzled expression crossed his face. Pinching his lips together, he peered down at Suzanne but said nothing.

The farmer wiped his brow with a cloth. "She's French, isn't she?"

"Oui." Suzanne stared up into his almost colorless eyes.

"Huguenot?" He spat into the dirt.

She wanted to slap his arrogant face.

"Husband!" A young woman emerged through the doorway of the wood-framed house, a baby on one hip and a toddler clinging to her leg.

"What do you need?" His brusque question was addressed to Johan, whose smile now wavered.

"My uncle is a priest at Aachen."

What was that supposed to mean? Suzanne peered at him, but Johan's expression was blank. He'd already told her that they weren't going to Aachen but to his home.

The farmer's expression softened and his shoulders relaxed. "You're making a journey?" But this was no pilgrimage, which is what the man meant.

"Ja." Johan rocked back and forth.

She smiled, realizing she'd learned what this habit meant—he was forming his opinion of the farmer and deciding what to do next.

The pretty blonde woman drew near.

Her husband pulled her against his side and took the baby. He kissed his wife's forehead and then the baby's red cheek. The toddler leaned against her mother's leg, sucking her thumb. This farmer's wife appeared only slightly older than Suzanne.

Did Johan have a wife? Possibly even a child? Suddenly hot, Suzanne raised a hand to her neck.

"I miss my family, when I see one so happy as yours." Johan bent and touched one of the toddler's golden curls, and the girl hid her face.

Suzanne squeezed her eyes shut in disappointment. She'd been *très stupide* to think Johan was unmarried.

"Marta, can you help them?" His eyes were full of love for his wife. "Can you get these travelers something to drink, my darling, while I look at their horse?"

Blushing, Marta seemed pleased with her husband's endearment.

He released his wife, scooped up his little daughter, and headed toward Fury, singing a nursery rhyme.

Johan's eyes followed the man, his countenance reflecting a deep longing.

Suzanne's stomach clenched. *He must miss his own wife and sweet babes.*

Marta disappeared into her house and returned with a large pitcher and two surprisingly pretty delftware mugs.

"Has your wife ever been to Aachen?" the woman began shyly.

"She's not my wife." Johan seemed downright cheerful about this assertion.

Her cheeks began to burn as she realized the young mother might wonder about her morals, seeing that she was bounding around the country with a young man.

Marta's smile faltered.

In rapid German, she and Johan discussed something that brought a peal of laughter from him. He was probably talking about his wife and children.

Somewhere in this country, a young woman like this one waited for Suzanne's traveling companion to come home. Her mouth went very dry.

"The well is right there." Marta pointed.

"Merci, madame."

"I'll go fetch the water." Johan patted her hand, and the compassion in his eyes brought tears to her own.

"Come on," Marta urged, gesturing toward the porch. Following the woman's long strides wasn't so difficult in the breeches she wore. Pity she'd soon be back in skirts.

Within a few minutes, Johan crossed the yard, half of the water sloshing from the pitcher onto the dirt. He set it near the porch and poured a cup for Suzanne. "Drink."

She greedily gulped down the cool, sweet contents.

He wiped his thumb around her mouth. "Might want to wipe the dirt from your face."

Back home, his wife likely kept an immaculate appearance. Shame swiftly raced after that thought. Dirty, dressed in boys' clothes, and smelling bad, too— she was altogether unattractive. She pulled away and crossed her arms.

"I'm sorry about your brother's horse. I know he means a lot to you." Johan reached around to pat her back. *As though I'm a child.* "I wonder about my goat back home—raised her from a baby."

His goat? He was only concerned about his

animal. What about his family? She exhaled. And to think she had thought him…what had she thought? Her mind suddenly lost what her opinion of him had been. It didn't matter.

Then why was she thinking about how nice it would be if he lifted her up onto the new horse when they left in a few moments? Why did she remember the warmth of his neck beneath her hands the last time he had done so? She'd have to pray a hundred prayers of penance if she kept recalling his touch.

After they'd rested, the farmer returned and showed Johan the horse he'd exchange for.

Although Suzanne followed them away from the house, she couldn't watch as the man led Fury off to his barn and Johan returned to her with the farmer's mare.

"Come on. Mount up." Johan helped her into the saddle.

"Were you trying to trick those people into thinking you're Roman Catholic?" She glanced beyond him to the farmhouse, where Marta had taken the children back inside.

"No, I never said that. I said my uncle was."

"It's a lie of…" She couldn't recall the German word for *omission*. What a hypocrite she was. That was exactly what she'd planned to do—omit sharing information that might cause Johan's family to reject her. She would stay with them a short while before she departed for Amsterdam.

He inhaled loudly. "This duchy has suffered much. Living this close to France, this family never knows if King Louis may send his army to burn the harvest. Kill their livestock. Bring starvation. Even though they're Roman Catholic. They've done nothing to bring this about." A muscle tensed in his check beneath his beard as he circled the mare, examining her.

"Johan, maybe they're cautious because too many Huguenots have taken advantage of their kindness. Endangered them." So many people helped her in the past few days. Had she put any of them in peril?

"Ja. Exactly." He frowned. "One day, anyone can worship as he pleases."

Not in France.

Johan gazed up at her, his mouth set in a firm line. "The Quaker from Pennsylvania in the American colonies came here. Penn's mother was from this duchy." His French and her German had improved over the past several days and she was able to understand most of his words. "I wish to go there one day, to Penn's land. I think that's why Mama sent me to Uncle Vincent. It's almost time for the next group to leave."

Would she go with them? And would he accompany her? Of course not—he may have his wife and children to care for. But perhaps they, too, would come. Sadness overtook her.

Johan sighed. "I hope you understand we had to leave your brother's horse, Suzanne, but you know what he said. Fury has to rest. We'll try to come back for him soon." He mounted the farmer's horse, muttering something that ended with "my wife."

Jolted by those words, she almost dropped from the saddle. A wife. He did have a wife. Well, why shouldn't he? A capable woman. Her heart sank. She'd just left behind Guy's horse and now she felt as if she'd lost her only friend. When they got to his parents' farm, what would they do with Suzanne?

Johan continued talking and she tried to pay attention.

"Want a dozen children."

Thank goodness it wouldn't be her bearing those twelve babes. She frowned, pretending to be serious. "Only a dozen? Why not make it twenty babies?" Suzanne stifled her laugh.

"If God wills it."

For heaven's sake! The man sounded serious. He had seated himself and began to move on when she was pelted by something. A rag, wadded into a ball dropped into her lap.

"Maybe we'll have thirty children." He tipped back his head and gave a deep, rolling belly laugh.

His poor wife. She'd have to put up with his nonsense. Suzanne rolled the rag and threw it back at Johan, laughing with satisfaction when it hit his head.

How would she, Johan and his wife, his brother, and his parents fit into his home? And would their cottage be larger than that of the woodsman's?

She had a sudden image of thirty little children hanging out the sides of the windows, swinging from the shutters. And their lovely mother, managing them all.

6

Palatinate

Traveling with what she now surmised was a married man made her nervous, too self-conscious to take time on their stops, to be thorough in her cleansing. Moisture clung to her garments as the heavy mist increased.

"Not much farther now." Johan's low voice caressed her ears. How his wife must have missed that masculine voice whispering endearments.

Her mother would never hear her father's words again, nor would she. Did people speak in heaven? Shivering, she imagined words of love from the Father to be ongoing, never ceasing. She cleared her throat. "How long do you think?"

A two-story farmhouse, framed in cream-colored wattle and daub, came into view. Her grandmother would have called the home a foursquare house, four generous rooms on the bottom floor covered by another four sleeping rooms above. She smiled in anticipation of a bath and clean clothes.

"My home." Johan's voice rose.

The barn lay beyond the farmhouse, a wide stretch of new, bright green grass separating the two large structures. A modest carriage nestled under an overhang that extended from the side of the tall barn. Cows mooed from the barn.

She exhaled in relief.

A man with steel-gray hair emerged from the dark square opening in the barn, out into the drizzly day. With broad shoulders like Johan's, and the same toothy grin, he was no doubt Johan's father. He stood almost a head shorter though he exuded the same strength. "Maria! Come, Johan is home. And he brought company." Waving, he moved toward them.

Suzanne clutched the slick reins while Johan dismounted and came for her. He searched her face as though memorizing every feature.

She arched her back to relieve the ache. She'd love to jump down into Johan's arms but refused to allow herself such intimacy. A large raindrop plopped on her head and she shook it off.

"What's wrong?" Johan's horse snorted and stamped one foot.

She shuddered. She couldn't have Johan's wife come out and see Suzanne dropping into her husband's open arms. "No!" Clenching her jaw, Suzanne sat as straight as her painful back allowed.

Lines furrowed Johan's father's wide brow as he moved to the opposite side of the horse from his son.

She sensed the same rosy tint that blossomed in his cheeks painting her own, as well.

"Why is she angry with you, Johan?" The older man held his arms up for Suzanne.

As she slid into his father's strong arms, she spotted a dark-haired woman coming through the red door of the farmhouse. Overhead, blue sky and sun peeked out from beneath the dark clouds.

"I don't know, Papa," Johan called out, over his shoulder.

The man helping Suzanne smelled of sausage and onions and wood—sawdust perhaps, not unpleasant, but different.

Her stomach growled.

A half dozen chickens pecked at the mud nearby, getting their own dinner.

"I'm Adam, Johan's father." The older man held her at arm's length and scrutinized her. Then turning, he tucked her arm through his, the coarse cloth rubbing against her hand, as his son led the horses away.

Suzanne blinked back the raindrops continuing to fall despite the sunshine. "Thank you for your help."

Johan returned, his face crestfallen. He should be happy. Seeking out his wife. Maybe he knew his helpmeet wouldn't come out in the rain. Her heart clenched. Or was she nursing a baby? Their baby? *And all this while I keep thinking about those warm arms of his, wrapped around me.* Scorching heat blazed up her neck, not extinguished by even her wet hairline.

"Johan!" Silver streaks painted the dark hair of the woman coming their way. His mama, likely, but her looks were more French than German.

Where was Johan's wife? The young woman she imagined was beautiful, tall and voluptuous, with long, wavy golden hair. A vision from one of the paintings at court. Suzanne's hands clenched tightly, her nails strafing her skin. She forced her hands open and flipped them palms up—but no cool rain soothed them. The mist and rain that had clung to them for the past two days ceased falling.

Not much taller than Suzanne, his mother opened her arms to Johan, who picked her up and whirled her around.

"Son!" she gasped. When she was set down, the woman patted Johan's cheeks. "I'm so glad you're back."

"We were so worried." Adam's bass voice boomed. "I almost went to Aachen to get you."

"I am sorry, Papa, Uncle Vincent asked me." Johan ran his tongue over his lips. "Took longer than I thought. To, well…"

His mother interrupted his explanation by hugging him, and he engulfed her in his arms.

Suzanne wouldn't have another such embrace with him being a married man.

"My goat? Did she birth?" Johan called to his father.

"*Nein.*"

His goat again! What about his wife? He stared intently at her, a question in his eyes. She exhaled. Johan was probably thinking how to explain this filthy girl to his beautiful wife.

Annoyance flashed over his mother's face. "Now come, tell us, who did you bring?"

"Suzanne. She was…a neighbor of Aunt Louisa's." Johan fixed her with a frown so stern that any comments were silenced before they formed on her lips. He'd deliberately not mentioned that he'd gone to Aunt Louisa's home.

The two men exchanged glances.

Johan's mother cocked her head to the side. "We'll talk later, son." No mistaking the warning in her voice.

Suzanne took a deep breath and exhaled. Already, she'd brought trouble with her. Johan wasn't supposed to have gone into France. When she got settled, she would pray Grand-mère's rosary three times through.

"Suzanne, why didn't you let me help you down?" Johan's loud voice scattered the chickens across the yard. He turned toward them. "Still afraid of me, are you, chickens?"

She stared at the red farmhouse door, wishing his angelic spouse would appear.

They paused under the small overhang by the door.

"I, uh"—Suzanne loosened the tie on her cloak—"your wife."

"Your wife?" His mother gripped Johan's arms. "You're too young, Johan. How could you?"

"What's going on?" His father's voice boomed like her father's had when he'd discovered her plans to attend the ball at Versailles.

Johan removed his hat and massaged his head. "Suzanne, what are you talking about?"

Feeling foolish and uncertain, she shrugged. "I thought your wife would be waiting."

"He has no wife." His mother's plaintive cry of relief held an edge suggesting Suzanne lacked all common sense.

"Not yet." His father patted him on the back.

"And no means to support one," a cold male voice called out from behind Johan.

If she thought Johan handsome, this man looked carved from the same mold and then gilded with golden hair, given more sharply defined features, and trimmed to a leaner physique. But when the artist finished his face, he forgot to smooth the edges, to soften it, and to turn his lips and eyes upward instead of down.

~*~

Being clean had never felt so good. The simple dress Maria gave her hung like a sack, devoid of trim. Maria had gotten most of the dirt and debris out of

Suzanne's hair, but it had been an ordeal. Suzanne sat in the small parlor in the front of the house while her hostess cooked and the men finished their work. She counted the tomes in the book cabinet, stopping at one hundred.

Rubbing a finger over the rough, worn and cracked leather of one of the dark covers, she contemplated reading one after dinner. Perhaps one of the great philosophers. Her stomach growled loudly and Suzanne stood, rearranging the fabric of the dress.

Savory aromas of beef, salt, and herbs mingled and drifted toward the front of the house, drawing Suzanne toward the cozy room used for cooking and meals. Never had she been so hungry. She caught Maria's eye.

"May I?" When Johan's mother nodded, Suzanne pulled a rush-seated chair from beneath the heavy wood slab table. It was squeezed in close to the wide, arched brick fireplace.

"This is where you will usually find me," Maria said. "After we break the fast, until the nooning hour, I prepare the midday meal. It has to last them through the rest of their afternoon chores. A long day."

For everyone. I pray I don't collapse into my food and make a fool out of myself.

Johan slid onto a trestle adjacent to her, and she jumped. His broad smile and eyes full of mirth mocked her. He patted the empty spot next to him. "My wife, she sits here." He laughed. He lowered his voice. "I try not to sit on her, too."

Suzanne couldn't stifle her laughter.

"Johan, don't tease." Maria tried to be stern but she, too, started chuckling as Adam joined them, easing his way around Suzanne to the head of the table.

"Might as well ask the cock not to crow." He wagged a thick finger at his son. "Girls aren't used to that. Be nice to our guest."

Setting the plates, bowed slightly up to contain gravy or juices, in front of Johan, Maria ladled out root vegetables in broth thick with chunks of meat. Johan's fingers touched against Suzanne's as he handed her a bowl, giving her a start.

"Merci."

He waited expectantly. "You need to pass down the table to the end, to Papa."

"Oh, yes." This was what she had observed in the servants' kitchen when they'd allowed her access. She extended the steaming bowl to his father. Somehow, she must fit in here. Be absorbed into this family. At least until her brother found her or until she could get to Amsterdam to sail.

Adam cut a loaf of crusty bread and placed the slices onto small blue plates.

The door behind them opened. A cool breeze accompanied Johan's brother.

Her stomach churned.

He came around the table and kissed Maria on top of her head. "Mama, how are you?" The young man's gentle voice sounded nothing like his earlier growls.

Suzanne wasn't sure exactly what Johan and Nicholas had been arguing about after her arrival, but she suspected it had something to do with her. Well, not her exactly, but about Johan and why he couldn't marry. She rearranged her napkin in her lap, suddenly mindful that she had no chemise on under her dress.

"Did you wash your hands, Nicholas?" Maria patted her mouth with her napkin.

Suzanne held back a giggle. He needed more than his hands washed. If she had her way, she'd dump the whole bucket over his head. How dare he talk to Johan that way in front of her when they had just arrived? Even if she couldn't hear exactly what he'd said. How rude. *Get control of yourself, you are tired and exhausted. Sit up and behave like a lady.* The voice in her head sounded very much like her mother's, and she complied.

"Don't ask him, Mama, he's a grown man now." Adam tossed two thick slices of yeasty bread atop Nicholas's stew.

Settling himself uneasily on the trundle bench across from Suzanne and Johan, the brother ran a hand through the top of his golden hair. It was gathered back into a loose tail at the base of his long neck. His dark-blue eyes were identical to his father's, and his smooth skin was sun-darkened from outdoor work.

Suzanne tried not to stare at him, but he was a most handsome man. Not attractive in the same way as Johan, but interesting to look upon, like an especially well-executed statue one might appreciate.

Adam slid the fragrant bread in front of her.

Suzanne smiled at him. "Merci."

He returned her smile with a grin.

Across the table, Nicholas gazed at her in curiosity.

Why do I expect he'd show me any interest? Devoid of jewelry and powder, with her hair coiled up like a commoner's and in this sack of a dress, the only attention she would have received at court would be a cursory glance, perhaps an assumption that she was a street waif sneaking inside the palace at Versailles. Her cheeks burned.

Johan's father tapped a wooden spoon on the table. "Nicholas, will you say the prayer?"

Suzanne wished Adam would say it. His rich bass voice eased her memory of her father. She blinked back tears.

"Of course." In a voice purer than his disposition, Nicholas recited an unfamiliar prayer, finishing with "bless this food. Amen."

Johan leaned close, his warm shoulder rubbing against hers, and whispered in her ear, "I wanted to say the prayer. To thank God for our safe homecoming."

Suzanne squeezed his warm hand. "Next time."

Nicholas glared at them.

Stiffening, she sat straighter.

Even with the disgusted look on his face, Johan's brother was *très beau*. Perfect, even features were set in a square-jawed face. No Roman would have been prouder of his strong, straight nose. If Nicholas were at court, the girls would throw themselves in his path. Yet she found Johan more attractive, although not in a way she could fully describe.

She wanted to melt into him. To disappear into his strength and allow him to carry her on to where she needed to go. He was nothing but kind to her, and undemanding. *I really must get my sleep.* Suzanne yawned

Maria quirked an eyebrow. "We'll get you straight to bed after dinner."

"Boys, you help your mother tonight. I'll prepare the grandparents' room for our guest."

Nicholas's head jerked up from his plate. "You're giving her grandmother's room?"

Suzanne flinched.

A muscle in Adam's jaw twitched, and he held his spoon in midair. "That's what I said, son."

The muscles of Johan's upper arm tensed against her own. His knotted fists were ready to deliver a blow. Would he hit his brother? His thigh and knee brushed against hers, seeming to anchor him there so he wouldn't strike.

Their father rattled off something so fast that she could discern only the words *sanctuary* and *mother*. They were talking about her. Her German needed rapid improvement.

~*~

Moonlight filtered through from the window on the far wall, touching a simple cross and trailing a pool of light across the heavy quilt. Yeasty bread was rising somewhere. She must have fallen asleep as soon as she'd been tucked into bed. Low voices woke her.

Someone chatted in the kitchen on the other side of the fireplace, which supplied the heat for both rooms.

"Did you talk to Nicholas?" a deep voice inquired. "About keeping Johan in the room?"

"I told him to secure the door and he said he would." Johan's mother spoke.

"Good. We'll talk with her about his problem tomorrow if he gives Nick any trouble tonight."

"And we've got to tell the two of them soon about our decision, Adam. They need to know."

"This complicates things." Suzanne heard Maria's loud inhalation. "A French girl?"

"Like you, mademoiselle?"

Maria's throaty laughter recalled Grand-mère's.

Suzanne scooted under her bedclothes.

"As I was, you mean."

"You'll always be that lost girl to me." Adam's rich voice reverberated through the wall.

"I'm a woman now." Maria's breathy voice sounded young.

"Ah, that you are."

There was a long silence. Might they be kissing? She pulled a pillow over her head—she shouldn't be listening to their conversation.

"So God is answering our prayers?"

"For a daughter? Wife, it might be too late for that." He chuckled.

Maria's throaty laugh echoed. "For a wife—for Nicholas."

The bed suddenly seemed to sink beneath her.

"Maria…"

Please, dear God, don't let them think she was admiring that boorish oaf.

"Nicholas needs settling down. A good wife would do that." But the tremulous words rang false.

"Maybe he needs help." Suzanne almost felt the man's loud sigh.

"Our guest—have you considered that she might be an aristocratic lady-in-waiting to the Queen of France?" Maria's voice took on a singsong quality. "Perhaps she worships as a Catholic? Or would consider our son like dung beneath her feet?"

Suzanne stiffened and then sat up. What did they know of her? Nothing.

"What about an operatic singer?" Adam's tone was stern but held love. "A runaway from her parents?"

"Oui, what would someone do with a girl like

that?"

Johan's mother a singer? And French?

A breeze rippled through the woven curtains at the tall window, bringing the sweet smell of wet earth.

"Ah, who really knows why she is here, save the Lord himself."

"Exactly. Come on back to bed."

Steps groaned in the ancient farmhouse as the two climbed upward.

Nicholas. Rude, coarse, and mean. She wanted to gag. Only a simpleton smitten with his handsome face could overlook those defects.

She needed this place, was all. For now, until the next group of sojourners departed for the colonies. Why didn't that seem like the truth, then?

7

Cobwebs and mist entangled Suzanne as she stumbled through the cobblestone streets of Paris.

Guillame rode off through the crowd, away from her and Maman, who wore simple black woolen hooded cloaks covering their heads.

Her mother pulled her close. "I love you, Suzanne." The safety and security of her arms quelled Suzanne's fears.

Rustic smells distracted her—baked apples, bread, and eggs. Cringing, Suzanne kept her eyes closed. If she opened them, her mother would disappear.

Steps drew closer, and with them the memory of where she was. And recollection that her mother was dead. The long trip she had made. And the young man who'd brought her to his home, avoiding the French soldiers. A rap on the door sounded and she yanked her quilt up to her neck.

"Come eat," Johan called.

The door swung in.

She stiffened. Although they'd traveled far together, he shouldn't come into this bedchamber.

Drawing near, his face moved dangerously close to her own. His clear blue eyes changed from aqua to gray, like a stormy sea. His eyes weren't hungry, as Etienne's, but kind. A sheet of golden brown hair fell toward her face, tickling her nose.

Would he try to kiss her?

Her heart performed a strange flip-flop within her

chest.

Pinning her with an arm on either side, Johan jostled the bed. "Be a good girl and get up."

From beyond him came the sound of a throat being cleared. Maria, whose dark hair and eyes seemed more like Suzanne's than her son's, stood in the doorway to the room.

"Come join us for our morning meal," she announced in French.

"Oui, madame."

"You must excuse my son, he was accustomed to coming in and out of this room as he pleased." Maria hesitated and then pressed her lips together.

The thin chemise Suzanne slept in wouldn't cover her, and her dress had been hung outside to air. Her cheeks flushed. "*Une robe*? To cover me?"

Maria pulled a simple wrap down from a strip of pegs and handed it to her. "Can you help me with the chores after breakfast, Suzanne?"

Chores? Dread slunk up and laughed in her face, spitting in her eyes. "Oui, madame," she croaked as she stood and pulled the robe on.

How long until they realized she knew nothing of housewifery? Well, perhaps then they would abandon the notions of her as a prospect for Nicholas.

Maria straightened the quilt on the bed.

Embarrassment stung her. She should have seen immediately to making up her own bed.

"Suzanne, today is baking day. Can you make bread?"

Johan answered for her. "What girl doesn't know such a simple thing, Mama? You insult her. But I'll show her how to milk a cow. She hasn't done that before."

Cheeks heating, Suzanne kept her mouth shut. Maria would find out for herself. Feeling in her pocket, her hands closed around her beads. Her tension eased. *I still have something of Grand-mère's.*

Hours later, her rough dress scratchy, feet aching, and covered with flour, Suzanne was summoned by Adam to their tiny parlor, triggering a bout of irritability she tried to quench. She'd not slept through the night during her whole ordeal. Never had she been subjected to such conditions, which resulted in a short-temper she continuously had to keep at bay. Her fingers might wear out Grand-mère's rosary.

Adam gestured to a chair. "Sit down." He and Maria exchanged a nervous glance and then sat across from her on the bench.

"We need to tell you something about Johan."

What was so serious they needed to talk to her alone? "What is it?"

"Do you know what is a *schlafwandler*?"

"I have heard of people doing this, *somnambule*. A sleepwalker."

They'd slept alongside each other, needing each companion's warmth through the night. Neither slept for long, disturbed by the woods' sounds and their need to be on guard. If Guillame were here, he'd have pressed for wedding banns to be announced. But he wasn't there, and Johan's parents hadn't asked. Why was that? They mustn't have thought he'd traveled far.

Adam eyes darted around the room and he shifted in his chair. "When my father died, my mother used to let Johan come sleep with her in the grandparents' room downstairs."

Suzanne sank down in relief into the cushion on the seat. She'd been so worried they were upset with her. "Where I now sleep?"

"Ja." Adam cleared his throat. "We wanted to warn you. Johan walks in his sleep and ends up in that room." He hurriedly added, "Not often…"

Maria clucked her tongue. "Not in a long time."

"That we know of," Adam gave Suzanne a cautionary look. "Don't be alarmed if he rattles your door. It doesn't lock, so place a chair underneath to keep him out."

"Should I be afraid?"

"No." Maria sighed. She rose and retrieved a platter of tarts from the sideboard before offering them to Adam. "He wouldn't harm anyone. But having a *grand homme* suddenly in your bed, hugging you tight, might startle you."

Did she know how they'd had to huddle together at night on the trail to stay warm?

At first shaking her head as Maria offered her the treat, Suzanne relented as Maria's eyes begged her to accept one of the diamond-shaped confections they'd worked on together. "Merci." She nibbled on the almond filling at the edge. She wanted to giggle at the idea of Johan coming into the room, swinging his hands as he tried to hug her. An unbidden thought sobered her. *I trusted Etienne and look how he behaved.*

Adam clapped his hands together. "His brother will watch over him."

Johan hadn't wandered away in his sleep, during their travels. Why would he start now?

"I'd better go learn how to milk the cows. Merci for advising me." Suzanne hitched up her skirts and headed outside. Chickens scurried past. She shuddered at the thought that she might have to prepare one for cooking.

Johan headed toward her and clasped his large, rough hand over hers. "Come on, I teach you to milk." He practically dragged her to the barn. Once inside, he pulled the milking stool close to the animal and sat down. "Watch." He scrunched his long legs under him.

She pushed his shoulders. "Let me try. You're too big to sit on that stool. You'll break it."

"I've been sitting on this thing since I was this high." Johan held up his hand to Suzanne's shoulder.

"You're not that short anymore."

He didn't move, and when she pushed him again, he tipped over backward, bringing her with him. Horrified, she landed atop him with a thud. Heat coursed up her chest. Pushing with her hands against his shoulders, she tried to rise up, but her skirts were tangled in his boots. Preparing to apologize, she ventured a look at him.

He chortled. Had he allowed her to knock him over?

The cow mooed.

"What exactly are you teaching her, Brother?" Nicholas's voice mocked. "She probably learned how to do more than that back home. N'est-ce pas?"

Johan lifted her off him before rolling to his side. He jumped up and jerked Nicholas off the floor.

"Put him down, Johan." Suzanne covered her mouth. Would he hit him?

Nicholas's face blanched.

Adam's boots crackled on the straw. "What are you doing? Haven't we had enough death on this land? Johan—your brothers, all gone...stop at once."

Johan released his captive.

Face contorted, Nicholas grabbed the milk pail and dumped the contents on Johan's head before pushing past his father and out the door.

Johan shook off the liquid, grabbed a tub from a peg, and headed toward the well.

Suzanne's heart hammered. She'd never witnessed family members fighting like that. Guy argued with her, but he'd never touched her in anger. But if Nicholas had said those words in front of Guy? Her brother was a godly man, but she had no doubt what he would do. And the blow would hurt for a long time.

8

A rattling sound broke through Suzanne's thin haze of sleep.

The noise repeated and the wooden legs of the chair placed under the doorknob screeched softly as they wobbled against the floor. She hesitated.

Nicholas was tasked with securing Johan in their room overhead. Who was trying to enter the room? Nicholas?

In her fog, she searched for the rapier she'd forgotten at Aunt Louisa's home.

"*Oma,*" Johan's low voice called out, accompanied by a light rap.

Thank God, it wasn't Nicholas.

Suzanne forced her limbs out from under the quilts. *Johan would never hurt me.* Even in her exhaustion, something in her spirit recognized this truth.

"Please..." The gentlest voice from such a large person.

It broke her heart. Suzanne pulled the slatted chair away from the door, and it swung in. Johan slipped into the bed. She clapped her hands over her mouth.

"Nice and warm here."

She stared at his strong profile, reflected in the moonlight. She tensed as she realized what she'd done. In her exhaustion, she hadn't considered. She shouldn't have opened the door.

"Get in."

She stayed rooted by the door. *I've made so many bad decisions.* Suzanne hesitated. But she'd opened the door. "Wait. Be patient."

The wide chair sat in the other corner of the room.

She could sleep there. Stumbling slightly, she made her way around the bed to the other side.

"*Schmusen.*"

What did that mean?

He rolled to his side and held his arms out before tugging her hand, outstretched to pull one of the quilts from the bed. She toppled forward into the bed, landing on top of him with a thud. She gasped.

Johan pushed her off.

Her heart pounded.

A low growl accompanied his words. "What are you doing?" He rubbed his forehead, frowning. Certainly, he didn't look like a man intent on harming her. There was something both frightening and tempting about remaining there by his side. Johan rubbed his mouth. "Suzanne. I'm sorry. I don't know what…"

"It's all right." She eased out from beneath the covers and slid her feet to the floor.

He groaned. "I don't know what happened."

Even in her confusion, she knew. "Nicholas left the door unlatched." But why?

"Ja, he must have. I'm sorry."

~*~

"Did you rest well, my dear?" Johan's mother pressed her palms against each side of Suzanne's face and brushed her lips against Suzanne's forehead; cinnamon scent pleasantly reminded her of Grand-mère's kitchen.

"Oui," but her hands shook as she clasped the mug of warm milk between her hands.

Johan sat across from her, instead of beside her on the bench. "Morning, Mama." His voice was low, tentative.

"Why don't you sit by Suzanne?" Nicholas demanded, as he ambled into the kitchen and kissed his mother. When there was no response, Nicholas slipped in next to Suzanne, his hard thigh nudging hers.

She moved as close to the edge as she could without falling off.

Johan's sea-blue orbs fixed on her. He lowered his head, chewed his food, and then stared back at her. He seemed positively addled today. Perhaps the result of his episode.

But she didn't want to ask Maria. She'd talk with Johan later. "Johan, will you show me how to milk the cows again today?" Suzanne gave him her sweetest smile.

He took his plate to the dry sink, came back to the table, and removed Suzanne's before returning, taking her by the hand, and pulling her free from the bench. "We try again, but this time we sing to them. Make them relax and let down their milk."

"I see." She didn't. Singing to cows? "Before I forget, what does schmusen mean?"

Three pairs of eyes turned upon her.

Johan quirked an eyebrow at her. "Means cuddle. Like a child on a parent's lap. A good word. Why do you ask?"

Johan's mother gave him a pointed look. "After the milking practice, send Suzanne back to me."

Half an hour later, she returned, washed up and slipped on her work apron.

Fruit bread, baking in the hearth, wafted its sweet aroma as Maria sat chopping vegetables for the next meal. "I'm surprised you mother didn't teach you to bake."

She needed to change the subject of cooking. "I can stitch a good seam."

Maria smiled at her. "Yes, Johan told me. You can help me make his new coat."

Her stomach sank. "I'll try."

"We'll start in a little bit by measuring a new waistcoat for Johan. He has outgrown his good coat. Noel, his cousin, has a new baby and the baby will be baptized soon." Dark eyes surveyed her critically. "We'll teach you to cook, bake and to eat what you make. We'll fatten you up, child."

"I haven't eaten so much since before..." Tears pricked her eyes. "Maman had gotten sick." Maybe not since she was a child at Grand-mère's, before all the secrecy of what was required of a Huguenot family at court.

Had her brother been killed? Or had he started a new life without her? Was Guy in Amsterdam as planned, while she waited here until the next group of people could leave for the colonies?

"I miss my French family, also—an aunt and uncle I love dearly." Maria set her knife down on the chopping board.

The door flew open. Cold, earthy morning air preceded Johan into the room.

"Suzanne!" Heavy boots splattered clumps of mud across the wide, wooden planks of the floor. "Come see the baby lambs."

Amazing how he could communicate in a few words exactly what she needed to know. She laughed.

Johan turned and exited, slamming the front door.

Maria threw her hands in the air. "Put on that coat from the peg, Suzanne, and go ahead."

Suzanne slipped into her boots, put on the heavy, coarsely woven coat, and fled. Rich, springtime earth greeted her, and she tilted her face toward the warm sun.

A warm hand grasped hers and Johan pulled her toward the barn. He lifted the largest of the new lambs, offering it to her.

She hesitated, humbled by the tiny creature's exquisite construction. A divine hand formed such beauty. She tucked the lamb into her arms.

"All perfect, Suzie." Warmth, love, and *joie de vivre*. How could one young man roll that into just three words? Johan could probably convert King Louis. So charming, yet he didn't realize it.

"Suzanne," she corrected him. The reduced name had no dignity.

"Ah, let me call you Suzie."

His slow grin caused her heart to catch in her throat. She couldn't let him affect her like this.

"No, I refuse." Suzanne lifted her nose in the air as his nimble fingers tickled her through the back of her coat. "Stop that!" She shrugged off the assault. On second thought, the king was safe in his faith.

"Come, bring your lamb with you."

Not her lamb. Tempted to place it back with its mother, instead, she followed Johan.

"Time to tend the horses."

Leaning against the doorframe of the barn, clutching the baby lamb, Suzanne watched in the

Carrie Fancett Pagels

shadows as Johan retrieved and rubbed liniment into the horse's knee. His touch was gentle, but thorough, and the motions soothed Suzanne, too.

"There, not so hot now, girl, *ja*?"

She coughed, the dust in the barn thick. "What's wrong with her?"

"I'm not sure, but that knee keeps swelling."

She had to ride the horse again, to get back on her journey. Their group didn't depart for weeks, but she wouldn't wait that long.

Pipe smoke, sweetly cloying, trailed Adam into the barn. "Let me look."

Johan unkinked his long frame and loped to her side, but not before giving the half-smile that always sent shivers up her spine. *Stop*, she instructed her quivering knees when she sensed the wonderful heat coming from him in the chilly barn.

He frowned before wrapping an arm around her and pulling her close. "You're cold. Go get one of Grandmother's shawls before you come back out."

But she didn't move.

And he didn't release her. He stroked Suzanne's arm as his father continued to feel along the mare's front knee. "Not lame, Suzanne, but she will be if she doesn't rest."

"I'll get the other horses ready for the trip to Noel's, Papa. How much meat should we bring them?"

"Danke, we'll need both horses ready. With that new babe on the way, I want to bring extra for his wife. Maybe some venison and ham."

Suzanne placed a hand against the mare's side. "Would anything else help her heal more quickly?"

The skin between Adam's eyebrows puckered. "Only time will help."

106

Johan affected a fatherly tone and patted the horse. "No long rides for you for a while."

Suzanne bit back disappointment. Maybe Guy was coming for her. Reaching into her pocket, she fingered the smooth beads. Her hands shook. But Grand-mère's rosary no longer provided the immediate balm it once had. She'd get out one of Grand-père's coins, too. She recalled Jeanne once stating, "Between your grandmother's faith and your grandfather's riches, you have quite an inheritance."

Jeanne. She'd get word to her. If anyone knew where her brother was, it was her old friend. Guillame was angry with Jeanne—he hated that her friend disregarded his advice about Pierre. But surely, he would forgive Jeanne. He'd always had a soft spot in his heart for her, no matter what she'd done.

The tight queue at the base of her neck vexed her. She pulled the ribbon from her hair, shaking her head and releasing her hair. For now, she'd stay put. She'd rest and ready herself.

Johan smiled down at her. "Will you help Mama make my new coat?"

"Oui."

Observing as Johan exited the gate and bisected the yard, she ascertained that his infernal pregnant "pet" was munching grass by the fence. She sped after Johan, hoping the ornery animal wouldn't bother her.

The nanny goat ran toward the gate, blocking it. "Maah!" Green grass hung down from the goat's mouth as she bared her long yellow teeth.

Nicholas whistled tunelessly behind her. "Afraid of a nanny goat?"

Suzanne didn't bother to turn around. She was to help Maria with Johan's new garment. She'd been measured many times herself and had been with Guy when the family tailor had come to their apartment. No animal, nanny or not, would prevent her from getting to the house.

The nanny chomped on more grass.

Suzanne motioned. "Shoo!"

Nicholas laughed. "She's not a fly."

Suzanne shook off the chill that dripped down her spine, and moved toward the goat. She didn't fear the nanny, or Nicholas. No, she feared herself and her reaction to the young man whose coat she would soon be fitting. Wrapping string snugly around Johan's broad shoulders. Standing close to him, absorbing his warmth.

The door to the house opened, then banged closed behind Johan. "Ready?"

~*~

Mama left to talk with Papa, leaving Johan alone in the kitchen with Suzanne.

"We need to finish measuring you." Suzanne gestured for him to raise his arms up and out.

Such intimate contact felt awkward, but he complied. Her lip was twitching. Was she nervous? He cleared his throat. "You've done this before?" He desperately needed a new frock coat. He'd not be a laughingstock at the christening of Noel's new babe.

She shook her head and passed the paper strip behind his back with her right hand. She leaned in.

When her chest pressed into his, he tensed and sucked in his breath. He took hold of her shoulders and gently pushed her away from him even as he imagined pulling her closer.

Pink spread across her pretty face.

"You should have walked around me, Suzie."

She seemed speechless.

"Here. Let me have the end." He held the strip to his chest. His heart pounded against the fragile paper.

Her head bent low. She closed the end piece and cut the paper. Standing only inches from him she looked up, the centers of her eyes wide and dark against the amber rim.

He inhaled her sweet scent. What a good wife she would be. A good mother. His face heated as his mind followed that thought. Ja, but her face was as flushed as his probably had to be. Did she share his feelings?

A life together as husband and wife required more than strong emotions, though. What a shame the poverty she'd endured had left her lacking simple skills. Tonight, she'd prepare dinner again. Suzanne's mother must have been ill for years and neglected her training. But thank God, Mama had taken her under her wing.

Maybe they did have a chance together, after all. Only time would tell.

9

Finally, Suzanne had prepared dinner without any disasters.

The Rousch men sat at the table, staring up, reminding her of baby birds waiting for a worm to be dropped in their mouths.

She stifled a laugh. Suzanne offered the tray of poultry to Johan and he flipped a piece onto his plate. The right side of his mouth lifted up in mischief.

His mother wagged a finger at him and shook her head.

Nicholas ladled out his portion of roasted chicken and vegetables. A muscle in his face twitched. "Nothing burnt, Suzanne."

Suzanne glared at the handsome wretch as she pulled the pan away and brought it to Johan's father, her head lifted high.

Johan grabbed the wood cutting board, knife, and a loaf of rye and began to slice large portions. His gaze met hers as though they both felt the tension in the room, which was thicker than the heavy bread he now cut.

Nicholas made room on his plate for the cabbage Maria moved from her plate to his.

Adam cleared his throat. "You did a fine job delivering the baby goats, Johan."

"Danke, Papa." His cheeks grew pink at the praise.

She smiled at him.

"Your best meal yet, Suzanne." Johan passed the

bread.

"Merci."

"Ja, it's good. Tender. My teeth aren't in danger tonight." He opened his mouth and clicked his teeth together.

Of all the nerve! Easing onto the trestle next to him, Suzanne stomped his toe with her boot.

"Ow. Why did you do that?"

She dropped her voice. "You know why."

Nicholas snickered and placed bread onto her plate. "He knows. Don't let my brother's innocent face fool you."

Suzanne rolled her eyes in exasperation. "How is my horse?"

Johan wiped his mouth and set his napkin in his lap. "Do you miss riding?"

Miss riding? Is he crazy? Perhaps he'd not realized how far she'd ridden across France.

After he swiped another bread slice, Johan slathered it with butter that she and Maria had churned.

Suzanne rubbed her still-aching arms.

Adam smiled indulgently at her. "Perhaps another week, then a practice ride."

Suzanne tried to ease the dismay from her face. *A week.* "I see." She clamped her teeth together trying to prevent a scream of frustration. Might she take their little-used horse?

Adam brushed his hand across Maria's cheek.

The woman blushed, and Suzanne's face grew warm with pleasure at their simple display of affection. She'd never see such acts of devotion between her parents again. *I'm an orphan.* She must fulfill the vow she'd made to her mother. She must discover if her brother had survived. Suzanne turned toward Johan. "What part did you do delivering the goats, Johan?"

"I saved the smallest baby goat—she's a feisty one."

Adam beamed. "I'm proud of you."

Nicholas's handsome face twitched as though in insult.

"I pulled her out. She was stuck." Johan combed his fingers through his beard. "That's what it took, Suzie."

His familiarity caused her spine to jerk up as though a string pulled her from the top of her head, like the marionettes she'd watched as a child. "Don't call me that," she hissed into his ear before adding, *"s'il vous plaît."* It was improper to use a diminutive name with her—she of the noblesse ancienne. Yet this man she'd allowed into her room, into her bed the night he'd sleepwalked. Regardless of the fact that she wasn't in bed *with* him, intimacy was there. Warmth spread across her chest under the ties to her blouse. She felt like tugging the garment up over her head and tying it there.

She'd been here much too long—Johan was becoming much too close. But could she really leave them with no horse? Nothing for transportation in the event of an emergency? She smoothed out the full apron over her costume. She was playing the part of a farm girl in a theatrical performance, but she wasn't on a Paris stage. And she was developing alarmingly real feelings for Johan.

Nicholas tore off a huge chunk of bread and stuffed it into his mouth. From beneath heavily fringed eyelashes, Johan's brother seemed to take her measure. "Where did you say you grew up, Suzanne?"

"She lived near Aunt Louisa, remember?" Johan glared at Nicholas.

"French—probably a Catholic and not a Huguenot at all," he muttered.

Suzanne stiffened.

Maria shot him a stern look. "Nicholas! Don't be rude. Why would she be here if she were not a Huguenot?"

Her stomach clenched.

"Perhaps she didn't realize Papa would never tolerate a Catholic under his roof."

Only a few more weeks' shelter before the group leaves. These good people wouldn't put her out, would they? Suzanne dropped the pewter utensil to the blue stoneware plate and brought her napkin to her lips.

Nicholas pointed his knife at Johan. "Suzanne needs a female friend."

Yes, she needed a friend in the village. Someone who could help her get a message out without these people knowing the letter was going to Versailles.

"Someone her age?"

Johan stopped chewing and set his fork down. "Greta is older—ready for marriage. Right, Nick?" He winked at him.

Nicholas's face flushed. "Too bad she has to wait." Jaw clenched, he bent his head back over his food.

Suzanne exhaled in relief. A large hand crept over hers.

"Are you all right?" Johan whispered.

His touch felt like a warm cloak had been arranged around her shoulders.

But she had to resist the emotions he stirred in her. She'd get to town, somehow, and get a message out.

~*~

Johan hoisted the full bag over his shoulder. These rabbits would make a fine stew. Mama would be so happy that he had caught so many, especially with another mouth to feed. But he didn't want Suzanne to see what he'd caught in his traps, didn't want to go through yet another explanation.

Somehow, she didn't seem to understand that they owned their woods. Insisted that they couldn't. She couldn't grasp that the copse of trees by the river was their portion of family-owned lands, passed down for generations. He sensed her presence even before Suzanne spoke, the hair on the back of his neck prickling.

Her voice was soft. "I need a favor."

Wiping his hands, he took a deep breath. He avoided looking at her. Mama's cooking and the country air seemed to agree with her. The former angles on her body were now womanly curves.

"What is it?"

"I, uh…for heaven's sake, Johan, why won't you look me in the eye anymore?" She lodged one fist against a newly rounded hip.

His gaze settled there, sensing the flush in his cheeks. Her amber eyes were wet. He hated the sinking feeling he got in the pit of his stomach whenever he saw her distressed. Cupping her face with his hands, he wiped the wetness under her eyes away with his thumbs.

"What is it? *Leibling*, what can I do?"

"I need to go to town." Her words carried away with the breeze.

He clutched his hat to his head. "Tomorrow I go to market. Come with me then. What's so important?"

"There's something I must do." Suzanne adjusted the scarf around her neck, covering the skin exposed by the dip in the neckline. Soft ivory skin.

He took a deep breath before escorting her back to the house. Her words stayed with him through the milking, the plowing, and at night as he helped Suzanne clean up from dinner.

"What do you so desperately want from town?" He knew what he wanted. The blacksmith had promised to let him watch and learn a new technique. He wanted to master this skill and go to the village himself.

"I...need a friend." Her words saddened him.

"You have friends here." That came out wrong. He sounded jealous.

She ran her tongue over her lips, a movement that unsettled him. "Your brother mentioned Greta—I wish to meet her."

"Ja. I'll take you there. And Mama knows?"

She barely nodded, but he decided to take that as an affirmation. He couldn't help feeling that he should be concerned. So he prayed. For the remainder of the day he struggled with the notion of exactly why Suzanne needed a friendship with Greta, the merchant's daughter. And as he settled into bed, across from Nick, he wondered what Greta saw in his brother other than his handsome face. Was that all a woman wanted in a mate? He'd grown up knowing Nick was the handsome brother, not he. But with Suzanne, he felt as though he was more appealing. And something inside him changed.

His eyes seemed to have just closed when the rooster crowed. Must have slept uneasily again. Beneath him, the bed seemed larger, softer than usual.

He spread his legs wide but couldn't feel the edge of the mattress. *It can't be.* But it was. He was in his grandparents' bedroom.

Suzanne's chamber. Opening his eyes, he spotted her, curled into a ball in the chair, a blanket wrapped around her. He must depart before Mama caught him, but he couldn't leave Suzanne in the chair. She'd get a crick in her neck.

Slipping from the bed, he lifted her. Inhaling her sweet fragrance, he placed her yielding body under the covers on the bed as her golden-brown eyes opened.

"Johan…"

He exited as fast as he could, afraid of his wandering thoughts. Ja, he wanted a wife, one that smelled like flowers and felt so good in his arms. But not yet.

10

With Suzanne's soft body pressed against his in the small cart, thoughts of talking with her about his plans flew from Johan's mind. He tugged at his collar. "A little hot today, ja?"

"I think it's cool. Damp, too." She pulled Grandmother's shawl up higher around her smooth neck. "But you look flushed."

When her hand settled on his forehead, he leaned back in the seat, and then breathed in her floral scent. "I'm fine." He enfolded her hand, keeping his reins in the other hand. It felt good, wrapping her small fingers in his own.

Under her cap, Suzanne's cheeks turned pink.

He'd been wrong to do that. He released her hand. "I'm sorry about last night—coming to your room again." He removed his hat, his scalp burning.

Silent, Suzanne stared at the floorboards before they hit a small bump and she grasped the seat. "No harm done. Your parents warned me. I shouldn't let you into the room, but..."

Why did he always have to be different? Sleepwalking, his difficulty learning to read. He sat up straighter. He waited for her to begin her usual chatter, but today she was silent.

The sun warmed the earth as they rode onward. Soon they passed the markers for the village.

They hit a rut and she bounced, but he threw an arm around her shoulders and held her in the seat.

Was she the one? The answer to his prayers? How could someone who mangled the easiest of household tasks make a home for him? He couldn't help chuckling, remembering how her roast was so overcooked it could have been brought into town and given to the shoemaker for leather.

"What are you laughing at? Do I look funny?"

"No, you look fine." She looked pretty in his grandmother's green dress. "Was thinking about something I forgot to bring for Greta."

Her eyes narrowed in suspicion.

He whistled. "I don't think she would have wanted it anyway." Johan maneuvered the horse close to the hitching post, planning to tie it up.

Suzanne grasped his forearm. "Please, I'll go by myself. Don't worry." She gave him a tight smile as he held the horse in check for her to get down from the cart. "Merci!" She picked up her skirts and almost ran.

Why was she in such a hurry?

He slackened the reins and clucked his tongue for the large horse to move on. Before long, he was at the watermill. Johan removed the baskets of new wheat from his cart, running his hands over the varying textures—so different, yet all part of one plant. He toted them into his cousin's mill.

Cousin Phillip turned, his eyes red and his face puffy.

Dropping the containers to the floor, Johan grasped his older cousin's shoulders.

Phillip pushed him away, and then began patting the many pockets in his vest, as if trying to locate a handkerchief.

Johan handed his own cloth to Phillip. "What's wrong?"

"I got terrible news about Aunt Louisa. She's gone, Johan, we got word this morning."

"Gone? Aunt Louisa is dead? How?" His words echoed inside the stone building, along with the dripping of water.

His cousin's worker, the young man at the grindstone, glanced up.

Johan was about to say that he'd just seen her, but since he wasn't supposed to have been in France, he clamped his mouth shut. The large room chilled him with its clinging moisture.

"Don't yell. Your voice is like a cannon booming. Come outside and we'll talk."

"Ja." He kept his voice quieter. Inside his gut, his breakfast strudel seemed to be churning round like grain inside the mill.

"She was found in her cottage."

"When?"

He could barely hear over the grindstone's rumble.

The miller wiped his hands against his apron and motioned to his laborer to continue.

Back out through the entryway, his nose full of the scent of grain, Johan exhaled.

"Stabbed." Phillip placed his hand over his heart. "With a rapier." His cousin cleared his throat.

Two women carried sacks of rye grain inside.

"Come here, Johan." They trod down the grassy bank to the water and sat on two large boulders. "It happened near the time you arrived with the French girl."

"Her name is Suzanne." Could the murderer have been after her? His vest suddenly grew tighter. "Was it robbers?" Ridiculous, since Aunt Louisa owned nothing valuable.

Phillip shifted uneasily. "Cousin Noel said the blade belongs to an aristocrat—the cut was made by something extremely sharp but light."

A nobleman. With reason to find Suzanne. Who would want her that badly that he would take a life of an innocent elderly woman?

He swallowed. "Did Noel find her, did he see anything else?"

"No, the groundskeeper from the estate checked on her. Found her body."

Johan had to find out if Uncle Vincent knew—and if he was safe. And he had to talk with Suzanne. Needed to know why such a thing would happen.

"Your parents want to send Nicholas to the colonies." Phillip narrowed his eyes and gave Johan a hard, cold look, his voice suggesting suspicion. "Why not send that girl with him? What do you really know about her, anyway?"

Johan closed his eyes tightly to block out Phillip's face and held his fists down at his sides. *Patience, Lord, please help me not to beat him to a bloody pulp.* He flexed his fingers and opened his eyes to see Phillip backing away from him, his hands held up, palms facing Johan.

"I'll be back to get our flour later. With Suzanne. Good day, cousin."

~*~

The bell above the door jingled as Suzanne entered the shoemaker's shop.

The young woman inside wiped her hands on her apron.

With a smile so welcoming, Suzanne immediately

wanted to trust her. Magnificent auburn braids encircled her head. Could this be Nicholas's paramour?

"*Guten tag.*" Her deep voice held suppressed laughter.

An older woman, silver hair plaited and wrapped around her head, stood behind her.

Suzanne licked her lips. The scent of new leather reminded her of Guy. Of his many pairs of polished boots ready for use in the army. "Are you Nicholas's intended?"

Greta's already rosy face took on a pinkish glow around her eyes. "I...uh..." She pulled off her white apron and turned toward the woman seated on a tall stool behind the counter. "Mama, might I take a little walk?"

Her mother looked up from her work. "Nicholas tells everyone but us that he will marry Greta."

Suzanne chuckled. "Oui, madame."

When Greta's mother glanced in her direction and frowned, Suzanne regretted that she hadn't used the woman's own language. *Too late.*

The young woman nodded toward the door. "Come. I'll show you where Nicholas and I meet when he comes into town."

"I see." But she didn't. Had Nicholas even bothered courting this girl?

They exited the shop and Suzanne and Greta walked side-by-side toward the village center.

"Tongues are wagging. They say he'll marry you, not me." Greta laughed. "Of course, he's never said one word to me about being his wife. Talks a lot about how he doesn't know how he and Johan could both keep families on their farm." Stopping at the corner, Greta handed a small coin to a girl holding a bucket of tulips and pulled out two flowers, one red and the other yellow, from the assortment.

"Danke." The child grinned up shyly at Greta. Her hazel eyes widened when she surveyed Suzanne's face.

They continued on and Suzanne leaned in toward Greta. "I love another..." She covered her mouth. The words slipped out before she'd considered. How many times had she told Jeanne that she loved Etienne? Greta reminded her of Jeanne. A crawling sensation ascended her neck. She hadn't referred to Etienne just now. She meant Johan. "Nicholas said he plans to marry you soon."

Auburn eyebrows worked together for a moment.

A group of girls walked by, their disapproval of Suzanne evident on their faces.

Greta took a deep breath, her eyebrows raised as though she was deciding whether to share her opinion. "I don't understand Nicholas."

Suzanne patted her shoulder. "It's all right. If you don't feel the same way you should tell him."

"But I do!" Greta wrung her hands. "I don't put up with any of his nonsense and he respects me."

Unusual basis for a marriage. "Do you love him?"

"Of course. Always—since our schoolroom days. He was so smart. So sweet and shy."

Sweet? Shy? Greta's flawed opinion startled her but she'd not express that. Suzanne needed to depart the Palatinate and be on her way. "I won't be here too long with his family. And...I need help."

Greta linked her arm through Suzanne's and they strolled toward a statue of a mounted cavalryman in the village's central plaza. A fountain flowed in the circle beyond it, surrounded by flowers and greenery. Greta stopped. "What kind of help?"

"Can you get a letter out for me?"

A man on the corner, selling sausages on thick crusty buns, offered Suzanne one, and she declined. She was too nervous to eat.

"Perhaps. Where to?"

Suzanne retrieved the missive from her bag. Could she trust this girl? Nicholas said Greta's parents sent packets into France regularly. What would one more letter matter? "To Versailles." She stared boldly into the other girl's green eyes, so reminiscent of Jeanne's. She always thought Guy would marry her best friend. Now it would probably never be. A weight of sadness settled upon her.

Greta's pretty lips parted. "Versailles?" She bowed her head. "I won't ask you why. It would do me no good and could do harm." Greta was both kind and discerning. No wonder Nicholas cared for her. "I'll put it in with the other packets my parents send out."

"Merci, Greta. It's very important to me."

A stout man carrying a stack of leather squares smiled at Greta but averted his eyes from Suzanne.

The pit in her stomach opened up. She was French. The man probably thought of the despised French army. She turned to look at the tanner's back as he continued on. Leather. Boots. Guy. She peered back at the statue of the Palatinate general on horseback. Rochambeau. He would be her next line of attack in her search for her brother.

~*~

"Suzanne?" Now was the perfect time for him to ask while they traveled back. She couldn't escape him.

Seated as far away from him as possible, she

stared off into the distance, a line worked between her eyebrows. "What is it?"

He wanted to tell her about Louisa. Would wait. "Tell me about yourself." *Dear God, was she from the French nobility?*

Her long eyelashes fluttered. "What do you want to know?"

"Who are you really?" She wasn't a Huguenot peasant.

She clutched the front of the bench. A rut bounced her toward him and she grabbed his arm. "Oh!"

"I want to know everything." He wanted to know what it felt like to kiss those pink lips. To tell her he'd protect her. But an aristocrat wouldn't want that. Not from him.

"What did the priest tell you about me?" By the twitch in her cheek, and the way she pursed her lips together, he knew he needed to choose his words carefully.

He sighed. "Father Vincent is my mother's uncle."

She began to work a knot into her apron. He'd have to get firm with her, no matter how good she smelled with those flowers in her hair. No matter how he wished to pull her even closer to him. "Tell me everything."

Sitting up higher, her posture rigid, she gazed beyond the golden wheat fields.

Toward France?

"I am Suzanne Richelieu, my parents were Huguenots. Both are dead. I don't know where my brother is, and I'm supposed to go on to Amsterdam and sail from there to the American colonies."

Heat flared up his neck and he clenched the reins. *"Nein."* He knew his voice was hard, but he needed to know if she was from one of those ancient French noble families. Too good to even love the likes of him. *Love.* He'd allowed himself to think the word.

"Oui, I already told you."

"Don't mock me." He hadn't meant to raise his voice so loud or to cause those bright spots of color to appear on her cheeks. The muscle in her cheek tensed—an indicator that she was about to become silent. He wouldn't allow it. A family member had died and maybe from something she hid.

"Who would kill my Aunt Louisa because of you?"

Her face blanched. Suzanne squeezed his arm hard. "No! She cannot be dead."

"It's true. She was murdered."

"*Mon Dieu,* no." She clung to his arm, a look of horror on her face, and then buried her head against his shoulder, moisture soaking through the cloth.

He let her stay there, even when he sensed her pulling something from her pocket, a string of round hard objects that clicked against his thigh. He spied the blood-red beads, garnets, linked by chain, as she clasped them into her hand and pushed them back into the pocket she wore over her skirt.

Nicholas was right. She was Catholic. *No, not Catholic.* Suzanne didn't seem to have any true faith at all. And that had been troubling him when he'd allowed himself to imagine a life together with her. She bowed her head as though in prayer, she asked questions, but Suzanne didn't seem to know his Lord. And he'd never marry a woman who didn't share his faith.

11

Suzanne repeated her confession so many times, she almost imagined it was she who had killed Johan's Aunt Louisa. And the more she wore her knees out on the oval rug, the more she almost became convinced she was responsible for her family's deaths, too. How, she wasn't sure, but it seemed to have something to do with the LeForts and DeMints. Or perhaps her best friend. No. Jeanne wouldn't have betrayed her—not even if Guillame had spurned Jeanne's interest. She shook off the unwelcome thoughts and finished pinning her hair up. But the vision of the rapier she'd forgotten, piercing the kindly woman's heart, couldn't be chased away.

The Rousch family was taking her to their Lutheran church, where they worshipped publicly. Her breath caught in her throat. Maman and Papa had never had that chance. They worshipped as a family in private, away from the prying eyes of court and of her Grand-mère.

After the short ride to the small church, the two women were helped down from the carriage and entered together. Grand-mère's beads clicked against Grand-père's coins in Suzanne's pocket. Her heart beat in time with them as she walked the short aisle, members gawking at her as she passed. Her rituals no longer soothed her and she was haunted by vague memories of her father's Bible lessons and the peace evidenced in his life.

Maria waved Suzanne toward the end of the pew. No incense burning here, just the scent of damp wool, fresh greenery on the windowsills, and newly hewn wood.

Adam joined them. "Johan made these pews." He smiled and slid his hand along the back of the golden wood.

"Truly?" Pleasant surprise warmed her.

He smiled. "Johan is very talented with his hands."

She eased into the pew, the coarse linen of the skirt scratching her legs. When she got to Aachen, she'd substitute the gown for one left at the statue of the Lady of Aachen. If the story held true—that women left their finery at the feet of the statuary.

Nicholas removed his hat, and then leaned in, his smooth cheek brushing hers. "Did you bring that fine rosary with you today, Suzanne?"

She clutched her handkerchief in her lap. He had to have been in her room. In her things. *Or he's watching me so closely, that…*

He prepared to settle himself on the pew next to her when Johan shoved him aside.

No, please do not let them come to fisticuffs in here. "Sit by Mama. I want Suzanne to sit by me." Johan's loud voice surely carried to the back of the small church.

Her cheeks heated.

"Of course, why not?" Nicholas shrugged. "Suzanne and I can talk later."

Not if I have anything to say about it.

Nicholas moved to the other side of Maria.

"That's better, ja?" Johan bestowed the first smile upon her since learning of his aunt's death.

Suzanne tried to get comfortable on the bench, but

worry made her jittery. The tittering of young girls a row or two back irritated her, and she couldn't relax.

Johan took her hand and began to massage the top of it with his thumb.

She pulled her hand away. "That's not proper."

"Why not?" He genuinely sounded perplexed.

She exhaled. "Not in church. With all these people here." Even as she said it, she recalled how readily she accepted his every embrace. Schmusen, he would call it. He hugged everyone, didn't he? Last week when they'd left town, they couldn't turn a corner without him being greeted by ladies with open arms. And he gathered into his arms every lady who wished a hug. She slid her hand back over to him, hoping no one would see.

His blue eyes, like a fathomless sea, asked permission before he took her hand and placed it between his own. "It's not proper to come into God's sanctuary and fail to worship him, either."

His words stung because they were true. Lately it seemed to her that God was trying to talk to her in her dreams. That He was calling to her. She wadded her handkerchief in her hands. "I...I mourn the loss of your aunt."

They rose to begin singing the hymns.

But all she could think about was Louisa. Dead. Because of her. The culprit might pursue the priest. She had to get to Aachen. To warn Father Vincent. Her stomach lurched—would her message to Jeanne be intercepted? Could she trust her best friend? She shouldn't have sent it. But surely, Jeanne wouldn't have anything to do with something so heinous. Was Pierre so obsessed that he'd kill to learn where she was? Even a monster like him wouldn't risk imprisonment or the defamation of his family should he be discovered. Someone else, but who?

~*~

If Suzanne kept chewing her lip, she might bite it off. And she'd worked her handkerchief into a knot so tight that Johan could have packed it into the end of a musket. He squeezed her hand to get her attention and then tapped his upper teeth against his lower lip several times. Her gnawing stopped.

The pastor's closing words boomed out. "Carry your faith to the new land. Like so many who have gone before you, start a new life. We regret that the parishioners who were to leave within the month will have to wait a little longer. Come up and speak to me after the service, and I'll tell you what I know."

Suzanne's shoulder, hard against his own, stiffened.

Nicholas shifted in the seat on the other side of him, and then craned his neck around to look at Greta.

Johan slapped him on the leg to get him to turn around.

It worked, but Nick elbowed him and leaned in toward him. "Are you going, Brother? Could be your opportunity."

Mama's eyes filled with tears as she gazed at Nicholas. Why did they plan to send their eldest?

Papa, too, dabbed at his eyes with a handkerchief.

Nicholas's arms crossed, his expression smug as he appeared oblivious to his parents' sorrow.

Johan couldn't think about the American colonies right now. Today, he'd have to tell his parents about Aunt Louisa, before anyone gossiped.

After the service, Suzanne followed his family out of the building. His strapping blond cousin and his wife met them outside the church, each of their arms containing their children, while another golden-haired imp ran around them. Little Sarah's unbound hair hung to her waist, unplaited. Such a simple task for a mother to perform, yet she apparently hadn't.

Beside him, Suzanne stiffened and seemed to add several centimeters to her petite height as color drained from her face.

Johan gestured toward his relatives. "Suzanne, this is my cousin Noel and his wife, Elizabeth. And these are their children."

Maria kissed Elizabeth and Noel and each of the children, grasping the oldest as she ran one more circle around them. "Sarah! Behave yourself."

The child smiled at her with a toothy grin. Noel always said Sarah looked very much like Johan.

He heard Suzanne draw in a deep breath as she took Sarah's hand in hers. "You are *belle*—beautiful."

Would he have daughters like little Sarah some day?

~*~

Johan had just gotten up good speed with the carriage horses when his mother called out.

"Pull over here, Johan." Mama hadn't made him come to the ancient graveyard in a long time, and never with Papa and Nicholas. Why stop there?

His father raised his voice above the slowing hoof beats. "Not now, Maria. Please."

"Oui, today. Stop, Johan. It is time."

From the shifting of the carriage, he wondered if

Mama was already getting up.

"Get out, sons," his father gruffly commanded once Johan had secured the horses. Papa had already helped Suzanne down. "You can come with us, too, Suzanne."

She tilted her head nervously and sought him out with her gaze.

He got down and went to her, taking her cool hand in his.

Mama and Papa both frowned.

Nicholas stood by the carriage, pretending to examine it.

"My brother doesn't go in the graveyard," Johan murmured.

His father cleared his throat. "One of you must go with the group."

"I'll go to the colonies and take Suzanne." Johan watched his father's jaw drop down, but he quickly set it again.

His mother began to cry and hurried on to the cemetery.

A wrinkle formed in question between Suzanne's eyebrows.

Johan cleared his throat. "My other brothers are buried there."

Nicholas ambled behind them. "The French soldiers killed them all."

Shock and horror washed over Suzanne's face.

Johan released her hand, and then put his arm around her shoulder, pulling her close to his side. He saw how she looked at Noel's family, at little Sarah. Suzanne wanted her own family, too. And he would help her. They couldn't replace what she had lost, but they could start over. Give her a new life. But he had to be sure she shared his faith.

Her whisper tickled his ear. "Why does your mother wish us to accompany her?"

Johan shrugged. "I don't know."

"I'm going in this time." Nicholas strode past them to join his parents.

Papa began talking to him, but his voice didn't carry over the gentle wind and the sounds of songbirds calling to each other.

They passed through the huge iron gate in the stone fence surrounding the cemetery. An assortment of embellishments on the ironwork—a skull, an angel's face, a rose, and a horse marked this plot as hundreds of years old. Beyond the bars lay rows of headstones.

Papa threw an arm around his oldest son. "Nicholas, we love you, you know."

Mama nodded, lifting her apron to wipe her cheeks, her handkerchief sodden. "You're so like your father. He was the light of my life." Her voice broke. "Our firstborn."

Papa pulled her into his arms and soothed her.

"What do you mean?" When their parents didn't answer, Nicholas turned to Johan. "What are they talking about?"

Johan stepped to a headstone nearby, one he'd always wondered about. He pointed to the name and dates. "This brother of ours—he was over twenty years older than you, Nicholas. And yet he bears your same name."

Nick bent and ran his fingers over the engraving and frowned. "Why did you give me the same name?"

"We didn't," their mother sobbed.

"Our son, Nicholas, was your father." Papa managed the words but went back to rubbing Mama's back.

Why hadn't their parents shared this information with them before?

"You're my grandfather?" Nicholas's mouth hung open. Then he ran from them.

"Mama?" Johan couldn't make sense of what his parents had done.

"You're our eldest and only living son, Johan. I can't let you go."

~*~

Earlier that day, Suzanne had watched the Rouschs and understood.

Johan was his mother's only child remaining, born of her own flesh.

Suzanne couldn't let him leave his parents. How horrible that would be for them.

That night, as she prepared for bed, she tried to imagine traveling without her brother. Without Maman. Without Papa. She must get to Amsterdam and see if Guillame had stopped to claim their travel funds. But she drifted off to sleep with an image of her brother's slumped body atop a King's Guard horse.

"Guy!" Suzanne sat up in the bed, sweat pouring down her neck, her heart pounding from the nightmare. Where was her brother? In her dream, he'd galloped through the streets of Paris, away from her. But it wasn't a dream. He had been outside Paris, with the soldiers.

Her breaths came in short bursts. Moonlight shone through the window, illuminating the dark wood cross on the white stone wall. She was in the grandparents' room of the Palatinate house. She hugged the soft down-filled pillow. With the early morning light streaming through the rectangular window, she could read the words of the simple plaque on the wall: "Bless one another with love this day."

She brought only destruction.

12

Suzanne squirmed beneath the covers. She wouldn't wait for the local group that would depart to the colonies. She'd make her own plans to travel to Aachen. She'd sewn some of the Spanish coins into the hem of the garments she planned to wear and the remainder she kept in the pouch.

Father Vincent could assist her from there.

The door to the stairs opened, and she heard two pairs of feet pad down the narrow staircase. Wood creaked against stone as Johan's parents settled at the table.

Adam's voice carried through the wall. "Your uncle Vincent sent word."

Suzanne's breathing quickened. Easing upon her elbows, she leaned toward the fireplace lest she miss his words.

The priest was alive.

If she remained at their home, she might yet bring them danger.

"Maria, your uncle Vincent was to have sailed the day he wrote the letter."

The priest wouldn't be at Aachen to help her. Suzanne's heart sank.

Silence cloaked the room, save for someone walking overhead—the creaking coming from the brothers' room.

Maria's exhalation could almost be felt on Suzanne's side of the wall. "Why? It makes no sense.

An old man like him. Adam, what was he thinking going to the colonies?"

"He seeks your old friend, the marquise's sister."

Tante Isabelle. She was Grand-mère's only sister and would inherit the title and estates if she could be located. Why would Father Vincent look for Isabelle in the colonies, though? Suzanne wished she could creep out of the room and hear better.

"Non. C'est impossible!"

"I thought he gave up that notion long ago. Maria, I'm sorry. You mustn't blame yourself."

What did Johan's mother have to do with her aunt?

"Only God can free your uncle from the idea that he alone can somehow locate her over the sea."

"God gave Vincent help—he received word from Montreal."

Dear Lord, could she still have family? Was her aunt still alive? Suzanne raised her rosary and kissed Grand-mère's gold crucifix.

"Montreal—where they first went—I wonder if she ever returned there."

"I don't know. He didn't say. Maria, he sent a very odd message, too."

"What was it?"

"Vincent said that he was very sorry. He underlined the word 'sorry' several times, and you know he doesn't ever do that. And, wife, it couldn't be true. He wrote he was truly sorry that Suzanne Richelieu, the girl Johan brought from Louisa's, was gone. Said he would have liked to have known the marquise's granddaughter better, and wasn't it a shame that the illness at the cathedral killed so many in such a short time."

He must be afraid that someone might intercept this missive. Had anyone taken Jeanne's letter? Would someone follow her here?

"Suzanne is the marquise's granddaughter? Isabelle's niece?"

"Apparently. But Father Vincent's letter makes it sound as though she died."

"Oui."

"And as though our son had been to see Louisa."

Maria gasped.

Suzanne took a deep breath, afraid of what she might hear.

"Johan wouldn't have dared."

"I don't know." Adam sighed loudly. His voice went to a lower register. "There's one more thing."

"What?"

"Louisa is dead."

"Dead? Oh, no. I wish we could have seen her again."

A sweet woman. Her life cut short. Because of me. An ache began at Suzanne's temples.

Maria continued, "She helped many faithful ones over the years. Such a dear soul."

Suzanne held her breath waiting for Adam to say she'd been killed.

Instead, she heard nothing. Until something scraped the floor in the bedroom overhead.

"I'll talk with Johan in the morning," Adam said, his tone mild.

"I'd better tell Suzanne. Oh, Adam, I feel terrible about how I have treated her, and she the marquise's granddaughter, friend of family."

Suzanne lay back on the bed. Recalling her father reading the Scriptures, those that advised against eavesdropping on others, guilt gripped her.

Adam coughed. "Johan is falling in love with her."

"She'll not take my only remaining son!" The kindness in her voice only moments earlier vanished.

"Perhaps she loves him, too."

"The marquise's granddaughter married to my son? No."

~*~

A soft rap on the door awoke Suzanne and announced Maria, her arms full of a ruby-colored silk gown, its bodice laced with silver cording with a sheer scarf to wrap around the shoulders.

Suzanne's breath caught in her throat. The ensemble appeared as fine as anything she'd seen at court, although an outdated style. "Madame?"

"I need to talk with you." Maria's downcast eyes avoided hers.

She swallowed, glad she'd overheard the conversation last night. "Oui?"

With the door open, the thunder of Nicholas and Johan's rapid descent down the staircase was almost deafening, echoing as it did from the stone on the entryway floor.

Maria closed the door. "They are loud this morning."

From beyond the bedroom door, a thump against the front door sounded as though one brother shoved the other into it.

Maria exhaled and closed her eyes. The muscles in her face worked much like Maman's did when Suzanne and Guillame had exhausted her patience. "Here." She displayed the gown. "I want you to have this. Very old-fashioned, but I could remake it."

Suzanne touched the fine quality fabric, its tight stitching suggesting the garment may never have been worn. "Whose was this?"

"My friend gave me this gown. Your Tante Isabelle. But I never wore it."

Suzanne's shoulders retracted. Even knowing the relationship between the two families, Maria's words surprised her. "So you know my secret."

"You remind me so much of Isabelle." Maria patted Suzanne's cheeks. "She had courage, like you."

A trait she lacked. Suzanne frowned. Her actions screamed survival, not courage. She clamped her lips tight.

"Sometimes it requires even more courage to stay put. Like Johan must." Maria averted her gaze. "He recognizes the eldest son must care for his elders. We can trust him to provide for us and we'll assist him and his future wife. Someone who shares his hopes and dreams—a young villager, like Johan, accustomed to our ways."

"I see." Part of her longed to argue with Johan's mother, to tell her that they were suited to one another. But it wasn't true. He belonged here with his family and she needed to find her own. And to return to some form of her previous life, not trapped on a farm.

Maria brushed her hand across the silk gown. "Your aunt, Isabelle, departed with my brother, who'd taken his vows. I believe her father intended for her to enter a convent in Montreal. Instead, she went missing from one of the forts and my brother has blamed himself ever since." She stared out the window.

"Maman said they assumed her dead."

"Vincent never gave up hope." Maria shook her

head.

"We should continue to hope. But regardless, my parents had planned for us to go to the English colonies, because of their...our faith."

"My family has always been a friend of your family." Maria laced her broad hand through Suzanne's narrow one.

"Merci, for you kindness to me."

"We want to help you get to the colonies. Nicholas can accompany you. We have many congregants who live near Philadelphia, and I'm sure any would take you both in."

Didn't they know about Greta? What about her? Suzanne sighed. "Oui, madame."

Maybe wearing the fancy clothing would make her feel like her old self. She needed to come to her senses and stop this infatuation. A completely incongruous match disapproved by Johan's mother.

~*~

The afternoon chores completed, Johan went to see what was engrossing the women.

He smelled burned bread as he entered the house and spied Suzanne in the keeping room. He pinched his nostrils and made a face.

Suzanne's cheeks reddened. "I got distracted and burned the loaves. Your mother is scraping them off, out back."

"You try so hard with the baking." He drew close and patted her hand.

Cuts marred the back of her hand on the calloused flesh. She pulled her hand free and rubbed at the crimson spots. When he first met her, she'd worn gloves that prevented her hands from chafing from the reins. The gloves hid white, tender hands unlike any he'd seen.

"It's no use." When she closed her eyelashes like that, the black of them so stark against her pale skin, Suzanne appeared frail, childlike. But with her dark eyes open, flashing at him, he saw the woman.

"What's no use?"

"For one thing, to fix this gown." She pointed to several fancy articles of clothing—completely impractical for the farm. "Where would I wear these?"

Was she asking him if she could stay there in the Palatinate? He took a deep breath and then exhaled. Why had Mama given her the garments? He stroked his chin as he examined her. His cheeks flushed as he spied the straining fabric over her bosom. "You need a new blouse for sure."

"*Excusez-moi?*"

"Too tight." When she blinked at him, he demonstrated, running his own hand across his chest. "Here."

Pink splotches started at the dip in the front of her blouse and spread up into her dark hair, pulled loosely atop her head. "You shouldn't discuss such things with me."

"Why not?" He bit back the desire to tell her that if she grew anymore and did nothing she might burst through the fabric.

"I'm a lady." Her fiery black eyes bore into his.

"I can see." What else could he say? Heat started in his own chest, and he turned away. She was right; he'd been improper to notice such things. But how couldn't he? He noticed everything about her. Enjoyed her wit and her concern for others. She never gave up.

And he wouldn't deny that her outside appealed to him, too. He faced her again, unsure what to do.

Suzanne's face softened. "Don't you want to be a gentleman?"

He wanted many things, but he'd always considered himself a gentleman. "Of course."

She smiled tremulously and rose up on tiptoe to kiss his cheek, her floral scent quickening his senses. "I'm sorry I'm such a trial for you."

Despite his mother's insistence that Nick would be going to the colonies, Johan hadn't given up on his dream—of going there and having land of his own, a big family, a place where he wouldn't have to worry about invasions. He couldn't imagine Suzanne surviving in the Virginia wilderness. Any attraction growing between them needed to stop. He cleared his throat. "I'm glad to help you." *While I can.*

Once he convinced his parents of the rightness of his plans, he'd be leaving, not Nick. In the colonies he'd find a good woman with excellent homemaking skills, who shared his vision.

Until then, he would help this girl any way he could. While he'd miss his mother and father, one brother must go. His parents loved Nick and him equally. Nick was just as much son, although a grandson.

His mother appeared in the doorway and eyed him coldly before addressing Suzanne. "Have you tried on your gown?" The sternness in his mother's voice took him aback, as did the flash of anger she shot in his direction.

"No, madame. I desire a bath before I don the clothing. So I won't soil it."

His mother motioned to him to leave. "Johan, get

more water from the well. Then heat it for a bath. And get the tub. Use the new soap, Suzanne."

~*~

Suzanne slid down into the water, determined to wash the dirt and her worries away. This room of the Rouschs' grandmother had become her oasis, but now her anxiety increased.

What was Maria up to? The woman continued to pour water into the tub. Perhaps Johan's mother believed this might literally throw water on the growing attraction between the two of them.

The warm water and scent of lily of the valley enveloped her. Her rose perfume bottle finally had emptied. She closed her eyes as Maria poured warm water over her hair.

"Let me help you." Maria's nimble fingers worked the soap lather into her thick waves, massaging her scalp and working out the tension there.

"My son may not be able to read and write well, but he possesses skills that will help him survive on this farm."

Did Johan know how to kiss? Her hand flew up to her mouth, as if she had uttered the thought aloud. She reached for the soap and washed her face, breathing in and holding Grand-mère's favorite perfume scent in her lungs.

Maria sighed. "Johan is a kind young man." A decent man.

"Oui, he is."

"Suzanne, you and Nicholas will sail in about a month. I hope you can overlook his…"

Tormenting, aggravating, arrogance? She bit back

those words.

"I'll leave you to your bath. Call out when you are finished." Maria slipped sideways through the door and reclosed it.

After a good soaking and scrubbing, Suzanne rose and dried off with a coarsely woven towel. Soon she stood before Maria in her chemise.

The older woman offered a tight smile. "Let's see if those pieces all fit."

Suzanne had forgotten how laborious dressing in the complete attire of a proper gentlewoman was, even with assistance. Maria laced her stays so tight, Suzanne struggled to breathe. Her benefactor seemed to be planning mischief. "Please loosen them."

"Certainly." She eased them out a bit. "Oh, no, I've forgotten the shoes."

The bedchamber door rattled as the front door was slammed shut. "Mama, I have come to see Suzanne in her dress." Johan's cheerful voice was followed by yet another banging of the door.

"Mama, please, we have chores to do." Nicholas's groan was followed by a *thwack*.

Their mother opened the door. *"Voilà!"* She gestured for Suzanne to move forward but her bare feet remained rooted on the wood floor.

The two young men gaped.

Johan's face paled. His Adam's apple bobbed.

Nicholas stood twisting his hat in his hand, without a glib comment for once.

"I present Mademoiselle Suzanne Richelieu, granddaughter of the marquise. And friend to our family."

~*~

Johan strode out to muck out the stables. Dressed in his shabby work clothes and his boots, he shook his head. Suzanne in the house dressed in her fancy gown and he about to clean out manure. He chuckled, but it sounded wrong in his ears.

"You look as if you've lost your closest friend," Papa called out from the wide door of the barn.

Ja. *I have.*

This new woman. This granddaughter of the marquise who held the vast property near Aunt Louisa's home. Suzanne was completely *verboten* for him. Yet in his heart, he sensed God telling him that his path entwined with hers despite her deficiencies.

"Papa, how did you know Mama was the right woman for you?"

His father's face lit up and he laughed as he handed Johan the pitchfork. "I'm pretty sure it was when she dumped a pan of strudel over my head because I wasn't paying enough attention to her."

Recalling Nicholas and the bucket of milk, he wondered if his mother and Nicholas were more alike than he realized.

"You can't ignore a woman as beautiful as your mother and not pay the price."

Had he paid enough attention to Suzanne? He rarely complimented her. Ja, he was aware of those fine golden eyes that followed him everywhere and of how her fingers twisted into her pretty brown hair when he looked at her too long.

"How did you make up to Mama?"

His father dropped to his knees, his hands clasped together and raised. "Oh, my darling Maria, I am unworthy. Take pity upon your humble servant and favor me with your affections!"

From behind, Johan heard a stifled giggle, joined by another louder laugh.

Mama and Suzanne leaned against each other, hands over their mouths.

He banged the pitchfork against the ground and offered his father a hand up.

Papa brushed off his knees and gave him a broad smile. "That's how it's done, son."

It was no use. The two women scurried to the house.

Stepping into the dark barn, he imagined remaining here rather than Nicholas doing so. A young woman of Suzanne's background would never adjust to such a life as this. He'd have to accept reality. And let her go.

13

She could fly. Inhaling fragrant lily of the valley, Suzanne flew to the middle of the palace at Versailles. A wind whipped through the courtyard, wrapping her burgundy satin dress tightly around her legs, and kept blowing until her loose wrap was pulled into the air. The red ribbon of fabric disappeared into the air, pulled by intangible hands. It floated toward the mountains illuminated over the spikes of St. Marie's. She, too, ascended after the scarf. Her mother and father embraced and waved good-bye.

Beyond the gardens, an army encamped in a field. Guy ran from a tent and called to her, but she couldn't hear him. The battlefield rolled up, as though it were a rug, and was tossed aside by a peasant tilling his fields. Lowering now to the ground, her feet touched on stone. Turning, she spotted Guy in a town square, a statue of Charlemagne behind him.

A warm hand took hers and guided her out of the courtyard. She couldn't see the person who led her, but the hand was familiar, comforting. A ship waited outside the square, a vast ocean surrounding it. The hand was larger now, pressed the lower part of her back, urging her forward. Beyond the ship blue mountains rose from the ocean. Her heartbeat hammered as a voice whispered to her heart that she was going home.

Surely, she would die.

She sat up with a start. Pressing her hand to her

heart, she tried to keep it from beating its way out of her chest. Someone was sitting in the rocking chair. It creaked as the person rose.

"Suzanne." It took her a moment to recognize the owner of the pleasant man's voice, dazed was she by the nightmare.

Johan's tender lips brushed the top of her head. "You're crying again."

"Oui, I had a bad dream." She exhaled and pulled the sheet up to dry her eyes. "Seemed so real."

Was it God who'd whispered directly to her heart, summoning her closer so she would hear Him?

"So many of these nightmares. I hear you in my room. Tonight, I had to come down and watch over you."

"How do you hear me if you sleep?" Her breath caught in her throat. She fought the urge to reach up and wrap her arms around his neck.

"I'm afraid to sleep some nights. Worried I'll sleepwalk." He was so matter of fact. So sincere.

"I'm sorry, Johan."

"Your crying—it's so *herz brechen*." He tapped his broad chest.

Heartbroken. That was what was wrong with her. She swallowed. "I'm sorry to trouble you." But she wasn't really. She wanted him to carry her in his arms even while she was awake. To whisper soothing words to her. She closed her eyes as hot tears tried to wash away that need.

~*~

Johan located the flint and struck it until he procured a spark, then lit the candle and set it on the nearby stand. "When you want to talk, I'll listen."

Instead of his words resulting in a reassuring smile from her, tears streamed down Suzanne's face.

He sat beside her on the bed and wrapped an arm around her. He pulled her close and let her weep, her soft frame trembling against him. *Oh, Lord, don't let her suffer like this.*

She sniffed as the tears ceased falling. Her hands trembled as she placed them on his cheeks.

He froze in place. He'd come to help her. Yes, he'd wanted to kiss her, but he wouldn't.

Suzanne pulled his face toward hers, his lips toward her mouth.

He couldn't do this. It wouldn't be right. She was distressed, fragile, and nothing good could come of this for her. He must leave her room immediately. Johan pulled away, turning his face from hers, but not before he'd seen hurt flicker in her eyes.

It required everything within in him to resist the overpowering desire to cover her sweet mouth with his, to pull her into his arms, to make her forget about the pain in her heart. He took a deep steadying breath and stood over the bed. "I'll pray about these bad dreams of yours," he whispered.

She took his hand in his. "Don't go. I'm sorry. I shouldn't have tried to…"

"Shush, it's all right. Don't worry about anything." He hung his head, not wanting to see the hurt etched on her pretty features. "I'll always think of you and your good first, Suzanne. Know that." He extinguished the briefly lit candle and then departed, closing the door behind him.

He stood outside her room, leaning against the door, his head bowed. *Dear God, make me strong so I can resist her. Help me be the man I told her I am.*

~*~

Another day, another load of laundry to hang. Suzanne laid the clean, wet clothes across the fence rails.

Nicholas joined her, picking up his and Johan's work shirts and handing them to her. He gazed at the blue sky overhead and sighed. "You don't understand my brother. He doesn't live in our realm."

Suzanne raised her eyebrows, surprised he could use a word like *realm*.

The corners of Nicholas's lips curled downward as if in distaste. "Johan dreams of marrying a capable young woman. He believes together they'll produce a dozen perfect children and live a happy life."

Suzanne un-wadded one of Maria's blouses and shook some of the wrinkles out. "What's so terrible about that idea?"

But she couldn't imagine any woman going through that ordeal a dozen times. Her cheeks heated as she contemplated how one conceived those children in the first place. The tender intimacy between a woman and her husband. Yet Johan had refused her offer of a kiss. Every waking minute since then, she'd imagined how Johan's kiss would have felt if he hadn't broken free.

Nicholas smirked. "There'll be no French army to invade Johan's world."

Did he know about Guy, too? Had he intercepted a letter from her brother?

"I cannot stomach him being crushed when his desires are denied."

"What do you mean?" She watched his face closely.

"Suzanne, you must see how he wishes you were his?"

"I don't know that." Suzanne took a shaky breath. Nicholas's words felt like an assault. She wasn't about to tell him that Johan had refused her kiss. She covered her mouth, embarrassed.

Nicholas tipped his chin down, examining her. "Did you know he wants to go to the American colonies?"

She exhaled. "He says God guides him."

"We should all listen to God's guidance, but Johan—he..." Nicholas shook his head. "Johan's dream is to settle in Virginia."

She thought the group was going to Pennsylvania. Virginia? She had a cousin there, near the coast, but she complained bitterly of the prejudice against anyone who wasn't English. "Why there?"

"He's heard there are vast land tracts available for purchase."

"I don't see how. Virginia has been settled by the English for over a hundred years."

"In the backcountry."

She'd heard there was wilderness in Virginia, which the Indians also occupied. She shook her head. He couldn't mean there.

"We have to settle what will be done about this farm."

"Such as?"

"Two families cannot live here. My cousin can barely feed his family on his section."

His parents were sending a lot of food to Noel's family.

Maria and Adam took smaller portion for themselves and moved food from their own plates to their sons'. What Nicholas said seemed true. And troubling.

She hung Nicholas's shirt. "Do you love Greta?"

A muscle in his jaw spasmed. "I intend to ask her to marry me—at the festival."

What about his parents' plan to send him to the colonies?

"If we both stay here..." Nicholas pulled out a pouch that hung from his neck beneath his tunic.

Did he have her money? Patting the heavy cloth pocket that hung beneath her apron, she felt the rosary and three of Grand-père's coins that she'd placed there.

His words were measured, his tone sly. "I may not be the best brother, but I'd never tell Mama and Papa about Johan coming to your room at night."

"Your brother has done nothing wrong." Her cheeks heated. "Since you were supposed to ensure that he remained in the room at night, you'll share any blame."

Aha! His face blanched. She had called his bluff.

When a slow smile crept across his face, her skin crawled. "But Suzanne, didn't you put the chair under the door? Since he didn't come back to bed, I assume you allowed him entry. N'est-ce pas? As the French say."

She spoke between clenched teeth. "I'm leaving soon, and you'll not have me for a pawn in your chess game with Johan."

"I'm the better farmer and have someone to marry here. I'm the elder and by right should receive the better portion of land."

When she didn't reply, he waved his hand

dismissively. "Instead, I'm the one Mama and Papa wish to send to William Penn's land. Their grandson."

"I'm sorry…" She draped one last item from her basket over the fence, then dropped her hands to her side. "Perhaps I'm supposed to accompany you."

14

The rising sun sent strong beams of light through Suzanne's window, waking her. She got up and retrieved her pouch. Nicholas hadn't taken anything. What then, did he have? Did she have enough money to pay someone to transport her all the way to Amsterdam? Counting out the Spanish coins yet again, Suzanne heard wheels rolling over the dirt drive. She pulled the window covering aside to see a fine cart with a bonnet pulling up, a woman at the reins—Greta.

From the barn, beyond, Nicholas hurried to help his sweetheart.

She dropped the curtain back into place and hurriedly dressed. Might there be word of Guy?

Greta, her red hair bunched on her head like a huge bread roll, was out of the cart. Adorned in a bright green skirt with a contrasting red bodice over a white blouse, she appeared radiant as she held aloft a square envelope.

Suzanne lifted her work skirt and ran across the yard.

Lower lip trembling, Greta passed the missive to her. "The letter was addressed to me and Mama..."

Its seal was broken.

"I'm sorry, but it has been opened."

After she removed the letter, Suzanne rapidly scanned Jeanne's scrawling hand. She slid it back into the envelope. "I'm going to take this somewhere and sit down in private."

"We have things to talk about." Nicholas led Greta off toward the house.

Greta called over her shoulder, "Suzanne, I need to talk with you later."

"Oui." She went to the barn. The tomcat paced back and forth in front of her. *He looks just like a royal guard, if he weren't so scruffy.* Settling onto the milking stool, she splayed her legs out in front of her. Light filtered through the open barn door, specks of hay dust floating down. *Lord, if You're here with me, make this news important to my journey. Please, I feel Your hand readying me to move.*

She unfolded the missive.

My dear friend, I'm so glad to finally hear from you. Happy you made it to safety. With great sorrow I must tell you — Guy was killed outside Paris the night you left.

No. Lord, no.

Tears dripped down onto the paper and she pulled back. She settled into her grief, unmoving. One of the young goats nudged her. Hands shaking, she folded the letter and stuffed it into the pocket hanging from a band around her waist. She'd finish it later. *Compose yourself, take a deep breath. Ah, Maman, I can still hear your words in my heart.* Closing her eyes, she placed her head in her hands, and let herself sink into an uneasy repose. *Gone, gone, all gone.*

Rising, she staggered to the barn door and leaned against it before stepping out into the sunlit day. Everything had been taken away, yet the birds still sang. The trills didn't mock her, for the poor birds were unaware of her plight, but those words from Jeanne were like the screams of demons tormenting her. Guy was dead.

Suzanne made her way to Nick and Greta, heads

bent over the baby lambs, frolicking in the grass.

She walked past them to the fields of golden wheat, swaying gently in the wind. She heard a death requiem for her brother with each step. On she went, skirting the edge of the forest, music continuing in her head.

The flowers had no right to give such sweet perfume. The apple orchard flowered with an effusion of delicate pinkish-white blossoms. So gorgeous, almost too beautiful to be real.

Gone. Everyone she held dear.

Not everyone.

A breeze blew over her. Through her. She went to Johan in the field. Tears streamed down her face. She stopped a horse's length ahead of him and stared, unmoving.

Greta and Nick walked behind her, but she took no notice of them.

Greta squeezed Suzanne's shoulder as she navigated around her and explained. "Her brother—dead."

Suzanne placed her head in her hands and sobbed.

Johan took two strides toward her and pulled her into his arms. "I'm so sorry, Suzanne. So sorry, my liebling."

She pulled away a little at his use of this last word but then settled back in, pressing her face against his chest. She shuddered with the intensity of her grief, finally broken loose from its bounds.

"I'll pray for you, meine Liebe."

Johan's love cocooned her and she never wanted to break free. But he couldn't go with her. He needed to stay and care for his parents. Guy wasn't coming for her.

She rubbed her arms. She felt like a canvas scraped clean of its paint. Her new portrait would begin with a wash of Palatinate blue, the color of Johan's eyes. Before she left, she'd do something special for Johan. Leave something to help him remember her. First, she'd stay long enough for Noel's baby's baptism. Then she'd take the boat with those leaving from the Palatinate. Without either of the brothers.

The afternoon passed quickly despite her mulling over and over Johan's words—he'd called her "his love."

She sat in the chair by the window, the chair where she'd slept several nights, looking out the window. Finally, she'd embroidered the last embellishments on Johan's silk vest, cut from the damaged gown she had worn when she escaped from Versailles. That seemed a million years ago.

The door creaked open.

"May I see it?" Maria reached for the vest.

"Oui." Reluctantly she released the garment.

"Magnificent!" Maria stroked the shiny material, one finger touching each starry ring embroidered on the waistcoat.

With every stitch, she'd prayed for Johan, for his future wife, for his children, for blessings and safety. She sensed that a master craftsman stood beside her, overseeing her work. This was supposed to be a special gift. Something to show how much she appreciated his friendship. To protect him, with her prayers sewn into the fabric.

Maria's eyes widened. "Oh my dear—did you make this for…" Her voice caught.

Suzanne dropped the vest into her lap and covered it with her hands.

Johan's mother's facial muscles seemed to be working something out. "Was this for Nicholas? For his wedding?"

"No!" Suzanne covered her mouth. "I didn't…"

Framed in the doorway, Johan's downturned mouth transformed to smug satisfaction. He knew it was for him. Johan cleared his throat. "Nicholas will be very happy to wear this on his wedding day."

"It's not…"

How could he?

"Suzie, he'll love it. I'm so touched that you would put all that effort into such a gift for my brother." The raised eyebrows, the measured words, and the nodding of his head told her what she had to do.

Resentment grew in the pit of her stomach and she closed her eyes. Johan knew it was for him and he was freely giving this gift to his brother. Nicholas wasn't taking anything from him. When she opened her eyes, he was tapping the area over his heart. Ah, yes, he knew.

Maria looked at each of them a long while, the silence hanging like a wet sheet on a damp day. "I see."

Johan closed the door as he and his mother left the room.

Suzanne moved to the edge of the bed. How could this prayerful labor been turned around into a suspect act?

Maria's ensuing silence and her dark eyes did the censuring for her. What had Suzanne been thinking by making such an elaborate piece of clothing for her friend? Such things were only done for people one…loved. *Please, God, if You can hear me, help me.* She'd pray aloud. "I have to leave Johan with his family. It's the right thing to do."

Why did this plan make her cry? Her father's words echoed in her mind. *The right thing is not always the easy thing, my child.* She didn't want to do the right thing. But she would.

~*~

Johan leaned against the wall behind the door, head bowed, wishing he hadn't heard Suzanne's words. He needed to act quickly. Had to confront his parents, make them listen to reason. He would go to the American colonies. Even if only to reunite Suzanne with some of her family there.

~*~

As silent as the mouse that skittered by on the darkened front stoop, Suzanne made her way through the dark velvet night to the barn, intent upon spending time with God's creatures. Since the distressing letter, she'd been comforted by the young animals, petting them and even talking to the little goats and lambs.

Someone stepped out of the shadows.

"Who…"

The man's scabbard bumped against her leg.

She tried to back away but he grabbed her arm. A scream stuck in her throat as the man clamped a hand over her mouth. He smelled of tobacco, horse sweat, and something bitter. His rough clothes scratched her, but his sword marked him as a gentleman.

"Mademoiselle, don't scream. I'm sent by a friend." The sound of her own language should have been a comfort but wasn't. "We've long searched for you. I'll receive a nice reward." He laughed but the sound was gentle, self-deprecating.

Dear Lord, please don't let it be someone sent by Paul DeMint.

"Rochambeau's aide sent a message. I'm the courier." His hold loosened. "If you don't scream, I'll bid you adieu and return to give him your location."

She hesitated. Was he telling the truth? Rochambeau must have felt terribly guilty for Guy's death. She nodded.

The man released her and slipped his hand inside his jacket. He pressed a heavily sealed envelope into her palm. The courier raised his fingers to his lips, whistled, and a fine black horse trotted to him, the saddlery gleaming in the moonlight.

Rochambeau would come for her. But then what? Would he take her back to Grand-mère's? Would Etienne then marry her? *I don't love him. I love another.* Just as she'd told Greta.

Once the messenger gained his saddle, Suzanne released a whoosh of breath, relieved the man had come but also glad he'd departed for the taste of fear overpowered her.

She scrambled toward the house. Movement in Johan's upper window caught her eye. What if he'd seen them? Heart hammering, Suzanne closed the door to her room. Her hands trembled and she couldn't get a spark to light the candle. She wanted to scream in frustration.

Stairs creaked and then the door slowly opened.

"Suzie?" Johan entered, holding a lamp. "Who was out there? Are you all right?"

"Oui, come, sit."

They settled on the bed.

Sitting close, his muscular thigh pressed into hers.

His deep breaths pressed his arm into hers then away. With his lips inches away from hers, awareness of a heaviness building low in her belly caused her hands to shake.

"What's wrong?" Light flickered in Johan's wide eyes.

What should she tell him? The tears started then. She gasped as he pulled her up onto his lap and into a gentle embrace. Sobbing into his neck, she felt his fast pulse beat against her cheek.

Rochambeau would offer to get her safely home to Grand-mère's estate, or he and his wife might take her–especially if he knew of Paul DeMint's treachery. Did she truly want to go back? Dare she defy her mother's request?

"Tell me." He patted her back. His warm hand could stay there forever.

Suzanne rubbed her forehead against the side of his head. He smelled like fresh hay, oiled leather, and his own scent. This was wrong. She'd allowed herself to fall in love with him and would be leaving. Going so far away, she'd never see him again. A new round of sobs broke free.

He squeezed her tighter. "It will be all right, whatever it is. We'll get through this together. You'll see, my little *doeling*."

She sniffed. Had he just called her a baby goat? Suzanne pulled away and wiped her face.

"Read it, Suzie."

He held the candle steady as she tried to decipher the bold handwriting.

Teardrops fell from her face onto the paper bearing her brother's handwriting but signed with their grandfather's two middle names.

Her heart leapt. *Guillame was alive.* He was coming for her. Soon. He would take her on to the colonies. When would he arrive? Tomorrow, at the fair, she'd enjoy her last moments with Johan. This was what she wanted. Why then, did more tears stream down her cheeks?

15

Her packed bag stowed beneath her bed, Suzanne dressed for the village's fair day with heaviness in her heart. What if Guy came to take her today? She went outside

Johan was readying the horse and cart. "Should be an exciting day." Johan wrapped an arm around her and they rode on in silence, Suzanne mulling the letter.

Outside the village's walls, farms encircled the town. Wheat fields extended to a forest line on the Rousch lands. An adjacent field yielded crops and beyond grazed a pasture full of livestock. As they came closer to the village, the scent of roasting pig meat became strong.

The carriage rolled on through the open gates.

Inside the ancient village walls, women in bright dresses clutched the arms of their escorts. Mothers holding children's hands waved at them. Throngs of people lined the walkways. Musicians played nearby, and scents of cinnamon and sausage emanated from each street corner.

Soon Johan had secured the carriage and led her into the plaza. The fountain stuttered in its spray. Elevated on a pedestal was the statue of a German soldier astride a horse, sword held high.

Uniformed French soldiers rode into the square on horseback.

Her heart froze in her chest as Johan stepped in front of her as though he could protect her from them.

She peeked out from around his broad shoulder.

In only moments, a French officer ascended the stairs, his black boots flashing. He stood atop the stage. That gesture—pushing back his hat and then his hair—just like her brother's. His movements, stance, and proud posture were those of Guillame.

She pushed through the crowd. "Excuse me."

"Suzanne, come back!" Fear laced Johan's voice as he barked the order, but she ignored him.

The officer, his jacket dusty from travel, could have been in his early twenties, but the dark circles under his eyes he made him look much older than her brother. An ugly jagged scar ran down one side of his face. His battered nose contrasted with his beautiful lips.

Suzanne pushed through the crowd and past Noel, who gathered his family close.

Little Sarah's eyes grew as big as saucers.

The French soldier's familiar dark eyes locked on her. He stuttered and then looked away before he continued his speech.

Guy. She reached up to her throat as though Grand-mère's jewels would reappear. This couldn't be good. If he'd come only to retrieve her, the soldiers would have stopped at the farm.

Guillame cleared his throat twice; his nervous habit.

Suzanne stood close to him, stared up, and willed her hand not to reach out and touch the soldier she was sure was her brother.

A sheen of moisture glinted in his eyes as he turned to another man immediately behind him. "Make the announcement for me."

The cavalier's eyes darted from Suzanne to Guy

and then back before he announced, "We're under orders to burn this region."

She gasped.

Voices raised in protest as Guy stepped down from the platform and came toward her, clasping her hands. "Suzanne?"

She nodded, swallowed. "Guy," she tried to say, but no sound came out.

"We're here to warn you so that you may make preparations." The Frenchman's voice rang out compassionate but firm.

Johan's cousin, the miller, and his wife, glared at her. Angry eyes of other villagers accused her, and people shook their heads in dismay.

"Come with me; say nothing." Guy grabbed her hand and pulled her through the assembled group and past the people who were streaming toward the square. It was him. Alive. But he brought a message of destruction.

It was her fault what was now happening to these people. "Can't you stop them? Can't you do something?" Pulling on his arm brought nothing but resistance.

They passed through a narrow alleyway. She was aware of the gazes following them, but no one challenged their progress.

Her brother stopped and held her at arm's length. "Let me look at you." Guy smiled, but only half of his mouth rose. "I know I look a mess." There was a little tremor in his voice, and she stepped into his arms.

"Oh, Guy." Suzanne pressed her wet face against the wool of his dusty coat but he pulled away, reaching into his pocket for a handkerchief.

"If you bemoan the loss of my handsome face, I

say only praise be to God I am alive. Rochambeau rescued me and took me to his chateau to recover, claiming I was his aide and that Guillame Richelieu was killed." Guy pressed the soft cloth against her face. "And now I use our grandfather's names."

"What about our plans?"

"If you can get to New York, I'll find you there." He grasped her shoulders.

"Can't you halt this—what the soldiers plan to do? Surely Rochambeau had no part in it."

"*Certainement.* He's gone to rescue Jeanne from those supposed friends of ours who now occupy our grandparents' estate."

"What?"

Guy drew in a deep breath. "Jeanne is with child. Madame DeMint and her son believe Jeanne's baby is mine and will inherit the estate. She fears they intend to do her harm."

Suzanne gasped. Never would she have believed her brother capable of compromising her friend.

He raised one hand. "We have little time to discuss this. But know that Pierre LeFort is no threat to anyone any longer. He died a soldier's death."

Her head began to swim. So was Pierre the baby's father? "Please help these people."

"I am doing something. I'm here warning you. I'd planned to get you within the week and depart with you, but now…" He held his hands open. "The interim commander ordered this cruel attack. I owed you and this family at least a warning, which he allowed. I'll be watched more closely now by my superiors. My plans to go to Montreal will need to be official ones. I'll need Rochambeau to procure an army assignment for me. From there I'll try to get to New York. Make contact with the Huguenot church there once you arrive."

"Guy—don't make me do this alone." Suzanne pressed her face into his chest and clung to him, grabbing his jacket with her fists.

Her brother clasped her shoulders. His voice was strained. "You won't be alone. You've never been alone. Look to God, Suzanne."

~*~

Johan observed as the scarred soldier talked with his Suzie, whose gestures and face expressed a multitude of conflicting emotions. He must be Suzanne's brother. These French soldiers planned to burn their countryside. *Dear Lord, no.* Why now? After all this time. Mama and Papa—it would kill them. Johan reached up and wiped the sweat from his brow. All their harvest, ruined. And him—he was no farmer. What had he been thinking even considering remaining behind? Foolishness.

If anyone could save the farm, could rebuild, it would be Nicholas, not him. But there would be no hope if they destroyed it all. Johan rested his head in his hands. He couldn't manage a prayer. Couldn't think. In such a time as this, he knew the Holy Spirit would intervene for him. And that would have to do. *Why, God? Why?*

"Johan?" Greta slipped her hand through his arm.

Behind her, Nicholas's face was white with fury.

Their wedding—could Greta and Nicholas post their banns with the village reeling under this invasion? He squeezed Greta's fingers. "It will be all right."

She gave him a tremulous smile. "You must come

stay with my family—take shelter in town."

Nick edged closer. "Suzanne cannot stay there. People will be too angry."

Greta tugged on his arm. "Come on. Let's go tell my mother and father and yours, too. They are discussing our wedding plans now. We must warn them."

They wove through the crowd as quickly as they could manage. Some of the inhabitants he'd known all his life glared at Johan as he passed. They finally made it to Greta's home and hurried inside, Nick lowering the wooden bar into place to secure the door.

"Come to the back." Greta waved them on as they ducked through into her home.

They finally stopped at a fine oval table set just outside the kitchen. Chairs, rather than trestle seats, surrounded it.

Papa raised his hand. "We heard the whole thing."

Johan peered down at his father and mother, both seated at Greta's parents' table.

"We've made some decisions, son."

"Yes." His father covered his mother's hand. "Nicholas and Greta will take over the farm."

Johan exhaled in relief. "I'm taking Suzanne from here now. There's no other way."

"Will you marry her?" Mama squeezed Papa's hand.

"Yes, if I need to do that to protect her."

"First you have to find her." Nicholas filled his future in-laws' kitchen doorway, crushing his hat in his hands. "Didn't you see her ride off on that huge black stallion? She may be leaving with the army."

Johan stared at his brother. Suzanne had ridden with him on such a beast, Guillame's, from France.

Papa frowned at him. "Where would she go?"

Nicholas glared at Johan. "Back to France. Probably to the army camp. They can protect her now. She's their problem, not ours."

"She wouldn't go to them." Yet he wondered.

Greta pushed Nick. "Let me past." She placed her hands on her hips.

Mama's face blanched.

Greta frowned. "We must get your animals to safety and remove anything that might burn in the house. Let's bring what we can into town. That's why they built that fortifying wall long ago. Let's make good use of it."

"I'm going after Suzanne." Johan was firm.

Greta took Maria's hands. "My father and other men are assembling to go to your farm and two others outside the village. We can bring the animals into the square or make room in the barn. Trunks can be stacked in the shop."

Tears rolled down Mama's cheeks. "Danke, Greta."

His father stood. "Johan, watch for the other soldiers. More may follow behind this group. One never knows." Papa hugged him tight and then Mama did, too.

Nick clapped him on the shoulder and Johan pulled him into his arms.

"Don't get yourself killed, brother," Nick murmured in his ear.

Would he ever see his family again? Perhaps not in this lifetime. Johan swallowed and tried to shrug off the stone's weight that had settled upon his shoulders.

"God go with you!" Greta called out, and the others repeated the blessing.

Johan strode out in pursuit of his future.

~*~

Clinging to Fury's mane, her head bent low, Suzanne galloped up the road to the farm. She'd leave immediately. Guy explained how to meet the bargeman and where. She'd be on her way to Amsterdam that very day. Clumps of dirt flew up, dirtying her skirt. Fury hadn't been ridden hard and should have no trouble getting her to the river, where Guy would retrieve him.

In her room, she grabbed her valise. Would Johan ever forgive her if his fields and his home were destroyed? He couldn't. She wouldn't forgive herself for not leaving sooner. *I'm a stupid girl.*

Suzanne peered around the room. Thoughts of Johan holding her tight made her shiver. She would never feel those warm arms around her again. Yet he'd never said he loved her. Perhaps he only pitied her.

Guy could promise her nothing. He told her to pray that some Divine intervention would stop this fiasco. He'd do his best to get to New France as quickly as he could.

Pouring out Grand-père's gold and silver pieces onto the bedcover, she counted out one set of coins for Nick and Greta, another for Maria and Adam, and a third for Johan. She tucked her note under the last set. If they were left with nothing, they'd at least have some money to help them.

Fury neighed outside, as though to hurry her. Should she stay and try to help them get their animals to safety? Wiping away a tear and choking back a sob, Suzanne steeled herself for what she must do. She'd get on the horse, get to the river where Guy told her a barge waited, and free these fine people from any encumbrances with her.

Her head ached with sorrow. *Johan—oh, God, bless him with a wife who deserves him. One who will bring him joy.*

Scooping up her tattered bag from the floor, she charged out of the house and across the yard, straight to Fury.

16

Rhine River

"Be good. Wait for Guy." Suzanne patted Fury's forelock.

Early summer air wafted cooler near the river. If only rain would quench the fires that the French army planned to inflict upon Johan's family and their neighbors. If only she were drenched in the cooling waters of God's forgiveness. Although Guy claimed a junior officer's ambitions brought on the disaster, Suzanne feared the torching stemmed from her own mistakes.

A beefy bargeman leaned on a pole by the bank, a family with three small children reclined against each other on a cloth on the nearby grass, eating fruit. Memories of eating *al fresco* in the countryside with her family floated through her mind. Thank God she still had her brother. Part of the rip in her heart had been mended. For now, that would have to be enough.

After paying her passage, she led Fury to a trough by the stable where her brother's horse was to be left. One more goodbye. She stayed with Fury, currying him and talking to him as though he'd tell Guy everything she'd said.

The stable boy brushed his feet through the sandy soil as he approached her. "They'll be leaving soon, miss."

"Merci. Take good care of him." She pressed a coin

into his hand.

After several hours' wait, the group was prepared to depart. The mother in the small family tried to corral her children, who were running in circles around their father. The handful of other travelers gathered in a queue on the bank.

Suzanne dusted her skirt off and bent over to retrieve her bag as a rider rapidly approached the stable. A tall man, whose sea-blue eyes held no reproach, dismounted. "Just in time. Ja?"

How had Johan known where to find her? She didn't care. She wanted only to throw herself into his arms and tell him a million times that she loved him. Instead, she gaped at him.

"I'll be right back." He ducked into the stables.

Johan returned smiling, took her hand, and brought it to his warm lips. "I'll watch over you the best I can. Get you safe to where you're going."

She snatched her hand away and placed it against her cheek. *So he means only to be my protector.* He didn't love her. Johan had never said the words. She sighed. *A duty, a responsibility. That's what I am.* Her hand moved to soothe the sudden ache in her stomach.

Johan searched her face. "All will be fine. You'll see."

"Oui. But first, we must pay your passage." She moistened her lips and led him toward the dock. "How did you find me?"

"I encountered three cavalrymen on my way. I prayed for God to help me." He gave her a cockeyed grin. "Your friend, Rochambeau, he directed me. And I have papers."

After they paid and boarded, she gazed upriver to what lay ahead. Their destinies would part when they reached the New World.

But Johan would guard her transit.

Would that be enough?

~*~

Amsterdam wasn't as Suzanne remembered. Her strongest recollection was of her mother's delight at this port city. Maman had purchased delftware for their apartments at Versailles and artwork and new tiles for Grand-mère's fireplace in the dining room. But Maman was gone.

On impulse, Suzanne pulled Johan into a portrait shop she recognized. "This is where I first became fascinated with painting." She recalled the long hours seated in a chair by the window, the shadowy shapes of the picture taking form over time until at last she could see a picture of herself, captured on the canvas.

"I didn't know you were an artist, Suzie."

Dare she tell him of the painting she'd done of him? No. That would be too humiliating. He'd decided he was her bodyguard. Her protector. Until her brother came for her.

"Mademoiselle, how might I help you?" The proprietor, Monsieur Daan, used to tell her that her eyes were golden like a lioness's. He stared. "Suzanne Richelieu?"

"Oui." She squeezed Johan's hand and felt warm satisfaction flowing through her. Here was a man who'd known her and all her family. Under his tutelage, she'd mastered many aspects of oil painting.

Flipping his hand over, Monsieur Daan exposed paint-streaked palms. "What a strange coincidence! Someone brought me a small portrait recently. I recognized it from the sketches of the young man that you'd completed here in this studio."

He'd given her help with Johan's likeness. But how could it have gotten here?

The proprietor's broad smile made him appear younger. "And the picture had that strange little signature you used."

Heat crept up her neck.

Please don't say it! She shot a look at Johan.

"The tiny lioness chewing up an insect. Wasn't that what you said it was?" Monsieur Daan laughed. "Such a strange sense of humor you had!"

Johan was looking at something over the artist's shoulder. "That looks like me."

The man narrowed his eyes at Johan, examining his face before turning around. He held the small gold-framed portrait out for them to see.

Suzanne tried to find her voice. "How…who?"

"Mademoiselle Richelieu captured your eyes and bone structure well. But otherwise you seem quite altered." The artist rubbed his short, graying beard while studying Johan. "You're a man now, not a youth."

If Guy had the painting brought here, he'd have told her. So either Pierre had done so before he died or possibly Madame DeMint or her son. Cold prickles surged up her spine.

Johan rubbed his beard with the back of his hand. "Perhaps I should shave."

If he did, Johan would be more easily matched to the picture.

"No!" Suzanne shouted and then covered her mouth. "Forgive me, it's just that…who brought you this painting?"

Johan's image had been left at Versailles. Someone deliberately brought the painting to this city. Someone who knew where she'd learned to paint, for the person to select this shop. Her chest squeezed tight.

"You painted me, Suzie? Why?" Johan's eyes had taken on a gleam.

She swallowed her building panic as she addressed the proprietor. "Were they looking for me? Or for the man in this picture?"

"Yes, some men from your grandmother's estate are looking for you." Monsieur Daan raised his eyebrows. "They want to bring you back. Said your godmother was waiting for you. She'd give you shelter. 'Knows you worship in the one true faith' is the phrase they used."

A lie. The DeMints meant to kill her as Guy told her they'd tried to do to Jeanne before Rochambeau rescued her from them.

Johan took her hand in his. "Do you wish to go back there, Suzie?"

Jerking her hand away, she turned to him. "No! You don't understand. They don't want me back there. They're looking to harm me."

"Surely not! Her own son came here to accompany you in safety." The proprietor tucked his chin in stiffly, his white neck cloth brushing his jowls.

"No, monsieur." Suzanne shook her head so hard she became dizzy and sagged against Johan.

The artist pulled up a chair. "Sit down."

Johan lowered her into the high-backed wooden seat. "Did they say where they might be staying? Where to contact them?"

"They're in the Renaissance Inn, and I was to send word to them."

Johan cleared his throat. "What inn is farthest from the one where they stay?"

An hour later, after explaining to Johan about the DeMints, Suzanne dropped into the ladder-back chair inside their room. "Can you get the tickets? It would be better in case Paul DeMint has any of his spies about."

Johan set his small trunk down and locked the whitewashed door. "I'll make a pallet on the floor."

Surveying the tiny room they'd share, she bit back the urge to tell him she was sorry. Sorry about everything. But in her heart, she couldn't have borne it if he'd left her. She grasped his arms and looked up, feeling anything but sorry that he'd come with her.

~*~

After departing the inn the next morning, Suzanne scanned faces in the crowd. Strong scents of West Indies coffee and hot chocolate tempted her from the small coffeehouses lining the street.

Johan squeezed her hand and gave her a tight smile. "This city is a busy place. So many people." He eyed the sweet pastries displayed in the windows. They went inside and purchased two slices of sweet cinnamon bread. Johan produced a battered tin cup and had it filled with *café au lait*, which they shared.

They marched on.

"Very pretty." Johan pointed to the blue and white tiles that surrounded many of the door frames.

Keeping a lookout for anyone suspicious, Suzanne tugged her head scarf lower on her forehead. As they got closer to the docks, seagulls squawked overhead before swooping down to feast on chunks of dark Dutch bread; the refuse of those travelers enjoying a last bite to settle their stomachs before departure.

Her own insides churned like the foam they'd soon witness on the seas. *I'm really doing this. I'm leaving.*

Mothers fussed over their children before charging on down the boardwalks, squeezing tiny hands to keep little ones nearby. *My mother isn't with me.* As remorse welled up in her, Suzanne sniffed and held back tears. Perhaps it was true that God was gracious in taking her mother so quickly and sparing her this journey.

Maman would have been terrified, looking much like the tall woman with the glazed eyes standing next to them. The brunette stared at the ships in the harbor, a daughter next to her, clutching her arm.

In Suzanne's imaginings of this day, her brother stood nearby. She looked up at Johan, the sun's rays illuminating bronze strands in his hair. This wasn't Guillame, but her brother would join her soon. With Jeanne, if all went well.

"Where's our ship, Johan?" Suzanne peered around the teeming wharf as carters pushed past, crates stacked high.

A loudly coughing man bumped into her, and she shuddered.

"The ticket master told me to wait for him by that wooden building down there. Said they verify our passage tickets, and then we board." Johan's voice held hesitation. He regarded the whitewashed structure.

"Looks like a storage shed to me." Boxes were strewn around it and bags randomly piled as though discarded.

His strong hand folded around hers and he drew her toward the building. Once they reached the shed, an elderly woman, the tails of her cap flapping in the breeze wailed, "My belongings—gone!" She covered her face with her hands. White hair escaping from his cap, her husband bent down and opened a battered trunk, its contents gone.

Fear prickled up Suzanne's neck and she pulled free from Johan. "Let me see the tickets you purchased."

Johan pulled the papers from his leather pouch. He looked around the area. "He isn't here."

The older couple approached them. "We've been robbed of our belongings. And we don't see our boat."

A porter with a stack of boxes on a cart stopped. "Oh, no, not that fellow selling fake passages again. I thought they put him in jail. Let me see what you have. Probably more of his forgeries."

Their money was spent on the tickets, with little left.

Suzanne scanned the names painted on the sides of the tall-masted ships. She and Johan needed to be on their way. Sensing threat, Suzanne turned and spotted Paul DeMint examining another man's dagger. Metal glinted in the sunlight as her stomach lurched.

"Johan, come, let's go down closer to the ships." She pulled his head down and kissed his cheek, then held his head there to whisper, "They've found us."

Johan almost dragged her along, and Suzanne struggled to keep pace with his longer strides. They stopped alongside a ship whose crew was loading trunks and checking lines and sails, men scurrying up and down the ladders with ease. A man leaning against a stack of wooden crates, with a pile of papers atop, lifted his quill from his ink pot as he looked them over.

Johan asked about how they could get to the

colonies aboard the vessel.

But their words escaped her. The sailors' noisy activities, the boat creaking against the wharf, and the fishy odors by the water felt as if all her senses were scrubbed with sand.

The Dutchman finally finished. "And so, if you wish to make passage, you must sign to be redeemed in the colonies."

Suzanne swallowed. She, the marquise's granddaughter, become an indentured servant? Offered transportation wherein someone on the other side of the ocean would make her their slave for up to seven years. She had only enough money left for one—not both—of them to get to the colonies. If Paul DeMint didn't have her killed first.

Johan shifted nervously. "But we'd be redeemed, chosen once we arrive. I'd be taught a good trade?"

"Yes."

"And we could pay this off earlier, too, ja?"

The ship's agent hesitated, before he nodded almost imperceptibly. "You could, yes."

Suzanne tugged at Johan's arms. "We must talk."

The lines of the man's hard face softened. "I hate to rush you, but we depart soon."

"I don't see what other choice we have. We'll return in a moment." Johan smiled at the man.

Suzanne stared at Johan. "Must we do this?"

"Come on." He tucked her arm in his and led her to a shady spot beneath a tree at the edge of the wharf.

What other options did she really have, as he said? She couldn't simply run to Guy's army camp. DeMint and his men would attack her and Johan before they ever left the wharf. And she had no time now to get word to Guillame that they sailed for Philadelphia, not

New York, as intended.

"Suzie, I think…"

Behind him, Suzanne spotted several men who were peering up and down the dock. In the center of the trio stood Paul DeMint, his hand resting on a leather sheath over his waistcoat. Her stomach knotted. "Johan, we have to get on that boat." She pulled up Maria's headscarf, tying it tight around her face.

Digging through the bag beside him, he pulled out the wide green-and-red woven cloth, just the thing a peasant woman would wear on her shoulders, and wrapped it around her. Heart racing, she clutched her bag to her chest.

Would DeMint dare to kill her there on the docks?

Johan bent over her. "You saw them?"

"Yes. Johan, I am now your German wife. Do you understand?"

Confusion, fear, and concern, mingled with a drop of hope, flashed across his handsome face as he took her hand and led her toward the ship's gangplank.

17

Finally boarded, Suzanne's stomach lurched more from the stream of passengers than from the boat's movement as it rocked in the water.

A blonde woman, lines marring her otherwise youthful face, elbowed past her and Johan.

"Excuse me," Johan offered, as he removed his hat.

Another passenger shoved past them, glowering at Suzanne.

A heavyset man in filthy clothes pushed by. His stench overpowered her, and Suzanne's hand moved to her mouth as she stifled the impulse to gag. *I cannot sail on this vessel.* "No," she mumbled, but she knew Johan wouldn't hear her over the sounds of the water, the passengers, and the ship's crew shouting.

Surely, this was why Maman and Papa isolated her from the masses, from the peasants and the villagers and the people who populated the cities. Her stomach clenched. She wouldn't let herself be sick in front of all of these people. "It's so hot," she told Johan.

He only nodded.

Fishing in the pocket hanging under her apron, she clasped the beads. She needed her rosary. *Not mine*—Grand-mère's.

More passengers crowded in.

A youth hacked as he joined the queue that streamed past. He covered his mouth with a dusty cloth.

Nausea from the body odor of the passengers and

the stench of rotten fish threatened to overwhelm her. Suzanne turned away.

How could Johan smile? *What have we done?* There must be some other way. She'd get off the ship now. Go back to France. Hide somewhere in Amsterdam until Paul DeMint had left. Contact someone else at Versailles and make her Catholic faith her salvation. Tell them that she worshiped as her grandmother had and not in her parents' Huguenot faith. Then she could return to Grand-mère's estate or stay at Versailles.

Your grandmother's faith was her own.

Suzanne heard the words in her heart almost as though someone had spoken them aloud. She turned around.

Johan's eyes were closed. He seemed to be praying.

The sounds of the port were drowned out by the sound of her heartbeat in her ears. She had just enough funds to take her back to France. But what of Johan? She squeezed his hand. She needed to hold Grand-mère's cool beads in her hands, needed Grand-mère's faith.

You need your own faith. This you cannot borrow.

Shivers coursed up and down her arms and she rubbed them. "No! Don't say that."

"What is it, Suzie?" Johan rested his chin on top of her head.

"I can't do this. We have to get off." She could not breathe in this place.

Johan squinted at her. "What?"

She opened her mouth wide and yelled, "I must get off this ship!"

Bewilderment clouded his eyes.

A swarthy deck hand passed behind Johan, his

crooked mouth amused, as if he'd seen this before.

She grabbed Johan's hand. "We have to get off. I can't do this." Hot tears streamed down her face. These horrible people, this awful place, this would surely kill her. God was punishing her for all she'd done. For her failure to seek Him out. For her borrowing a faith that she didn't truly know. *I will seek you, Lord, only let me off of here.* She just needed her freedom.

My freedom will be yours for the taking. Wait. Seek. Believe.

"My father died for his beliefs!" she shrieked at Johan. "I have lost everything. Everything, because of Papa's precious beliefs!"

"Ja, I know. I'm sorry." Johan wrapped his arms around her, his warmth dispelling the chill that overtook her.

Images of her father and her mother flowed through her memory and overwhelmed her. Death was everywhere. She felt it as surely as she knew that dread no longer shadowed her. He'd been replaced by the certainty that death waited on the open sea, arms waiting to swallow her up, just as it had in her nightmares. She trembled as Johan released her. "I won't survive this trip."

"You can't know that, Suzanne. Only God knows such things." Johan rubbed her hands between his own and led her to a trunk to sit.

"Haul up that gangplank!" a crewman bellowed.

Dear Lord, no. This was it, then. Would God have her die here, with strangers, on this awful ship?

~*~

"Sleep, meine liebe." Johan pressed a cool kiss

against her brow.

But if she closed her eyes, still there would be the soul-sucking despair she'd experienced when she was awake. "How many days now, Johan?" Her voice emerged as a croak. How long had they been underway, stuck in this hole? The darkness in the belly of the ship embodied an image of Hades, a creaking groaning vessel housing a miserable mass of humanity. Suzanne took short, shallow breaths, not wanting to inhale the fetid air around her.

Babies and children cried out all hours of the day, many sick with fever.

"We're underway for over a week now. Close your eyes and rest." Johan's voice seemed far away, although he touched her hand.

Sometimes those on board appeared to swirl around her, calling out for her to bring them comfort. What relief did they have? None.

Lately, when Johan fed her the thin gruel that passed for food, she'd pressed her lips tight, but he'd coaxed her to open them.

The man behind him, the one with the glow about his head, the shepherd, also nodded as though she must partake of the horrid paste she was fed.

She sank into a deep sleep filled with unearthly noises. Sometimes she woke.

The shepherd kept calling for his little goats to follow him—why did he call for goats and not sheep? And why did he now keep reaching his crook out to her?

When she remained awake, tossing and turning, Johan no longer knelt and prayed.

When he crawled into his bunk, she tried to rise.

"No, Suzanne, don't worry about me."

"I have to secure you." She rolled over and slowly pushed to her feet. "You can't sleepwalk on the ship."

She stood and he rolled over to face her, grabbing her hands when she began to slump. Dizzy. So weak. "Hand me the rope."

"I can tie it myself, love. Lie back down."

"Oui." She sank to the floor. She'd kneel and begin her prayers. Always they were the same. *God, help me, help me.* Perhaps she wouldn't die. Perhaps she'd only lose her mind. She crawled into her bunk. Suzanne tried to open her eyes as someone continuously called her name. Cool beads were pressed into her hand. Grand-mère's rosary.

"Mein liebe, if this brings you comfort, please hold it."

"Nothing." She rasped. Nothing brought peace. She threw the rosary at him.

The shepherd didn't like that.

She could tell by the way he slowly shook his head.

~*~

Johan gently wiped Suzie's brow. She thrashed in the narrow wooden bunk, but her eyes often remained open. He closed his eyes, longing for the fresh breeze he could take in up on deck. If he didn't get his beloved out of the belly of this vessel, he feared she might not regain her own will again. Day after day, he'd seen her slip into a place where even he couldn't reach her.

"You have to get up. The sea is calm." Johan tried to use a gentle voice, but there was no reaction on Suzanne's gaunt face. "They'll let us get fresh air.

We're the last ones down here." Finally, he hauled her up himself, her body molding to his own. A few weeks earlier, it would have brought him pleasure to have her cling to him; instead terror gripped him. She was so light, he feared a good ocean breeze could carry her away. He stood, arranged her in his arms, and then mounted each step on the ladder slowly, readjusting her body so they didn't hit the sides of the hatch.

"Don't let them," she moaned as he slid her off his shoulder, resting her against his chest as he grabbed a rope and braced his knees for the gentle rocking of the boat.

In the stern, the crew slid a body from a board into the ocean.

He turned Suzanne slightly so that she wouldn't see. He cringed. *How dare they do that while all these women and children are up on the main deck?* The next time the captain pressed him into duty, he would discuss the crew's insensitivity with him.

Johan leaned his head against Suzanne's, his arms clasped around her small waist. He would keep her there always with him, if he could. Didn't she know how much he loved her? Needed her. Imagined no future without her beside him.

Shuddering in his arms, Suzanne's wild eyes darted over his face. "Please, don't… let them… throw me over."

So she'd seen them. He'd finally gotten his love up above, and those *Dummköpfen* had to throw bodies in the sea. "No, my love." He pulled her closer.

Suzanne shook with sobs, but no tears flowed. "Don't let me die here."

Johan couldn't speak. He kissed her head.

Two men had lost their wives so far, three children

had been thrown into the deep, and the minister had unceremoniously been tossed into the water after his death last week. His widow hadn't spoken one word since, but sat rocking their two-year-old son all day in her bunk.

All who'd perished evidenced the same symptoms—high fever, dry hacking cough, and inability to retain anything but small amounts of fluid. Like Suzanne.

Even as these facts ran through Johan's mind, he refused to accept them. She would live. "God convicted me that we'll be together in the new land."

Had He said that?

Truly, he wished it with all his heart. But God had stopped answering his prayers—the ones that kept the French soldiers out of his homeland. A ball of *spaetzle* dough settled in his stomach. God no longer cared what Johan wanted.

But she wasn't listening. Suzanne sank into his arms, her eyes rolling back in her head.

18

His beloved drifted between the realms of heaven and earth, rousing and talking briefly before lapsing back into unconsciousness again. Suzanne's last words, over two days earlier, still speared his heart. "Could you really see a life together with me—a Catholic Frenchwoman? Someone whose brother brought an army to your village and burned your parents' fields?"

He hadn't yet asked her to marry him—nor told her how much he loved her. He should have but feared she'd make another excuse as to why she wouldn't marry him, a peasant with nothing to offer an aristocrat brought up at the French court. He couldn't answer her then, but he could now. His two days of sweat had nothing to do with a fever, but sprang from the unrelenting fear that he'd lose her.

Johan stroked Suzanne's hair, loose and wet, spread out on the pillow around her as though she lay in a river. He recalled the sun glinting on her hair as the barge took them upriver to Amsterdam. Easing into her bunk, he lay down next to her. *Dear God, forgive me for withholding words of love, of acceptance, and grace, when she needed to hear them most.*

The continual rocking and creaking of the ship lulled him into a stupor, and Johan forced his eyes open. *Oh, God, please spare her. Take me if You must, not her.*

His mind succumbed and Johan fell asleep, his arms stretched across Suzanne's body, his head resting on her torso.

"*Je vois*," she called out, the sound echoing through her body.

Johan jerked awake, lifted his head from her form. He would try to speak in French for her sake.

"What do you see?" He rubbed her hands, still cold despite the fever that raged in her.

She sighed and smiled. "They're waiting for me. It's time."

A chill passed through him. He wouldn't ask who waited. He tried to swallow, but it was as though his mouth was filled with spicy *pfeffernüsse* cookies that hadn't been dipped in strong coffee to soften them.

"Tell them they must wait, Suzie, tell them you're not ready." Johan raised the ceramic water jug to Suzanne's mouth.

She locked her lips against the intrusion and shook her head, but finally she relented, gulping down the liquid. He lifted her and held her with the water near her lips. She continued to drink. How he wished he hadn't fallen asleep. Each moment with her was precious.

When she finished, Johan gently laid her back on the mound of clothing piled into pillows.

"Johan?" Her lips were as pale as her face.

"Yes?" Wiping perspiration from her smooth brow, he allowed his fingers to linger a moment on her hot skin. This fever had to break soon.

"Can you help me roll over on my side?" Tremors caused the pale, blue muslin dress to move over her thin frame.

Johan hesitated. A few days earlier, she'd asked him to never place her in that position.

Suzanne had spent so many days leaning over a

bucket on her side, that she wished anything other than that. And the fact that the Englishwoman bunked on that side had full view of her plight, seemed too much for his Suzie to bear.

"Away?" he asked. Away from him, her back to him—was she trying to leave, or would it be more comfortable for her now?

Johan rubbed his hand across his head. Despair crept over him and settled heavy, made a home. His love, his very heart, was so weak she couldn't even roll over. He reached under Suzanne's back and rolled her onto her side, then pulled her legs up, bent, before lifting her head and positioning her arms. Locating her rosewater-soaked handkerchief, he placed it gently in her hands, her fingers closing around his, his cheek pressed against hers.

She whispered into his ear. "*Je t'aime.*"

A lump formed in his throat. Rightness of purpose blanketed him even while hot tears soaked his beard. Nearby, someone began a death rattle. Another whom the ocean would claim. *Not my Suzanne, though, not her, dear God.*

"I love you always." Johan's voice cracked.

~*~

Cool, fresh air blasted down into the hold. Johan squinted at the light coming through the open hatch. Never in his life had he endured such conditions. And sadly some couldn't survive the close quarters where disease jumped from one to another quicker than a hare being chased through the woods.

"I need help with the bodies," the boatswain's mate called down into the hold. "My crew is sick from your infernal diseases. Send me up three strong men to assist. This calm is our chance. Once we've dumped them overboard, you can all come up for a whiff of sea air."

Johan hesitated. He wished he could help above deck. Suzanne's skin glowed with an unearthly pallor. What should he do? She couldn't die like this. No family here. He knew how important that was to her. He wished to give her the gift of family—for them to be joined in life even if for only a brief time. *Pray God, let her survive. If she does, I'll trust you to make her ready for the life you would give us together.* Something urged his soul in a way he couldn't understand to form a union as man and wife so that she would draw from his strength. The two would be one, and she would benefit from God's blessing of their love. If she knew she wasn't without family, would it give her new hope?

A firm hand gripped his shoulder. "Monsieur?"

The ship canted and Johan caught hold of the man as he stumbled.

Suzanne muttered something that Johan couldn't understand. He bent over her and strained to hear her over the sounds of men clambering up the wooden stairs to the deck. Nothing.

Nearby, babies cried and the newly ill groaned.

"Monsieur, with your permission, may I give your wife her Last Rites?" The man's voice was deep. "I'm a priest."

Dying, leaving him? Johan recoiled as though the man had punched him low in his belly.

The man's clothing smelled foul, as did everyone else's. Dark, dirty hair and an unwashed, unshaven face—the man didn't look like a priest, wore no collar.

Perhaps he wouldn't amongst these Protestants.

If a stranger could see the end coming, a man of God...her faith, which she desperately tried to hide from him, was of no consequence now. He nodded. "But we aren't married."

"She called you her husband just now."

Johan shrugged his shoulders. "If it were possible, I would be her husband before..."

"*Je connais*, I understand." The man was a good head shorter than Johan, with a fringe of black hair and dark eyes that darted about. "I could marry you and this woman, if you wish."

Johan stared at him. There was only one minister on this ship. Johan took several short breaths.

The Frenchman leaned over and murmured in his ear. "Will you promise to keep my secret?"

"Ja."

~*~

Music swirled around her, beautiful angelic voices singing a Latin Mass. She was being given the Last Rites. The words enveloped Suzanne, lifted her, and the majesty of it humbled her. Shivers of pleasure and anticipation coursed through her body. Light as a feather, a sheer silver gown shimmered around her. She marveled that the exquisite garment possessed no seams.

A red velvet tapestry runner dropped from the brilliant blue sky and unfurled, extending before her.

"Come!" a distant voice commanded.

Her bare feet reveled in the plush velvet as it set down on a hard surface, a long aisle. Against the red carpet, her feet glowed as finest ivory. Incense wafted around her, drifting under benches that materialized around her and from the mouths of the winged people in the golden balconies above. Friends and relatives appeared on the long pews. Overhead the angel Gabriel's stained-glass image pulsed with light. Her wedding commenced in the cathedral.

The church buzzed, as though a living being.

The groom turned toward her. Etienne stood tall, a dark blue waistcoat expertly tailored for his athletic body. He unsheathed his *épée* sword and flung it toward a shadow behind him. As soon as the weapon pierced the dark form, a beautiful prayer came forth in song from the image. Transfixed, Suzanne allowed the beatific music to wrap around her. It called her toward the shadow person, but an unseen arm jerked her away.

Etienne shook his head and gestured toward himself. He intended to marry her. But his clothing didn't match her dress at all.

Winged creatures, such as she had never seen, minuscule but brilliantly colored, buzzed past her, spoke to her soul that her mate's apparel bore no consequence.

Etienne turned his back to her. Her annoyance was shushed away by the creatures.

She surveyed the pews.

A beautiful white-haired woman clothed in a simple white robe smiled at her. *Oh, Grand-mère, I have missed you so!* She longed to run to her, but Grand-mère lifted one gloved finger and pointed toward her groom.

The shadow man sang a new song, more thrilling than the last. His voice climbed one octave in an unearthly aria.

Etienne vanished, replaced by another.

Her betrothed, tall with golden hair, opened his arms.

Suzanne froze in her steps, looked back to Grand-mère, who disappeared, replaced by her mother. Maman's face was serious, not the happy face of the mother of the bride.

Where was Guillame? He would advise her about the new groom. She sought him out, but couldn't find her brother.

Grand-père smiled at her, joy in his eyes.

Tante Helene waved to her and put an arm around a young girl by her side--Suzanne's cousin, but she should be Suzanne's age now, if...if she had lived.

"Suzanne!" the priest called to her. With a young face and a fringe of dark hair on his head, he wasn't from the cathedral at all. Searching the dais, she saw only this man's dark eyes hovering in front of her, then over her.

The voices sang, urged her toward the altar. She shook, her skin chilled to the bone, as one end of the cathedral opened, revealing a turbulent ocean. Brisk salty air blew her memories, her family, her loved ones away, to the heavens, even as whispers of their love, their encouragement pushed her on.

"Choose!" the unseen voice commanded her. Everything within her wanted to draw closer to her Master, to join Him. She raised her arms to Him. "I accept you."

"No, stay with me!" a man's voice cried at the same time that her own soul radiated a rainbow of colors, ready to join the one she chose as her Lord. The voice belonged to the earthly being she most loved.

With her next choice, the invisible string broke.

She turned to join the half of her she hadn't yet acknowledged.

A thick silver cloak, a happy match for her gown, dropped onto her future husband.

"I am Father François." The man of God took her hands in his and directed her to the altar, his words alien, yet familiar. And she couldn't for the life of her grasp their meaning—only knew they were words of utter truth, deep things, meant for her good.

She and the priest moved forward, closer to her awaiting groom. Suzanne looked back at open space and water, an ocean of empty waves that didn't hold her—their grave no longer waiting to claim her. "Yes," she responded. When the choir echoed her, prompted her, she again called out "Yes, I will. Yes, oh yes!"

Flying, they joined arms around one another's waists. Cool, gusty breezes lifted them over the ocean. She and her groom laughed and kissed. They landed on a high mountaintop, blue haze all around them. Hands grasped tight, they gazed down into a deep valley and saw houses everywhere, curls of smoke rising from chimneys, sheep grazing on hillsides, crops growing in fields.

Johan identified all the people who lived in those houses, a dozen in all. Strange that he called them only by their first names and acted as though she knew who they were.

Then Suzanne slipped and fell off the mountain, far into the abyss of blackness, into the unknown space that waited. The sea would no longer claim her and she slept for the first time in many days, with a clear, sweet, peaceful sleep. And despair vanished.

~*~

Where was she? Suzanne lay atop something hard and the air smelled worse than her grandmother's stables. And the building swayed as though in a gale.

A man's deep voice rumbled nearby. "She may never be the same. You need to prepare yourself for the worst. Alive, yes, but who can say what kind of life she might have after this?"

Her head throbbed as though the top might come off. Had someone knocked her unconscious when she'd tried to escape the DeMints' stables? Maman, was she still with her? Was she yet alive? She had to get up and check on her.

Someone rocked her in a slow steady rhythm—no, it was a boat.

Amsterdam, yes, perhaps they'd made it there after all. How? It hurt to try to think about anything. Perhaps her brother had taken them there.

German voices chattered around her. What in the world? She strained to understand them. Someone was praying next to her bed, in French. Sliding her hand down, she grasped the man's hands, so small compared to the other man's. He continued his prayers, her palm pressed between his.

Where is Maman?

~*~

The dark-eyed man was so serious, so sincere in addressing Johan. "Monsieur, what you did, it was right. Someone will need to care for her when we arrive."

Johan had never told him that he wasn't Catholic.

Did it matter? He wasn't sure. But he did need to care for Suzanne. And he'd have to get someone, a woman, to help him with her.

"Where's Maman?" Suzanne's golden eyes opened and she stared up at the priest.

What was wrong with her? She kept asking for her mother, yet Suzanne had told him she was dead. Did she no longer remember what had happened?

Johan's heart seemed stuck in his throat.

"Don't worry about that, madame. You just rest. Get well."

But her eyes had already shut again.

"What will they do about her contract?"

"Surely someone who paid for transportation will accept her instead."

Johan wondered. He'd been told that some, like he and Suzanne, would have people bidding on them—like animals at a fair.

What would she do when she awoke and found some strange man bidding on her contract, which must be paid? And what kind of man would redeem the passage of a half-dead woman? Who in their right mind would pay for a servant who might never fully recover? How could her contract even be redeemed? Some wicked men enjoyed having mastery over weaker people. How could he prevent his beloved from ending up with such a man?

19

Port of Philadelphia

Above board, the ship at anchor, Johan settled Suzanne in his arms. "It'll be all right. You'll see." *If you'll just wake up again.*

The boat rocked and then jerked as it strained against the anchor.

"I've got your belongings, Johan," Phillip, a fellow Palatinater, called out as he pushed past them with the stream of passengers being lowered from the ship. "This could take a while. Do you want me to hold her for a bit?"

Johan shook his head. Phillip was a good fellow, but... "I'm strong as an ox, maybe two, and she's light." Those were braggart's words, not his own. Sweat broke out on his forehead. What had this trip done to him?

Phillip flexed his arm muscles. "The work up on deck has strengthened us."

"And made us browner." Both were dark as well-tanned leather.

Phillip, who, like Johan, was half French, smiled, his white teeth a crescent against his sun-darkened skin. "You should see yourself—you have yellow in your hair now."

"I'm glad we could help the crew, Phillip."

"Too many dead." His friend looked at Johan before placing a fingertip on Suzanne's cheek. "Not this one, though. God spared her."

"Ja." Johan swallowed and pinched his lips together, afraid his voice would tremble. But would she ever be the same again? The port doctor would examine her after they arrived. Sailors warned him she might be placed in a public hospital. His gut clenched. *Never—I'll never let anyone take her from me.*

Preparations surged into action for their imminent arrival, sending energy through the new arrivals. His fellow passengers toted their meager belongings above board. The calm Delaware River glimmered as the long queue of passengers began to disembark.

Johan shifted Suzanne's head, her sable hair cascading in a waterfall over his arm as he took tentative steps onto the wharf. His legs wobbled and almost gave out, but he righted himself.

A paunchy man wagged a finger in the captain's face. "How will I make any profit if you can't keep them alive?"

Beneath almost transparent eyelids, Suzanne's eyes moved as though she were trying to rouse herself. The sun's merciless rays beat down on them. With no hat to protect her face, the midday sun threatened to burn her ivory skin. Although her periods of consciousness had increased, she still mostly slept.

Was the captain right—no one would bid on a servant so ill? Or was his first mate correct, saying, "there'll always be a gambler amongst those who redeem the contracts"?

Seagulls taunted them, diving so close he feared one might peck Suzanne. Along the riverbanks, this city appeared so new, different, and busy—with carters and merchants bustling around.

A crowd of men gathered, some checking their

timepieces.

From the group, a young man emerged and strode in their direction. Although a little bowlegged, he rapidly progressed toward them, square buckles gleaming on his black shoes—both needing a little polish. A few years older than Nick, he possessed a face the ladies would like and stood a few inches shorter than Johan. Hair the color of wet sand queued sharply into a thick tail beneath his tri-cornered hat.

When almost to the captain and the ship's owner, the man halted by Johan. Hazel eyes widened as he appraised Suzanne. "Where's her son?"

Grateful that he'd listened intently to the English lessons aboard ship, Johan shook his head. "No son." When he pressed a hand against her cheek, Johan swiveled away. No matter how gentle the stranger's touch, this was Johan's wife.

The captain hurried over. "What are you doing, Scott?"

Other men approached their group, some even squeezing the men and women's arms.

Johan lifted Suzanne's head and rested it on his shoulder. No one was going to touch her. He'd hit them first. But what then of him? The stocks? A lashing? What good would that do her?

Scott's frown deepened. "I think this man has Christy's wife."

The captain shoved his hat back on his balding pate. "Don't you think I'd have recognized the colonel's woman if she was aboard my own ship?"

"Given that you've dragged other women to the Indies and back, I wouldn't doubt it at all, sir." Scott raised an ebony walking stick skyward, his irritation growing.

The captain's eyes blazed.

Would Scott pummel the captain? He certainly looked as if he had a good fight in him.

Johan pinned his gaze on the agitated young man. "Her name is Suzanne Richelieu." No, it was Rousch. She shared his name now. Guilt gnawed at him—what if she didn't remember? What if she refused to be his frau?

Other men strode in their direction. Johan must find someone who would let him work off both contracts. "Mister Scott, do you need a strong man to work? I'll do extra if you'd let me pay for..." He hesitated. The words, my wife, stuck in his throat. "Suzanne's transport as well."

The young man's face fell. "Christy might have scalped the captain, but he'd have been relieved to find his wife."

Scalped? Johan associated this English word with the savages.

The captain took Scott's elbow and led him away, the two of them arguing in English, something about just what it was that Christy did have need of. A gentle breeze wafted the scents of bread baking, fish frying, and the delicate aroma of strawberries. Johan's stomach rumbled. Sometime soon, he required nourishment, and he must get some food into Suzanne when she awoke.

A man of middling years with a pleasant, round face, dressed in Dutch clothing, approached Johan, eyeing him critically. "I'm the agent for Vann's Blacksmith and Carriage Shoppe. Do you understand?"

"Ja."

"Good. We've need of two strong men."

His evaluation made Johan feel like a draft horse at auction, and his gut clenched as he held his Suzie tighter. The man's questions were rattled off so fast he had to think for a moment. "Ja, I know some blacksmithing. A little about wheelwright work but not much. I can work hard. Enough for two, even." He glanced meaningfully at Suzanne.

The merchant frowned at this last comment, stroking his pointed beard. "Let me see what I'm able to do." He turned around and strode back, seeking out the bursar.

Johan exhaled. Perhaps this would be his new master.

A deck hand shoved a trunk down behind Johan and indicated for him to sit with Suzanne. He lowered himself onto the hard wood, the raised leather straps chafing against the back of his legs.

"Danke."

His wife groaned and rubbed her soft cheek against his own.

Closing his eyes, he tried to block out the sense of being in a market where instead of animals or produce, the human cargo was being examined and purchased. On the way to this new country, he hadn't imagined this process to be so demeaning.

Blessedly the clouds now covered the sun, and he focused on the sounds of the waves lapping against the wooden wharf in time with his beloved's gentle breathing. He still felt as though he were moving and rocking. And Suzanne, when would she awake?

When he opened his eyes, a gentleman dressed in fine attire was pointing at them, asking the ship's owner something. Aware of his own dirty and rumpled clothing, which was of an inferior quality to begin with, Johan was suddenly ashamed. How could he have thought he was worthy of Suzanne? When she revived and realized her folly, would she forever rue that she hadn't married a man like the one before him now? Everything about the merchant bespoke of affluence, from the gold cravat at his throat to the ornate silver buckles on his shoes.

The captain returned and stopped beside them. "It's been arranged for you. Report to Vann's Carriage shop in three days. He puts his new workers up at the inn at the end of the dock, and there'll be a room and three meals a day there."

But this beautiful woman he held in his arms? This lady from a noble family—to be a servant to such a man. To be bought. He shuddered that he might not have been able to care for his own wife, that she could have been purchased at a reduced price because of her sickness. Such couldn't be God's will.

~*~

Vann's Blacksmith & Carriage Makers Shoppe

Johan descended the inn's narrow stairs with ease now that he'd rediscovered his land legs. Scents of vanilla, strong coffee, and cinnamon greeted him at the bottom of the staircase in front of the proprietor's desk.

"Good morning to ye." Polly, the innkeeper's wife, held out a trio of cakes atop a pewter plate.

Johan plucked one covered with sugar. "Danke."

"Nay, they're fer ye. Take 'em all." She jiggled the plate. "Vann won't be callin' me stingy."

"Thank you."

"Sit yerself over at that round table, and I'll pour

ye some coffee afore ye head out."

Johan tried to fit his legs under the table but finally turned sideways so that he could stretch them out. He didn't want to break the furniture.

"Yer master is good, hard-working, and honest. But leave his daughter be," the innkeeper's wife had cautioned him. "She'll bring yer meals and ale in the afternoon. Don't be lookin' at her or Vann'll cuff ye. And his son will work alongside ye. Vann shows no favoritism to the boy over the workers."

Shouldn't Vann's own blood kin be treated differently—better? Johan hoped this meant that his master treated them all well—like sons. "Danke. I'll come back later to check on my wife."

"We'll watch yer wee wife. Don't worry yerself, eh?"

"Ja. Danke."

Johan exhaled as he stepped out into the cobblestone street. His steps lightened as he headed to his new job. Vann was a good master and Suzanne would be watched over. Watching for carts and riders on horseback, Johan crossed the street to his new workplace.

Vann's blacksmith and bustling carriage shop occupied almost an entire city block near the wharf. Johan ran a hand through his hair, surveying the impressive operation—not a country forge. What would the expectations be? He located the office, centered between the blacksmith and wheelwright shops. Inside, a big man, hat askew on his grizzled dark head, perched on a stool behind a high desk.

Vann's muscular upper body suggested that, unlike some shop owners, he still engaged in his craft. He stood and ambled to the entryway, attired in a stained leather apron whose pockets bulged with tools. With skin the rich color of Suzanne's café au lait, his master's Dutch features combined with African, resulting in a happy blend.

The blacksmith extended his hand to Johan. "You must be my new servant, Johan?"

Johan clasped the man's hand with both of his and bowed slightly.

His master gave him an odd look.

Johan's stomach squeezed. He'd done something wrong already, his first day.

The older man chuckled and Johan's face grew hot with humiliation. "I'm not laughing. I'm cheered a man from the continent would show such respect." He lowered his voice and set his mouth in a firm line. "We have trouble here sometimes, because of my skin color."

Johan frowned. "Why trouble? You cannot change how God made you."

Vann's large, dark eyes fixed on him, and Johan squirmed under his gaze. "I wish all felt as you do. Watch for any gangs of men, Johan. Tell me if more than three men are gathered out front. Learn our regular customers' faces."

"Ja." Johan exhaled. He felt himself itching for a fight, an urge he'd hoped he'd left behind in the Palatinate, with Nicholas. Now his fists pulsed with blood flow, readying for action.

Why? Anger toward God, despairing Suzanne might forever bear this passage in ill effects upon her body and her mind. But not her soul. If anything, she possessed a new peace about her that he'd never sensed before.

"Tell me about yourself. All I know is that you're

robust and willing to work hard and learn new skills."

"I want to learn many things. I hope to go to the frontier—to have my own land and a business." A family, he thought, but didn't say. "One day, that is."

Vann smiled in approval. "Are you Dutch?"

"I'm from the Palatinate."

"Not too far from there," Vann noted. "My mother was from Amsterdam. She bought me this property after she sold her land in what is now New York colony."

Which was where Suzanne was supposed to meet her brother.

Smoke and the smell of melting iron drifted in their direction. Metal clanged on metal.

"Come on. I'll show you where the servants keep their belongings." Vann strolled out front and led him around the ironworks area, the men lifting their eyes only briefly from the hot metal they melted in the forge.

Johan watched in fascination as one of the men deftly bent the metal into a fine large hook and then quickly twisted the other end, making it decorative.

"I'll work hard for you, Master Vann." Now wasn't the time to ask him about how much longer he'd need to work to redeem Suzanne's passage. But he needed to thank him.

Vann turned his head and smiled, his eyes agreeing with Johan's statement. "I have quarters here for single men." Vann placed his hands on his hips. "Do I understand you have a wife?"

"Ja." Surely the blacksmith knew, since he was paying their room and board at the inn. "Ja, danke for allowing me to work longer so I may redeem her as well."

Vann hesitated at the end of a long, low building. "My apologies, but I don't know what you speak of."

Thankfully, Vann had turned away and didn't see Johan's consternation and confusion.

"Come in and see the men's living quarters."

What about Suzanne? He'd have to broach the subject again.

Vann gestured down the long interior. "A hammock for each man, blanket, pillow, and trunk. The necessary is out back. We provide hot water daily. Most men bathe once or twice a week because of sweat. We offer wash water morning, noon, and night. Clean towel given daily."

"Very generous." He was surprised.

"A happy worker is a good worker, and a clean one is a healthy one."

Johan nodded. "My mother also had this saying."

Vann adjusted a trunk askew beneath a creamy rope hammock.

"Your married men—where do they stay?"

Vann straightened. "Never had one before."

Johan tapped his hat against his thigh. "There's no place here for us?"

"Afraid not. But let me see."

Birds chirped and flew into a cherry tree nearby, the pair small, likely only hatched earlier that spring. Didn't seem possible he'd known Suzanne only a short while. There must be a way for them to be together.

"Where do you wish to start—smithing or wheelwork?"

"I want to learn it all."

Vann laughed. "Most start with the easy jobs. But we have a large carriage wheel we must complete. Willing to try?"

"*Ja*, show me where to start."

A youth, dressed in work clothes that hung on his slight frame, joined them.

"This is my son, Abram. He'll take you to the master wheelwright."

Vann's son, a slighter version of his father, pressed his lips together in disapproval.

"How do you feel about belonging to a black man?" Abram's voice held a challenge.

Johan clenched his jaw, unsure if he understood the odd comment.

Abram repeated it.

"I belong to God, and I don't think He has a skin color." Johan replied. "But if He did, it would be like all of ours mixed together, because we're made in His image."

"You like your Bible?" Vann's jovial voice cut some of the tension. "You and Abram share faith then." His employer trotted out with great quickness for a man his size.

The younger man watched as Johan emptied his haversack into a wooden box that Vann had pointed out for his use.

"You may attend church on Sundays, but during the week you do what Father says, when he says it. Understand?"

Johan's neck muscles bunched. "*Ja*. I'll work for him like a slave works for a master."

The young man's eyes widened and he took a step back. "I didn't mean you're our slave. But Father owns your time for the next few years."

"Unless I can purchase my contract sooner." He had to, if he was to be together with Suzanne.

20

Utter darkness. How long had Suzanne's eyes remained closed? Her mind commanded her body to move, to revive, while another softer voice suggested that she lie still and listen. Long, slow breaths, eerily similar to winter's wind, stirred the air nearby. Someone else lay in this room, in a deep sleep. Not a single candle pierced the darkness. Where she sensed there should be windows, she could perceive no light. Was this purgatory?

No, she'd been in purgatory and now she was released. Those horrendous sounds were missing, the passengers' agony and their death rattles. *The cacophony.* A torment of groans that persisted for the longest time. The howls of Hades surrounding her. Groaning wood, people coughing, children crying, men arguing, women scolding, and the pious praying.

Now just a velvet darkness and silence other than a nearby companion's even breathing.

She should pray. Suzanne searched under the covers for her grandmother's rosary. Nothing. Must remain calm. No fever now, but she trembled. Someone in the soft bed rolled toward her. She lay back as a heavy, well-muscled arm wrapped around and clutched her waist. Had she not been so startled, she'd have screamed, but her very breath was sucked out of her. Stiffening herself into stillness, she heard the man's even breathing resume and carefully snaked her hand out from under the coverlet. She inched away from him to the mattress's edge.

Her eyes needed to adjust to the dark room, for she could distinguish nothing. Heart pounding, she took a deep, shaky breath. A vague recollection, of being thrown over someone's shoulder like a sack of feed, seized her. Had she been bought by this man?

"I'll be a good husband, I promise." The man's German words were sleepy, slurred, but his voice recognizable. But from where? The man rolled away, pulling the coverlet with him.

Was this her husband? When had a ceremony and the exchange of vows occurred? Her head ached as though someone had thumped it with a wooden bucket. But she was alive. Tugging at the quilts, she covered herself and lay there for what seemed like hours, drifting into and out of sleep.

At first light, Suzanne lowered herself from the high bed. With sunlight drifting through slatted shutters, lines illuminated a rag rug of vibrant colors that covered a large portion of the planked floor. She swayed and grabbed one of the elaborately carved bedposts, its grapes and vines similar to one she'd seen in Paris, a Caribbean import. The vague recollection of Etienne being sent to the islands came to her. They were to have married and gone there together. Hadn't they? She rubbed her head.

The shaggy golden head on the pillow didn't belong to Etienne LeFort. Glimpsing his broad back above the sheet, she saw no comparison with her beau. She patted her muslin nightgown. Had he dressed her? Undressed her? Heat sped up her chest.

Shaking, she went to the washstand, thankful when she spied water in the tall ceramic pitcher, its basin chipped but clean. Making her way, she almost stumbled, found her feet covered by a blanket and a pillow, as though someone had slept on the floor but had gotten up. Untangling herself, she continued to the wooden stand. Thank goodness, it was sturdy, for she needed to lean upon it for a moment to steady herself.

A ball of soap lay atop a stack of cloths. She slowly poured a modest amount of the cool water into the bowl. Then, lifting a rough square of fabric, she saturated it in the cool water before wrapping it around the fragrant bayberry soap. She washed her face slowly, deliberately, enjoying the feel of cleansing her gritty skin.

Dear God, I'm alive. Alive!

All of her needed a good washing, but not in front of this stranger. A sudden movement in her periphery startled her. The cloth and soap plopped into the receptacle, water splashing on her bodice. Suzanne backed away from the stand, wiping at her chest, the flesh bony and hard. Turning toward her left, she caught the reflected movement in a silvered mirror on the wall above a burlwood bombe chest. In the mirror, she viewed a woman whose dark hair hung lank around a white face, punctuated by dark circles under her eyes. Hollows in her cheeks made her appear much older than her years. Suzanne's hands flew up to her face. She looked dreadful indeed. *Très miserable.*

But she was alive. Still here. Pressing a hand above the beating of her heart, she closed her eyes and tried to steady herself as her legs began to tremble, unaccustomed to bearing her weight.

What kind of man would have wanted a wife such as this? So dirty. She must bathe. The basin water was cool. She'd request hot water for a bath.

"Good morning!" A man's deep voice boomed

from behind her.

Suzanne's heart seemed to drop into her stomach. Raising her eyes to the mirror, a smooth-faced young man reflected back at her. Blue-green eyes twinkled. Could it be? Was it the young man from the forest near Grand-mère's—only older? Her breath caught in her chest. The portrait had come to life. How? Rooted to the spot, she stared at him as he sat up in the bed. The coverlet fell, revealing his wide muscled shoulders and a slim torso dark from the sun. He smiled broadly at her, revealing large white teeth. Reaching behind her, she felt for the chair and lowered herself into it.

She averted her gaze from the mirror, her back to the woodsman's nephew, when she realized he could be naked. "*Arrêtez.* Stop. Stay right there. I won't look." Little good this sheer chemise would do her, but it was something.

"Ja, all right, but I have my sleeping pants on."

Suzanne couldn't help looking up at his bare back in the mirror. She barely noticed her own body, but now quickly ran her hands over herself. *Mince,* too thin. A wave of dizziness washed over her. She rested her head on her hands. How had they come to be together? With her eyes closed, she saw his face covered with a short beard. His face was fuller and his body bulkier. Johan—he'd ridden with her through the forest. "You're Johan. Oui?"

Silence. Another face flashed through her mind, similar to this one. The kind brother had a beard. The other one looked more like this man. *Please, Lord, don't let him say his name is Nicholas.*

"You don't know me?" His strained voice was the same as the one she'd heard in the horrible place she'd been.

He'd been with her there. Through it all. But no. She didn't remember. Even so, she had clarity that the One who also accompanied them was with her now. She wanted to keep Him always near. She was a new creation and belonged to Him.

"No, monsieur. I'm very sorry. I cannot say for certain."

An ache began on the top of her head and continued down through her neck. No, things were not the same at all.

~*~

"Ja, I'm Johan." His wife didn't know him. God was surely having a good joke on him. Why had the Lord turned his back on him? Was he being punished for being so foolish to think he might have a life together with Suzanne? He'd work as many extra jobs as he could to pay off her contract. He'd talk with Vann again today.

"Johan." She exhaled his name as though relieved.

"Let me help you back to bed."

"No!"

He couldn't help smiling. She must be getting better to already be resisting his suggestion. As he walked to her, he explained, "Suzie, you need to get your strength back. It's been weeks since you've walked."

"Weeks?"

Before she could protest, he slid an arm around her back and the other under her legs.

Her eyes searched his face.

"No beard. Do you like it better?"

"I..." She dropped her head back against his neck.

Wetness from her eyes dripped down his tunic's collar. He'd upset her. "I'm sorry. I don't mean to make you cry. I didn't want you to fall and hurt yourself."

"Merci." Her voice was a fragile as a robin's egg.

"The doctor will come see you tonight. He wanted to talk with you once you were awake again."

But she was already asleep in his arms.

After placing her back in bed, Johan departed for work, trudging toward Vann's. This wasn't good. But God would want him to be patient. He went about his work, surprised at the number of young ladies who frequented the blacksmith's shop. And all so friendly.

When he returned from work, Suzanne sat by the desk, which doubled as a vanity, and brushed her hair. Her hand shook as she laid it down.

He closed the short distance between them and resisted the urge to kiss her forehead. "Good to see you up. How are you feeling?" He reached to push a stray lock of her dark hair from her forehead, but she pulled away.

"I was able to dress." She frowned as she spread her skirt around her. "Whose clothes are these?"

She'd worn this outfit in the Palatinate. "My mother remade her dress for you."

"I see. It isn't comfortable and it's much too big." She held her arms out. The bodice almost flapped open and she pinched it together.

Johan felt his face flush. "Maybe pin it together for now."

"Can you pull the laces tighter on the back? That would help." She stood by the desk, turned, and rested her hands on the wood surface.

Yes, he could, but his fingers fumbled as he tried to unknot the lacing. Starting from the top, he pulled them in until he got to the bottom. He hesitated, taking care to not brush his fingers against the small of her back. He didn't want any more tears today. She seemed frightened of him. And a good puff of Philadelphia breeze would blow her back out to sea. "You have to eat your meal tonight."

She turned and narrowed her eyes at him. "You shoveled gruel into my mouth, didn't you?"

He'd rather have her angry than wetting his shirt again. "Ja, I made you eat."

She shrugged her bony shoulders. "I want good food. Not pig slop."

Oh, no. He swallowed. Was he supposed to provide food like she ate at court? Impossible. "Tell me what you want."

"Strudel and roast pork." Her pale hands flew to her pretty mouth.

He laughed. "Ja, that's good. You remember Mama's cooking."

To his relief she laughed, too.

Her shoulders rose and then fell. "I remember my efforts, too!"

He stroked his chin and chuckled. "Unforgettable."

She slapped at his arm. "I thought you were a kind man. That wasn't nice." She affected a charming pout.

He could kiss those pouting lips, feel her arms wrap around his neck. Carry his wife to the bed. He pulled away and cleared his throat. "No, I'm always getting in trouble with you for teasing."

Her brows worked together. "My head aches, Johan, when I try to think. I want to remember, though."

"You will, in time." He hoped.

She stared hard into his eyes. "Do you have any proof of our wedding? Something?"

He opened his mouth but had no answer. "I wasn't thinking of that at the time."

"The priest's name—can we find him here in Philadelphia and speak with him?"

"Father Francois." He pulled at a loose thread on his vest.

She tilted her head. "Father Francois, that's all?"

He shrugged.

"Johan, you told me the ship was mostly Lutheran Germans immigrating together."

He nodded.

"Why would a priest be on board?"

His breath caught in his throat. "I don't know. I didn't ask." He clenched his hands.

She pressed her eyes tightly. "Why not?"

"I had more important concerns at the time!" He shouted. He'd never raised his voice to her before and he felt his cheeks heat in embarrassment.

Suzanne's eyes flew open and pulled away from him. "Are you preparing to hit me?"

"No! Never." He exhaled in frustration.

"You punched your brother."

Johan dropped his head. "Ja. He insulted you." Implied she was a harlot.

Amber eyes pierced his in accusation. "Get me the evidence of this wedding." She turned away, but not before two glistening teardrops fell.

He'd failed again. Made her cry and had shouted at her. "Suzie, I'm sorry. Please forgive me." He left to get the doctor, closing the door behind him. The lock was quickly bolted on the other side. Would she let him back in?

Soon he returned with Dr. Gill, a Welshman, who spoke in such a thick accent that Johan could barely understand him. But it sounded as if he said that in time Suzanne may recover her memory. And that she should get her strength back.

But it almost sounded as if he'd asked if she was with child.

Johan had been tempted to reply that it would only be possible if there had been some miracle. But he thought better of making such a jest. How miraculous that she was alive. And if she never regained her memory and if she wished to be free of him, then he'd need to seek advice.

He'd sent word to her brother and to his own family of where they were. Perhaps they could help him sort this all out.

He'd never felt so alone in his life.

21

Every noise, even Johan's slow steps in their room, caused Suzanne's head to pound. Although three days had passed, since she awoke, her recollection of the time since her mother died was like a mosaic that had shattered. Now she picked up the pieces and tried to force them back into a picture frame. Fragments, perhaps dreams, intruded that didn't belong in the artwork.

Johan placed water on the side table and a plate of bread and cheese.

She pushed her head into the pillow as he bent to kiss her good-bye, his warm lips barely grazing hers, but sending a shiver through her nonetheless.

He opened his eyes and looked into hers as he pulled away, frowning.

The memory of standing at the altar with Etienne must have been an illusion. But she remembered him asking her to marry him. Gripping Johan's arms, she pulled him closer. "I was promised to someone else. I don't remember marrying you."

He leaned in, his weskit brushing against her chemise, the heat from his neck warming hers. Johan whispered softly into her ear, "I promise you'll remember in time."

Suzanne gasped at this intimacy, taking in short quick breaths. When he was this close, she yearned to be well. To accept what he said were truths.

"You must eat what they bring up today, *frau.*"

"Oui," she heard herself whisper as he drew away from her.

"Good!" He brushed his warm hand against her cheek.

She must look a fright. But why should she care if he saw her like this? As she drifted off to sleep, she had another recollection. He'd seen her worse—in pig slop. They'd lived on a farm together. And heavens! He'd come into her room at night. Why would she have allowed such a thing? And if she had...no, surely not. But had they been intimate? Was she with child? How could she ask him such a thing?

He seemed to be such a good man. From experience she knew things weren't always as they seemed. Not recalling why, Etienne was the man she associated with that understanding. Not Johan.

Where was her betrothed now? As she drifted off to sleep, she pictured his plantation in the Caribbean— where they'd hoped to live. But in her dreams, he stood at a dock, with his arm around an island woman. When she awoke, the light filtering through the wooden shutters suggested that Johan should be home soon. Home? This place? She laughed. Still, she admitted, this room was better than that foul ship. That horror.

Suzanne gingerly rose from the bed. Forcing herself to avoid looking in the small mirror, she stepped to the basin and wet a cloth, lathered it with the new ball of fragrant soap, and began to wash. She inhaled its scent, recalling a warning onboard ship— "You'll be housed in rough quarters." Stiffening at the thought, she shook it away. What a blessing that she hadn't been sent off to work in servitude. Staccato raps at the door startled her and she jumped.

"Who is it?" she called out.

"It's Jemmy, miss, I mean missus, come to change your sheets, if you please." The maid sounded on the verge of tears, her voice tremulous.

"One moment, please!" Suzanne slipped her feet into the delicate leather slippers that Johan had secured for her since they had arrived. They were soft and had molded perfectly to fit her feet. Still a little dizzy, Suzanne crossed the floor and pulled open the door.

Indeed, there were tears in the chambermaid's eyes. She sniffed behind the pile of sheets she clutched in her arms.

"You'll not complain because I'm late, are ye, miss? I mean missus? Or because I forgot to wake yer husband?"

"He isn't...no, I..." She clamped her mouth shut.

The young woman looked her up and down and smiled in approval. "That did fit ye well, after all. T'was a struggle for Mother and me to get it on ye! And those undergarments yer man bought ye."

Relief ebbed through her as she took a deep breath and then exhaled. Johan hadn't dressed her. "Thank you for your kindness."

Jemmy pursed her lips as though considering. "Yer master, miss, he's in town for a bit..."

Master? Her knees sagged, but Jemmy dropped the sheets and caught Suzanne before she sank to the floor. *Oh, Lord, no.* That memory was real—they had redeemed their passage. And God hadn't removed this cup from her.

"Oh, miss! The colonel is a good man. And generous, oh my, yes." Jemmy released her. "Well, at least that handsome ward of his is—Wyatt Scott." The young woman assisted Suzanne up and led her to the padded settee before the hearth.

"Merci. I had…" Suzanne couldn't tell this young woman that she had no intention of serving as a slave to this man, no matter how good. Guy would redeem her shortly. And where was Etienne now? She should send word to him.

"I need to send a letter." She smiled up at the young woman. "Can you help me?" Suzanne frowned as she recalled Greta's face when she'd made the same request. She'd posted to Jeanne. She rubbed at the ache on the side of her head. Guy and Jeanne—were they together?

Jemmy nodded. "Aye, miss. Let me just fix up the bed, and then I'll take care of that for ye."

"Merci." Suzanne wished to lay her pounding head down.

"Miss? Are ye a'right?"

No, she wasn't. Might never be again.

~*~

Suzanne awoke the following day to Johan's heavy steps tramping up the stairs, jarring her from a dream of him and Nicholas on the farm. Heavens, he sounded as loud, solo, as the two did together pounding down those stairs beside the bedroom where she'd stayed.

She remembered more each day. Purposefully, she closed her eyes. Let him think she still slept. He'd told her the night before she must try to get up as soon as he departed for work. Today she'd go to the market and buy a few things for the innkeeper.

Johan strode to the bed. His lips tickled as he whispered in her ear. "Come back to me, my doeling." She heard his intake of breath, waited for him to add something, but he only kissed her cheek, the action bringing heat to her face.

Extending one hand out from beneath the covers, she stroked his cheek, almost unaware that she was doing so. "I want to remember."

Was this to be her life for now—waiting for him in this room? Until Guy made arrangements to pay off their redemption contracts.

Somehow, she'd make sure Johan had enough to start his farm when he was ready.

He leaned in toward her again, his shoulders straining the white linen fabric of his shirt.

She marveled at the change in his appearance. "Get me more fabric and I'll make new shirts for you." *That's what a good wife would do.* "I can't let the seams out further."

Pleasure and relief washed over his features and his eyes shone. "Ja, that would please me." He pressed a kiss into her palm.

She shivered and pulled her hand free, wishing his warm lips didn't have such a strong effect on her. She felt his kiss all the way down to her toes.

He placed two cold coins in her hand, dampening her pleasure. "For your shopping."

She groaned. "I don't want to go."

"You need to get up. Stretch your legs. Get some sunshine."

She glared up at him.

Johan stroked her cheek. "You might meet some interesting people."

~*~

As she approached the market, the crowds

thickened. Suzanne approached the first stand in the square. The scent of fresh tomatoes wafted up from the bushel basket as Suzanne squeezed two of the fruits. With a little basil and fresh butter, these tomatoes could make a savory sauce.

"Madam Christy?" A tall, heavy-set man with reddish hair stood ten paces from her near a stall equipped with all manner of fresh herbs. He stared at her, his light eyes wide, eyebrows raised as if in disbelief. The thin line of his mouth spread to a relieved grin as he trudged determinedly in her direction.

Suzanne glanced around her to see who the man sought. Dizziness caused her to sink. A firm hand clutched her elbow, steadying her.

Stale tobacco emanated from the man, and a hint of licorice. "You're not..." The deep voice held a Scottish burr. A frown furrowed its way between his straight eyebrows. His patrician nose sagged, joining his mouth in sadness. "I'm sorry if I frightened you. I simply mistook you for someone dear to me. A lady I've nay seen in some time."

Suzanne settled her skirts around her. "No, monsieur, I don't know you."

He tipped his hat and left her.

Who do I know? Struggling, she recalled Maria and Adam. Greta and Nicholas. She missed them, which confused her. Every recollection of Johan was of concern and friendliness on his part. Yet glimpses of her own feelings ran much deeper—more akin to the loving way he treated her now. Suzanne chewed her lower lip and moved on to another stand. Onions, potatoes, and an odd-looking bumpy vegetable.

"What is this called?"

The pockmarked youth laughed, revealing several missing teeth. "It's corn. What some call maize."

Good! This I know I have never seen before.

22

Birdsong drifted through the open window as Suzanne settled at the desk. Johan's Bible glared at her. Dared her to read it. She touched the leather cover, took a breath, and opened it. Inside, nestled letters written in a magnificent flowing script. Powerful, but lovely. Who had written these?

She looked out the window to the street, trying to tamp the temptation down, like Johan's father did with the tobacco in his clay pipe. Another memory. Odd, but for a second she considered Adam her father. Had Johan received missives from home?

Taking a breath, she pulled her gaze back to the first missive to read. Perhaps Adam sent good news. She scanned the note, noting many errors in the German words, making it difficult to decipher it.

We're home now. Thank you, God. The French girl, Suzanne, is safe. She's not so smart and I worry for her. I don't find all the French words to say, but I know what she speaks of. Yet she tries to teach me! I'm glad she's learning more German words because I have no more patience. She knows so little about basics. Nicholas is very angry. He thinks I mean to marry her. How silly. She knows nothing useful. But I pray for her now.

Johan wrote this weeks or months ago. And he was writing about her! Her cheeks burned. Was this how he really felt? She closed her eyes, the sensation of riding through the woods with him flowing through her, the memory of his smile as she said a German word correctly. The furrow in his brow when she spoke to him in French or took too long responding. He'd thought her an idiot! And the worst revelation was that she was ignorant. Not at all mindful that using fancy phrases or reading esoteric books didn't make a person intelligent.

Johan was right. He did understand better than she did.

A tear dripped onto the page. He'd sacrificed his future with a "useful" bride for her. But no document proved they were wed. She'd relieve Johan's burden. Perhaps the "priest" who'd supposedly married them was a pretender who hoped to ease Johan's pain when she died. But if she was such a burden, why did he care so much? Because he'd failed. And God hadn't answered his prayers. A guilty conscience nagged him.

She would set his conscience free.

~*~

Suzanne's cheeks still burned as she pulled her gloves up and approached the innkeeper, the pleasant scent of lemon oil teasing her senses.

"Good day, mistress." The balding man nodded at her, his shiny head fringed with a ring of silver hair. Ruffled shirtsleeves were pushed up as he rubbed beeswax into the wide oak counter top. "Good to see you up and about." He ceased dragging the rag in circles. "Going to the carriage shop?"

"Yes, I'd like to see…" What should she call him? "Johan." She'd get this over with.

"Can you bring him some of these little cakes? He enjoys them as much as I do." He handed her a small, but heavy, canvas bag.

Suzanne frowned as yet another recollection came—Johan savoring his mother's pastries. "He has a good appetite."

Mr. Tarpley's round stomach spoke of his wife's good meals. "Do you know the way to Vann's shop?"

When she shook her head, he walked her to the door and pointed straight down the street at a sign with a carriage painted on it. "Best carriage maker in Philadelphia."

"Philadelphia?" A bout of dizziness attacked her and the innkeeper grasped her arm to steady her.

"Yes, mistress, good old Philadelphia."

"How far am I from New York?"

"New York? That's a far spell from here. Why do you ask?"

"I...I hope to go there one day." Soon. Her head began to ache again. "Merci, monsieur, for the directions. Suzanne stepped out into the sunlight, bright against her eyes, with no hat to cover her head. At Versailles, she possessed a great many hats, jewels, and other finery.

Guy would replace those items once he made it to New York. But she must get there, too. For now, she had trouble enough simply walking.

Unaccustomed to so much exertion, her heart hammered as she strode down the hard-packed dirt pathways adjacent to the cobblestone streets. This colonial city seemed so *nouveau*, so new. Horse carts passed in the roads, the drivers holding their whips lightly in their hands. A frontiersman dressed in tan buckskins rode a fine black horse down a narrow side street.

The smell of horse flesh, molten metal, fire, and sweat carried across the street as she reached the intersection near Vann's popular business. Suzanne lifted her skirts and crossed the street, dodging manure piles and avoiding two small drays that rumbled by. With each step, the pins in her hair loosened and her curls tumbled down her back. Suzanne almost collided with a tall gentleman dressed in a gray waistcoat.

Elaborate silver buttons lined the front, reminding her of some on Etienne's clothing. His breeches were also in the French fashion. "Mademoiselle?" He lifted his hat and bowed, his eyes dancing.

Casting her eyes down, she stepped around him and into the building where Johan stood beside the forge. Johan's muscles bulged beneath his tight shirt as he hammered a metal rod, glowing orange from the fire, until it flattened. He lifted his bronze-and-gold head and turned toward them. His broad white smile contrasted with the tight smirk of the gentleman. "It's madame, not mademoiselle." He seemed happy to make that announcement.

But why? She was his burden. She lifted the bag. "I've brought you some *gateau*."

Johan grasped her hand and brought it to his lips, lingering there.

For a moment, Suzanne almost felt the Palatinate sun shining on them in the wheat fields. Smoke from the fire reminded her of something...she tugged her hand free.

French soldiers marching across the fields, setting fire. It was a fleeting thought, not a painting in her mind. "Johan?" She swallowed hard. Had they come to the colonies together because of something she'd done? *Dear God, had anyone died? Would the villagers starve this winter?*

Vann appeared in the opening behind them. He

wiped his large hands on his apron. "Do we finally get to meet Johan's beloved?"

His beloved? Did he mean Johan's ignorant Frenchwoman?

Johan clasped Suzanne's hand. He pulled her closer to him and tucked her arm in his.

Her heart seemed to have moved up into her throat, and she couldn't speak to tell him to stop. His handsome face begged for a kiss. Yes, she was foolish, she'd fallen in love with a man who didn't respect her. Who considered her beneath him. No proof of their marriage. Now that she was well and they were still sharing the same chamber—how terribly improper. And how uncomfortable for him to sleep on that pallet on the floor. Not that it stopped him from getting into the bed once he started sleepwalking.

"What brings you here, my doeling?"

"A goat? Again you call me a goat?" At least she now knew why.

"Suzanne, I mean it as sweetness, an endearment."

Nothing endearing about being thought stupid. Now that she was recovering, she'd have to do something to bring this charade to an end. And get to New York.

~*~

Johan pulled Suzanne in closer and she squirmed. He needed to move into Vann's quarters to end the temptation he nightly faced. His mouth grew dry. "I need a drink." Releasing her and retrieving a mug, he strode to the well and pulled up a fresh bucket of water. He dipped in and then poured the water over his head. Needed to cool down.

He refilled the tankard and drank his fill, turning

to see Suzanne staring at him with a mixture of longing and fear on her face. Why must she struggle so, always, with her feelings toward him? Somehow, it made him feel less of a man. But he'd prove himself worthy.

Suzanne suddenly bent over, her head low and her arms gripping her knees to steady herself.

He set the mug down and strode over to her, lifting her up as she sank into his arms. "This was too much effort for you. I'm going to carry you home."

"You cannot!"

"I can and I will." *I'm your husband, woman, don't you understand?*

"Mr. Vann! Please tell him he cannot do this."

Vann peered up from beneath his magnifying spectacles, his expression sour. "Madam, seeing as I cannot carry you, I suggest you allow Johan to do so. Or you may lie here on this cot."

Suzanne raised her head from Johan's shoulder, her dark hair brushing his cheek. The silky curls smelled of lilac water, eliciting a strong reaction within him. He wanted to kiss her and demand that she accept him as husband. He closed his eyes and prayed for release from his impulses.

"Madam, should you stay, you could thus gaze upon our customers and they upon you as you recline. Johan, I believe it might well increase our business." Vann's booming laugh apparently didn't agree with Suzanne, for she gasped and slapped Johan lightly on the back.

"Let me down, Johan. I can walk home by myself. You cannot humiliate me by carrying me down the street." She was right.

People passing on the sidewalk frowned, the

women clucking their tongues.

"I'll watch you walk, then."

Setting her down, he tried to rearrange her curls, but his big fingers poked holes in the strands, causing a bigger mess.

"Stop."

Her frown looked just like Mama's. He chuckled.

"Am I funny?"

He shook his head. "No."

She opened her mouth as if to protest then closed her eyes and shook her head. Shaking her tresses, she turned and walked away.

"No good-bye for me, Suzie?"

She made a noise of disapproval. Watching her wander onto the pebbled walk, he noticed the gentle sway of her dress. She wasn't wobbling anymore, but her feminine curves and the way she moved caused his heartbeat to become erratic, his legs almost as unsteady as when they'd first boarded the ship. He wiped his wet forehead, already hot again. "Suzanne?"

She froze and then turned, her mouth set in a line. "What?"

"Vann has housing for only me here. Can you ask at the inn about their charges, please?" Johan felt his shoulders slump. "For only your room and board."

Her pretty mouth hung open, her eyebrows knit together in disappointment. Then her features worked to feign nonchalance, something he'd seen her do many times when she was hiding something. "Oui. I'll see to it. And you—see to finding that priest."

~*~

According to everyone with whom Johan had

spoken, no French priests were to be found within the vicinity of Philadelphia. Among the many people who strolled the street of the city and those before him on the grassy area near the wharf, he'd never set eyes upon such a cleric.

But if Suzanne could be shown some proof, then surely she would come to her senses. She acted as though he'd fabricated the wedding and the administration of the sacraments of Last Rites. He wasn't that imaginative. Suzanne should at least remember that fact, if she recalled nothing else. Solid, hardy, a rock—those were descriptions his family and friends might give him, but not prone to making up fairy tales.

Phillip pointed out a level spot where they could sit on the Delaware River's bank. His friend blessed their midday meal and began to eat the fine cheese and bread that Vann had provided.

A group of people assembled to depart on one of the small clippers that crossed to the Jerseys on the other side.

One slight, dark-haired man peered toward him, his hand shielding his eyes, before pivoting and boarding the small vessel.

Johan eyed him. "Phillip? Have you ever seen that man before?"

The stranger resembled the priest who'd performed the marriage ceremony.

"Told Vann he's a new surveyor." Phillip grabbed a hunk of golden cheese and bit down.

"Surveyor?" *Not a priest.* Johan's appetite departed along with the boat as the small party sailed into the river.

"He comes into the shop now and then."

"Next time he comes, would you get me? I want to meet him." He squeezed the roll in his hand until it crumbled, and a bold seagull landed beside him, then proceeded to devour the bread.

Had the Frenchman on board the ship simply wanted to bring him comfort? What if he was this surveyor? If the man wasn't a priest, then the marriage wouldn't be valid in Suzanne's mind nor his own.

Johan finished his repast and returned to his work, grateful to be kept busy. He'd just finished a project when he was called to see the owner.

Vann's prominent features gathered in a frown as he gestured for Johan to enter the office area. A young man in rumpled linen clothing, cut loose in the German style, sat atop an empty barrel across from the carriage maker. The stranger averted his pale blue eyes when Johan joined them.

"Do you know this man?" Vann's expression seemed doubtful.

Sparse beard covered the young man's chin. "Sir, he doesn't know me." He twisted his soft cap in his hands. "You're Johan Rousch, aren't you?" He spoke in the Palatinate dialect.

"Ja. Who are you?"

"Albert Shacht. I work in a stable not far from here. I was a friend of your cousin, Noel."

"Ja?" He'd heard nothing from the group that he and Suzanne were to have joined in coming to the American colonies.

"Sarah, his little girl, said they lived in the same village as you. They came with some of the money you left your parents."

"Came here?" Mama and Papa—they gave the funds to Noel? His heart sank. "I don't understand."

The younger man stretched his fingers open, palms up in appeal. In an anguished voice, he told him, "Noel's family. They all died from the ship fever. Except Sarah. She asks me to find you."

"Only Sarah?" All her family gone? Johan ran his tongue over his dry lips. "The baby, also?" Noel's infant had only just been baptized. *Dear God, no.* Johan lowered himself onto one knee and pushed a hand back through his hair. His queue unloosed and he bent forward, his hair flailing his cheeks. Turning to Albert, Johan asked, "Where's Sarah?" She was his responsibility now. How he'd care for her—he didn't know.

23

Johan returned to Vann's after a quick visit with Sarah at the Schacht's small rented house.

The young man from the docks rode up on a sleek horse and dismounted. He passed his reins to Johan. "Wyatt Scott here to check the progress on my carriage."

Vann motioned to Johan as he secured the magnificent gelding to a hitching post. "Can you help him?"

"Ja. Come with me." He tipped his head toward the wall, where a fancy carriage wheel hung.

Alert hazel eyes, set high in a handsome, even-featured face, examined the wheel before Scott reached to touch it. "Your craftsmanship is astonishingly good for a newcomer." Scott's voice held a touch more English accent than many of the colonials Johan had met. His smile was infectious.

Johan grinned back at him. "Danke."

Vann joined them. "Johan's the best craftsman I've had yet."

Scott turned toward the proprietor and shifted his weight so that one hip jutted against his closely cut waistcoat. "Shall I be able to leave for Virginia within a fortnight?"

Vann rubbed his chin. "Master Scott, methinks you'd slap this lovely wheel on your carriage and leave on the morrow if it suited you."

Scott laughed. "But I'm not yet ready." His voice

dropped. "And I fear leaving Colonel Christy's home vacant when he's about to return home."

Vann frowned. "Imagine you'd want to say your goodbyes, too, if you're leaving."

"Of course," Scott quickly agreed. "And I've his new indentured servant to get settled." Scott seemed to be a lively fellow and wasn't much older than Johan, but had lines around his eyes and the look of a man accustomed to being out of doors. Chestnut hair escaped from beneath his cap. His clothing, while looking costly, was disheveled, as though he were the type to rush about. Impulsive. Might make a decision without thinking it out.

How many young women's hearts had this man broken?

Scott stroked his jaw as though mulling something over and then asked, "Is your wife able to work now?" His cheeks reddened.

Johan wasn't sure what he meant. "Ja. She walked to the market this week."

Scott averted his gaze. "We could use her help whenever she is ready. Our cook left us."

"Your cook?" Johan blinked at the man. He must be confused. He laughed. "Do you have a strong stomach?"

Scott raised his eyebrows. "Yes, why do you ask?"

"I want to know the same thing. Why do you ask about my wife?"

"I, well…Colonel Christy holds her contract. I don't wish to sound petty, but the innkeeper's daughter told me she was recovering and may be able to work…"

The man might as well have slammed an iron rod against his chest. His wife…bought her as a servant.

Oh, God, don't fail me now. This will kill Suzanne. Please, please take this cup away.

~*~

Suzanne stared at the innkeeper, sure she'd misheard him. He shoved a chair beneath her as she sank. "Merci."

"Colonel Christy is a good man and so is Mr. Scott. Don't ye worry yerself none now."

Purchased. "And he's been paying for my room and board?" Although she had money left, it wouldn't last long at the rate the innkeeper quoted her.

"Yes, mistress, that's so. Well, 'tis Wyatt Scott what brings the money by, but it's from the colonel." He shook his head as though agreeing with himself.

How much longer would this stranger pay?

"Merci." Her head began to pound. "I'll begin my preparations." With that, she departed, heading up the narrow stairwell as quickly as she could. But when she slipped inside, she secured the door, went to the bed, and collapsed.

Hours later, she heard Johan's distinctive footfall draw near. "Johan?" Suzanne rose and opened the door. Pressure built in her chest; she wished to be held in his arms, but she stepped back and allowed him past.

He removed his hat. "What's wrong?" Johan looked so tired, his face so sad and discouraged.

She couldn't burden him further. She'd get to the bottom of this claim. "I...I am very hungry tonight. Can we go to the tavern—get some German food?"

This brought a slow smile. "Ja. I'd like that."

She turned away from him, trying to fix her face

into a calm expression. Tomorrow she would tell him. "Do you have your pouch?"

"Nein." He crossed to the bureau and dug beneath his work clothes to retrieve his money.

The quick image of her grandfather's money and Nicholas waving a pouch flashed through her mind. Frowning, she watched as Johan checked the coins. What had happened to the silver and the gold? An ache began at her temple. If only she could remember everything. With a heavy heart, she and Johan departed to the nearby tavern, a favorite of the Palatinaters.

"Smells good, doesn't it?" Johan grinned as he opened the door to the establishment, releasing the scent of roast pork, cabbage, and apples.

A pretty serving girl nodded in their direction as she carried platters of steaming potatoes and meat to a large oak table, around which sat a dozen men almost as big as Johan and all laughing.

Beside her, Johan stiffened. He gestured to a small table for two on the opposite side of the room. "They look like troublemakers. Let's find a quiet place where we can talk."

The dizziness had returned and the next half hour passed in a blur.

Johan would begin sentences only to be cut off by the serving girl and the noisy diners. Finally, they'd finished their schnitzel dinner and were served a cup of spiced tea.

"Danke," Johan smiled up at the girl and she blushed all the way to her white mob cap.

Suzanne appraised the man across from her. Tanned, golden hair falling in waves to his shoulders, and handsome and fit. No wonder the girl's face was flushed from his brief attention. She felt her own face grow warm as his hand covered hers.

The servant finally departed.

His Adam's apple bobbed as he swallowed. "Suzanne, there's something I need to speak with you about."

"*Moi, aussi*—I also need to speak but you go first."

"First I want you to know I don't blame you for things that happened at home."

She frowned and watched as he rubbed his lower lip. What did he mean? She lifted the mug of fragrant tea to her lips and began to sip.

He drew in a deep breath. "There's a girl I must tell you about…"

Choking, Suzanne almost dropped her mug to the table. She tried to regain her breath but she'd drawn the hot liquid into her air pipe.

Johan rose as all around looked in their direction. He patted her back and finally the fit passed.

The tavern keeper scurried over. "All is well?"

"Ja." Johan paid for the meal and then assisted her up and out of the tavern, worry etched on his face.

A girl. He wanted to speak of a girl yet he claimed he was married to her. She was so weak that the effort of coughing had worn her out. Regardless of any other woman he pined after, she needed this man's assistance now. Later she'd figure out what to do.

When they'd returned to the inn, she couldn't manage the stairs by herself and Johan carried her up. Once inside the room, he lit the candle and then settled her on the bed. He removed her shoes and stockings, and pulled the covers up to her chin.

She was like a child. No wonder he'd be looking for another.

After washing, Johan blew out the candle, changed into his sleep clothes in the darkness, and settled on the pallet on the floor.

~*~

He'd mangled his attempt to discuss Sarah with Suzanne. But another day had begun and a beautiful pink sky illuminated his way to the carriage shop. Before long, he finished his first job and sat down for a break.

A fine horse trotted in so fast that several of the other customers, as well as Johan, were startled.

"Many pardons!" Wyatt Scott dismounted and secured his mount. The young man removed his hat and bowed to two older men before purposefully striding past them in Johan's direction. "How're my wheels coming?"

"Just as you wished them, Mister Scott." Johan gave a tight smile to the other customers who were glaring at them. "I made them sturdy—so they last."

Vann ambled over. He scowled, his eyes fixed behind where they stood. "Sarah's keeper is here."

"Ja?" Johan turned.

Albert stood with Sarah, the child's eyes wide in fright, the clear red imprint of a hand visible on her fair cheek.

"What's this? Who struck you?" Johan rushed to the girl.

Breaking free from Albert, Sarah launched herself at him.

Johan lifted his cousin's little one into his arms. "What happened?"

Sarah sobbed into his neck, her tiny hands

clutching at his leather apron neck strings.

Customers gawked at the spectacle.

Johan conveyed her out of the sun to a private spot behind an elm.

Vann and Scott's agitated voices clashed with Albert's behind them.

"Please, Cousin Johan. Don't make me go back there," Sarah wailed.

Above Sarah's plaintive cries, Albert's loud voice carried. "My mother has no patience with the child's constant questions. And Sarah breaks things every day."

Vann and Scott exchanged more words with Albert.

Scott strode toward Johan. "I have a solution."

Johan raised his eyebrows at Vann's customer.

"Is your wife well?" Scott's handsome face reflected concern.

"Better. Why?"

A furrow formed between Scott's dark brows. "You do believe me that the colonel redeemed her contract?"

Johan nodded.

Scott splayed his hands open. "Your wife could bring the child to work with her."

He appraised the other man. Scott was a handsome man, a gentleman. He owned a plantation in Virginia. If he and Suzanne didn't have a valid marriage, might she be free to marry someone like him? His breath left him. If the man who called himself a priest was really a kind-hearted surveyor, what then?

The well-dressed young man smiled at Sarah. "The colonel was waiting until he returned to have me fetch her. Why not bring her and the girl to the house now?"

Now? Because he wasn't willing to part with his wife just yet. Suzanne hadn't told him about the fees for the inn yet. And he hadn't discussed Scott's claim, either.

Scott pulled a bit of sugar cone from his pocket, knelt down, and offered it to Sarah.

Johan held the child closer.

Sarah sniffed and accepted the treat with a shy smile. "Does he have any children?"

Scott forcefully exhaled a puff of air. "Yes, a young son."

"Is he there?"

"No. But I expect Colonel Christy to return shortly. Having another child in the house might cheer William up." Scott was eye to eye with the girl, placed one finger under her chin, and then wiped a spot of dirt from her cheek. Scott surprised Johan by picking the girl up as though she weighed no more than a feather, and set her atop his right shoulder, bringing a peal of laughter from her. "Have you a good view up there, Mistress Sarah?"

An iron grip clutched Johan's shoulder, and he turned to face Vann.

"They're good people—Scott and Christy. None better. You can trust them." Vann nodded.

I hear your prayers.

A chill went through Johan and he rubbed his arms. Suzanne's contract to pay off. And now Sarah's support. How would he earn enough money to care for them all?

Trust me.

Had he just taken on a daughter? This tall-for-her-age blonde cousin wasn't at all like the little version of

243

Suzie whom he'd imagined as daughter. Was this the first of the houseful of children he'd wished for? He bowed his head in disappointment that he couldn't suppress. Suzanne might not be the mother of his children. And his future—when he owned land and had a home and a trade to support his family, was unsure.

Vann waved away smoke that drifted from the forge. "I'll give you extra work. Just make sure you rest and get your meals regular. Don't be running around with men prone to drinking and carousing." His eyes twinkled.

Johan grinned back at him. "Ja, I'll stop all that running around the town I do. No more nights swilling ale at the Barnacle. Or running naked after carriages down the street."

Wyatt winked at Sarah. "You won't catch me making that promise."

~*~

Suzanne perched on the end of the seat in front of the table, her hand itching to open Johan's Bible and read another of his journal notes. She wanted to know what he really thought of her. How could he act so loving if he really thought her incompetent? And now with this illness and this long recovery.

She bit her lip and blinked back tears of frustration. With God's help, she would get well. She inhaled slowly and reached inside the Bible. With effort, she read his misspelled German words.

Strange to admire someone who knows so little. Suzanne tries so hard. Sad she grew up a poor Huguenot but cannot perform most basic chores. She's very pretty, but what good—if her husband can't eat her cooking? She's knocked the milk bucket over, caught her dress on fire, and the clothes are still dirty after she washes them. She doesn't seem prideful or as though she refuses to learn. Maybe she is like Magda in the village.

She cringed. Magda was a mentally disabled woman whose family had to care for her. Suzanne slammed the Bible shut on the letter. Well *this Magda* was going elsewhere, to her new master's house. Why would she know menial tasks? Obviously, Johan placed great value in them or he wouldn't have written about it. Johan wasn't the accepting, kind man she'd thought. Instead, he'd judged her harshly by his own standards. The differences in their social classes were too wide a gap to bridge. She went to the armoire and began to pack her clothing.

24

Suzanne looked up from her stitching as Johan leaned his head against the door to their room.

His mouth worked into a frown. He grabbed the doorframe as though to steady himself.

"What's wrong?"

He kissed her cheek and then entered, closing the door behind him. "Do you recall my cousin, Noel, and his family?"

Snipping off some loose threads, Suzanne met his gaze. "I remember."

He squeezed her hand. "The baptism?"

"Oui. The baby? Do you have some word?" The hair on the back of her neck prickled.

He swallowed. Releasing her hand, he removed his soft work hat and squashed it into a ball. "They died."

She gasped as a weight seemed to settle on her chest. "Died? How?"

"They came with the group we were supposed to leave with."

"Oh, my! We could have died, also."

"You almost died, my liebchen." He caressed her shoulder. "Like our ship, many became ill with fever."

Tears pooled in her eyes. "All of them? Did the family perish?"

"Sarah lived. We can take some comfort from that."

Oh, Lord, not another. Not another life she'd ruined.

Suzanne squeezed her eyes shut. More people dead because of her. Had they come because of the burning by the army? Noel's farm was outside of the walled village. No, Johan said they'd already intended this journey.

A muscle in Johan's jaw jumped. "Suzanne, I have to tell you something else."

His countenance suggested he had something awful to share.

She sank down onto the chair.

"We cannot stay here together anymore."

She nodded, waiting.

"Vann has his workers stay in the servants' quarters."

"Moi?"

Johan ran a big hand through his hair, and then knelt by her, bringing one of her hands up to his lips. "No."

She pulled away.

"Your contract was purchased. They expect you to come there. To help with Sarah."

Her pulsed raced.

"Colonel Christy will keep Sarah in his household until you and I can take care of her."

Was he the husband of the woman she resembled? Would it cause the man distress to have her there? She brought grief with her as real as the dread that used to accompany her days. "You blame me, don't you?" She shouted at him. She brought a fist to her mouth.

"No." He clutched her hands in his. "Why do you think such a thing?"

"Now you have Sarah to care for?" He was right, she was responsible for Noel's family dying. "Oh, Johan, the baby." Sobs shook Suzanne's body. She resisted as he pulled her close, but then clung to him.

Johan kissed the top of her hair, piled atop her head in swirls. He trembled as though he was holding himself back from her.

Quick steps stopped in front of Suzanne's door, and Jemma stepped inside. "I sent for him like ye asked, and he's to come for you hisself, straightaway." The servant beamed at her.

Suzanne's hands flew to her neck, groping for a topaz necklace that was no longer there. She crossed her hands over her heart. Jemma couldn't mean Etienne. And why did the idea of Etienne coming for her now frighten her so?

"Colonel Christy? He's here?"

"Not him, but Wyatt Scott. He'll take you to the colonel's home. It's the biggest house in all of Philadelphia."

Suzanne's shoulders relaxed in relief. And she realized—she was more concerned about the idea of Etienne's arrival than of becoming, for all purposes, a slave to someone for the next few years. And how would she get to New York? To await Guillame?

"Mister Scott came hisself, he did."

Suzanne stood, trying to imagine one of Johan's iron rods making her backbone straight. This wouldn't be easy. She glanced back at his Bible, tempted to take it with her.

"Merci. Can you carry that one?" She pointed to the smaller bag, but Jemma grabbed the larger valise, fixing her with a wide grin as she carried it off down the stairs.

"Mister Scott! Can you take this one?" The young woman's laughter floated up the stairs, accompanied by a man's.

Suzanne stiffened at the air of familiarity the servant assumed with Scott. Then heat from humiliation stole up her neck. She'd need to assume the role of obsequious servant herself. *God, help me. I can't do this alone.* As she closed the door behind her, moisture pricked her eyes. For the first time in months, she'd be without her Johan. Hers. She blinked her eyes. She wasn't a suitable wife for him.

A young man bounded up the stairs toward her.

Her breath caught in her throat.

Wyatt Scott was undeniably handsome. And his broad smile suggested a cheerful disposition like Johan's. "Let me take that, dear lady. Your husband would be furious with me if you strained yourself on my account."

Her husband. Furious? A hazy image of being clutched in his arms, sun beating down, this man, Scott's voice demanding that she, Suzanne, was someone else's wife. Someone's mother.

"Are you all right?" He clutched her elbow to steady her.

"Oui, I just…we have met before, have we not?"

Dark, well-formed eyebrows collided over alert hazel eyes. "I mistook you for someone when you arrived in port."

"You argued."

"I did. With the captain." Scott's lips twisted in disgust. "But not about you." He smiled, one of those charming courtly attempts to cover some truth and divert attention.

"Another man mistook me for Madame Christy." She remembered being unable to keep her eyes open that day although she'd heard people talking.

"Christy won't be confused, you can count on

that." Wyatt Scott snorted as he assisted her down the narrow stairway. "He notices everything. I swear the man can identify something wrong or different from a mile away. That's what has brought him success as a military officer."

Like Rochambeau? And Guy? Was her brother making his way to her even now?

"Monsieur Scott, why did the colonel purchase my contract?"

Wyatt Scott's forehead turned pink beneath the brown waves that bounced with each of his springy steps. "He didn't."

She grasped his forearm. "I don't understand."

Scott nodded at the innkeeper and headed out the door with her trailing behind. "I paid."

Wyatt Scott drove like a madman. They lurched around every corner in the open carriage until finally halting at a turn into a lane that entered property occupying an entire square city block.

Her heart hadn't beat this fast since the night she and Maman escaped Versailles.

"Runs like the wind, doesn't he?" Scott grinned at her. He'd jostled into her so many times that she wondered if he hadn't broken one of her ribs with his elbow. "I race him on Saturday nights. Not far from here. We close off the street and place bets. Drayton almost always wins."

"Drayton?" She tried to catch her breath. She chewed her lower lip. So different from Johan. So careless and rash.

"My gelding is named Drayton."

Scott pulled to the end of the path to a carriage house, got out, and assisted her down.

Taking her luggage, Scott motioned his head

toward the back of an imposing three-story brick structure.

Mullioned windows reflected the midday sun. A herringboned brick path ran alongside the property and led from the large carriage house and stable to the house. Substantial grounds contained gardens, a terrace, and a private pavilion despite being within the city. The perfume of roses drifted to them on the light breeze.

She raised a gloved hand to her chest. "*C'est très belle*. So beautiful."

"Your new home, madame." Scott gifted her with another of his sunny smiles.

While his smiles warmed her heart, they didn't have the same effect upon her that Johan's did. Scott's mouth, his eyes, held a harsh knowing that troubled her. She'd seen that look before. Of having experienced trials beyond one's forbearance.

Scott's features relaxed. "Sarah's already been set up in a room next to yours. Seems anxious to see you."

One of the double paneled doors at the back entrance flew open, and the child ran to them. Sarah threw herself into Suzanne's arms, almost knocking her over. "Gone. *Alle*! Gone." The child sobbed.

Tears threatened Suzanne's eyes. She knew that refrain well.

"Not all gone, Sarah. Johan and I are here. We'll take care of you." Could they?

A short time later, waiting in the parlor of Christy's opulent home, she could well believe that the colonel was the son of a nobleman as Wyatt Scott told her. Everything was so new, though, from the Chinese porcelain figures on the mantel, to the fine woven rugs on the floor. Nothing there to link him to a family across the ocean. Adrift, like her.

Suzanne reached out to touch the portrait of a little boy, set atop the mantel, framed in dark mahogany. The child's almost-black eyes were haunting. How she missed the opportunity to paint, would love to do a portrait of the child herself.

The elderly servant cleared his throat before entering the room. He unlatched and lowered a tilt-top table with one hand before shakily lowering a tray of treats onto its dull surface. *Something in the room not so new.*

"The shop delivered young Mister William's painting today."

Wyatt Scott, dressed in a silk brocade coat, eased into the room. "Colonel Christy should return any day with his son. I've missed them mightily."

Her heart squeezed in her chest. How Adam and Maria must grieve Johan's absence as well. And it was all her fault. And Sarah—would Johan's little cousin blame Suzanne, too? "We must pray for safe travel home."

"Indeed. We've prayed for him constantly these many months." Wyatt touched the portrait. "Too intelligent a child to keep occupied in the backwoods forts."

~*~

Night was falling by the time Johan paused before Christy's imposing brick home. A mansion really. And more surrounding structures than he'd seen on one property since he arrived in Philadelphia. The long walk from Vann's to this lovely street lined with trees, parks, and gardens had given him time to consider his choices. As soon as he was able, he must try to assume the responsibility for Sarah's care.

No wonder many immigrants sent a few strong family members to the America colonies first, and then the women and children. Never had he thought he would turn a family member over to a stranger for help. Thank God, Suzanne could watch over her.

Approaching Christy's front door, he wondered if he should go around the wide three-story house to the back, where the servants would enter. He raised the brass knocker and rapped it three times.

An aging black man opened the door, his shoulders stooped and his eyes bleary.

"I'm here...for...to see...my Suzanne and little Sarah." The stammer that had left him years earlier reappeared.

Tinkling laughter echoed in the marble-tiled foyer as Johan followed the thin servant inside.

A man's low chuckle rumbled from an adjacent room.

"Guest for Mistress Sarah." The servant wheezed, turned his bleary eyes on Johan for a moment, and then moved stiffly toward the back of the house.

Johan stood, transfixed, in the entryway, staring at the massive stairway that curved upward. Wall coverings decorated the space, as did oil paintings on either side of the wide hallway. Aromatic bowls of cinnamon sticks and vanilla beans wafted his favorite scents toward him.

Sarah appeared as two paneled doors slid into the wall to his right. Dressed in a beribboned child's gown, his little cousin curtsied, and then giggled, lifting her fingers to cover her mouth. He stared. How on earth would he ever be able to provide for her as the colonel had? She ought not become accustomed to such finery. "Where is Suzanne?"

"She thought you might come. Wyatt gave her one of Mistress Christy's dresses to wear."

Suzanne had been accustomed to such a lavish home. She'd lost not only her family but her station in life. Would coming here open those old wounds? And to be brought here as a servant. He'd work harder to repay Suzanne's fee.

Scott swung an arm up in the air. "There she is!"

Johan swallowed. He was so grateful Mama had forced Suzanne to wear one of her aunt's beautiful gowns. If at this moment, he'd only first viewed this fine lady elegantly attired, he'd have run from the house. He was undeserving of her. Instead, he savored the sight of her dressed in a fancy rose-colored gown, a wide ribbon tied at her slender waist. She paused in front of him and he took her soft hand in his, raised it to his mouth, and kissed it.

Sarah joined them. "Wyatt is getting me a pony!"

Suzanne spoke first. "Sarah! You'll refer to him as Mister Scott." She leaned into Johan on the sofa they shared and looked up at him in question.

His gut clenched. By the time he could afford to purchase a pony, Sarah would be too old for one. She'd need a horse, especially because she was growing tall like that side of the family. "Sarah, your Aunt Suzanne is correct. And you cannot accept such a gift." He'd talk to Scott about this. Why would he tell the child such a thing? "Let's talk about some good news I had, Sarah."

But the light had gone out of her blue eyes.

They talked for an hour about what he'd heard about family members who had moved outside of

Philadelphia and closer to the region where many of the Palatinate families wished to settle—in the Shenandoah Valley of Virginia.

Suzanne's drawn face and questions about Indian uprisings and the difficulty of frontier life only furthered dampened Sarah's mood.

When the clock chimed, the servant came for Sarah and escorted her upstairs. The child almost ran from them—her sweet face twisted into anxiety.

~*~

"Johan, I have a request." Suzanne pointed to the portrait of a dark-haired boy. "Can we pray for safe travel for Christy and his son as they return? They're at a frontier fort."

Not far from an area the French army sought to fortify.

"Ja." Johan wrapped his fingers around hers and stepped in closer. His breath ruffled the wisps of hair on her forehead. "Father God, bring this child and his father home safely. Put your angels around him to guard them, to guide and protect them."

Suzanne peeked up from beneath her eyelashes to watch Johan's lips move. His eyes were pressed shut so hard that the muscles above them twitched. She resisted the urge to stroke the golden shadow of beard on his face. What a good man, a godly man. Her heart overflowed with love for him. And of all the times to want so bad to have just one kiss…

"Bring peace to this household as they await their master's safe return. And, Lord…"

Suzanne heard his sharp intake of breath.

"Please help me, help Suzanne, to find our way. I

ask this in Your own Son's name. Amen."

Johan's fervent prayer stirred her from head to toe, but what did he mean about the two of them?

"I need to tell you something." He cleared his throat. "I saw a man resembling the one who married us."

Her hands began to shake. "Oui?" Why did his brow furrow?

"Suzanne, he may be a surveyor. Not a priest." His voice was low.

"What do you mean?"

"I saw a man who greatly resembled him. And I was told he's a surveyor in the Jerseys."

"But you don't know for sure?" Why did he sound as though he was hedging about a wedding he'd insisted had happened?

"If that is so, you may be free to choose another as your spouse. Someone more appropriate."

How? Her reputation would be ruined after staying at the inn with him for so long. Heat sped up her chest to her neck. Her only recourse would be to go far from here, to New York where she was supposed to have fled, and hope that story didn't follow her. And that was the term he used in his writing—she wasn't suitable for him.

Conflicted emotions washed over Johan's face. "If that's what we discover, I'd want to make things right for you."

He doesn't want me. He was tired of all the trouble she'd caused. The deaths of his cousins, these few remaining relatives, had finally been more than he could bear.

She straightened, pursed her lips, and took a steadying breath.

Johan's visage became stern. "I'll take care of Sarah's needs as best I can."

Alone? Yes, he would. She blamed him not one whit for no longer wishing to provide for her. To be burdened by her.

He gave her a curt nod. "I should go."

"Oui." She couldn't keep the edge from her voice.

Johan stood and swatted his hat so hard against his thigh that he pushed the stiff felted wool through to the other side. "I'm not saying it right."

She couldn't argue with that.

His stomach gurgled and he placed a hand over it. "Not used to such heavy meals anymore."

A surveyor he now claims. This man had insisted they were married by a priest and had shared quarters with her for weeks. Her own gut churned.

"I'm working long days but I'll get to the truth."

She bit her tongue. Now she, too, spent long days watching his cousin and providing oversight for the kitchen and household staff. "I need to check on Sarah. Excuse me. *Bon nuit.*"

Head lowered, Johan departed.

Suzanne went to Sarah's room to check on her. How the child must miss her family. Despite being much older, Suzanne still mourned Maman, yearned for her comfort. The child's gentle whiffling breaths contrasted sharply with Suzanne's imagination of the child's family dying from the horrible disease that had almost claimed her. The seasoning, it was called, and Suzanne and Sarah both survived it.

She knelt beside Sarah's bed on the oval wool rug. Johan's heartfelt prayer moved her in so many ways. She loved him. Even if she hadn't begun to remember the many ways he'd cared for her, she'd have fallen in love with him again. But if they hadn't been properly wed, could she accept his offer to make things right—to once again have him give up his dreams for her? No. Guy could take her some place where the facts of her passage to the colonies wouldn't be known. She'd pray for all of them.

"Father God, protect Mr. Christy and his son. Bring them home. Help me be a good mother to Sarah…" Tears filled her eyes. "And Lord, if you wish Johan to be free of his obligation to me, I wish for you to make that clear." Sobs terminated her prayer.

If I have drawn you together, what do your differences matter?

Her flesh prickled as she looked around the room, almost expecting to see the Source of that message, as the lone candle glowed steady in the darkness.

25

Johan lifted the quill from the inkstand and carefully began his letter. *Dear Mama and Papa, I have bad news. Noel's family died enroute. Sarah alone survived the trip. She's in good care. Please write and tell me how you are. Do you have food for the winter? Is there still game in the forest after the fire? Please send your messages to me here in care of Master Vann.*

He tapped his fingers on the letter, careful not to touch the drying ink. Would this news distress his parents? Would it upset them to the point that they would cross that ocean that almost claimed Suzanne's life?

Grasping the edge of the paper, he brought it to the fire and dropped it in, the edges curling inward. He began again. Once he'd finished the missive, he placed it in an envelope and sealed it. Before he departed the inn, he left it with the keepers to post for him. Then he walked to work.

The day began well with Johan quickly completing his assignments.

His boss should be pleased. Vann joined him and settled on the bench adjacent. "Where are your admirers today, Johan?" the blacksmith teased.

Seated next to the owner, Johan continued work on the leather goods brought from the tannery. He wanted to show Vann how an application of an ointment he'd concocted worked better as both a preservative and for appearance. The stuff stank

259

terribly, but gave a lovely shine. "Who is that you mention, sir?"

"The ladies who now frequent our shop." Vann grinned. "Your beauty enriches my pocket."

"My beauty?" Tipping his head back, he laughed. "Nein, my brother is the handsome one." He hoped Nicholas and Greta would get word to him soon. Might they come here?

"Speaking of beauty, how are things working out for your wife?"

His neck stiffened. "I don't know." *She hasn't sent for me.* Suzanne required proof that she was married to him. In the absence of evidence, would she consider another suitor?

"Is it true that Mister Scott put her and Sarah upstairs in that big house?"

"Ja." Johan swallowed. He hadn't thought about how that might appear to others. "He has been most kind." Overly so.

"And Colonel Christy hasn't returned from the fort?"

"No." A handsome single man, an impulsive one, there with his wife. A wealthy plantation owner. And Scott was leaving soon. Would he run off with her?

He wanted to love Suzanne as God's word commanded—to put her needs before his own. Should he release her to another? But what of her reputation, since they had presented themselves as man and wife? If she left Philadelphia, if her brother arrived and took her to New France, he could establish her in a fine home and with society of her own aristocratic background. Suzanne could find a husband who was her equal. A fine gentleman.

As far as himself, his fondest wish was to own

much property; a farm with a forge or a tannery, and to have a large family. How had he ever imagined Suzanne would want that, too? He swallowed. But his dreams fulfilled without her? They'd be nothing.

"Tonight I'll go see them."

Vann clapped him on the shoulder. "Leave early today. Go get cleaned up for her."

"Ja. That's a good idea." And he'd tell Suzie what he'd heard about land in the Shenandoah Valley.

~*~

Sarah skipped into the parlor, where Johan waited. Fading purple and yellow fingerprints still marred the child's pale face but couldn't hide her wide grin. "Uncle Johan!" She stuck a finger in her mouth and looked up at Suzanne, who followed her into the cozy room.

"Uncle Johan? Don't you mean cousin?" By Suzanne's silence, her lips pressed together into a thin line, he presumed this was her idea. "Do you want to call me Uncle Johan?"

The little girl nodded. "Come sit at the game table with me and Aunt Suzanne." Sarah led him to the cherry wood table. The dark wood in the room shone and smelled of lemon oil.

He was afraid to touch the shiny surface.

Sarah, Suzanne, and he played cards for a while. His beloved kept her lips pursed and continued to cast him accusing looks. They switched to games of charade, Sarah's antics making him laugh until he cried.

Wyatt Scott joined them, bringing a steaming pot of hot chocolate and tiny ceramic cups to pour the liquid into and a tray of treats.

Suzanne finally began to relax. "Merci, Monsieur Scott." She tipped her head and gave Scott a slow smile that didn't reach her eyes.

The sun dipped low over the trees that bordered the property when the hall clock chimed.

Johan took Sarah's small hands in his. "Almost time for sleep." He kissed her cheeks. She smelled of rich chocolate, sugar, and vanilla from the cookies.

Wyatt Scott scooped the child up and made neighing noises as he bounded out of the room with her slung over one shoulder.

Suzanne laughed. "He didn't even wish us bonsoir!"

Johan stood and pulled her into his arms, hoping Scott didn't return. "He's high spirited." Did she wish he were more like that crazy-acting man? Maybe so. He wanted to show her what a passionate man he was, but this wasn't the time or place. When they straightened out their vows, when she understood they were a married couple. Then.

Fleeting pain skittered over her features and disappeared. "He's been good to me. I'm not treated like a servant at all."

Was she coming to care for Scott? "I think many of the people who wish to settle in the mountains of Virginia are bold like him." He pulled her a little closer.

Her eyes were wide. "Did you mean what you said to Sarah—that you intend to take us to this Shenandoah Valley?"

He licked his lips. If he leaned in, he could kiss her silly. "Ja."

"It's a wilderness. Not a safe place."

They'd talked about this on the journey over from Amsterdam. Her mouth narrowed into a line, and her lowered eyebrows accused him. She shook her arms and he released his hold. *She wishes to break free from me.* To marry a fine gentleman. Did she still seek to find the Frenchman she was intended to marry?

He stepped back. "Suzanne, when we first arrived here, the innkeeper told me you sent a letter out right away."

Her face was pained, guilty. "Yes." Her hands trembled. "I…in France, I was promised to someone. I remembered that." She looked down at her hands and squeezed her lips together in that way she did when she was about to cry.

Had she heard from him? His mouth was dry as the sand he'd sprinkled atop the letter sent to his parents. The woman he'd pledged his life to had summoned her old lover. He needed to keep too busy to be tormented by what he might do if her fiancé showed up. "I've accepted more work. I'll come when I can."

"I work here, too, you know. I perform the chores the colonel's wife would, if she were here."

With the colonel's wife apparently missing, would Suzie's presence put her at risk of being misused in this household? He'd have to trust what the others said, that Christy possessed an unsullied reputation.

"I'll be busy, but…"

Suzanne backed away from him, catching herself as she almost stumbled on her skirts. "I understand perfectly."

26

Brilliant autumn leaves drifted down outside onto the lawn and the brick herringbone walkway beneath Suzanne's window. "Sarah! Let's go for a walk."

"By ourselves?" Sarah brushed her hair in front of the silvered mirror, smiling at her reflection.

"Perhaps Mister Scott will accompany us."

Sarah snorted. "If he's up. He sleeps until noon. I don't know how he thinks he'll run a plantation."

"Well, yes…" Suzanne bit her lip. It wasn't her place to comment on Wyatt Scott's habits, especially since he'd purchased her contract, albeit because he claimed Colonel Christy would wish it. He'd said Christy had paid for several other redemptioners who'd been near death, even some who died, so they'd be buried properly.

Wyatt had dryly told her, "At least we didn't have to bury you."

"Do you think we'll be able to stomach the food today?" Sarah grimaced and set her brush down.

The regular cook and her husband were preparing to depart to Virginia with Wyatt and had taken a long holiday. Their temporary replacements, two redemptioners from Scotland, kept producing an oatmeal gruel with only a dab of butter and a pinch of sugar to sweeten it.

Suzanne had decided that beginning tonight she'd assist with the meals. "Let's not break our fast just yet," she suggested.

Sarah smiled. "Could we walk to the baker's shop?"

"Splendid idea!" Wyatt stood in the doorway, fully dressed—attired in his previous evening's clothing, now rumpled. Red streaked the whites of his eyes. "Shall I accompany you?"

Sarah made a sour face at him. "Have you been drinking ale all night?"

"Sarah!" Suzanne closed her mouth before she said something harsh.

Scott guffawed. "Quite right, Miss Sarah, but I'm fully capable of accompanying two beautiful ladies down the street. If you'll each take an arm, that is."

A fine gentleman all right. That was what Johan called him. If he only knew. But the plantation owner wasn't unkind.

Glancing quickly in the mirror before they left, Suzanne glimpsed a knowing look on Wyatt Scott's face, also present on her own features, hardened by sadness. She caught him staring at her. Had he seen it too? She suspected this man understood her far more easily than Johan would at this point.

~*~

Johan knocked at the entrance to the Christy mansion, clutching the bundle of flowers that Vann allowed him to cut from the gardens surrounding the men's quarters.

The elderly servant opened the door, sniffed, and then sneezed.

"The ladies gone a-walking with Master Scott. Come back later." The old man closed the door.

Johan stood there, dismissed. So Suzanne and

Sarah were warming up to Wyatt Scott. Burning anger suffused his chest. He'd go for his own walk.

Instead of making his way back to the carriage maker's shop, he strolled in the opposite direction, hoping he'd find them. Fuming, he marched on but soon found himself disoriented. Looking up from the narrow path along the street, he spotted several Quaker ministers heading in his direction. Johan stepped aside to allow them to pass.

The shortest of the three beamed up at him. "Can we help you?"

Should he admit he was lost? And that his sweetheart was off cavorting with another man?

"Looking for the Alms House?" another asked. They thought he needed charity.

Johan examined his shabby work clothes. In the Palatinate countryside, no one would have thought him poor. Scott likely wore elegant garments for his walk with Suzanne and Sarah. Shame sent a flush of heat to his neck. "No, but I should turn around."

A dark-haired man stepped forward from the back. Tough fingers seemed to grab Johan's heart, jolting him in recognition.

"Are you not Johan Rousch?" The Frenchman's deep voice was forever sealed in Johan's memory. "I remember you."

The priest who had married them on the ship—a Quaker clergyman? What of the surveyor?

"I...ja...danke." Disappointment drenched him, dousing his hopes. Aboard ship, Suzanne told him she'd agree only to a marriage performed by a priest in the cathedral. Granted, she was ill at the time. Would Suzanne recognize a marriage blessed by a Quaker as valid? Better than a surveyor, but in her mind no less valid a wedding

He felt both ill and yet suddenly filled with a rush of energy. He had to get away. "Excuse me. I..." His legs took on a mind of their own, twisting him away from the group and propelling him onward toward Front Street. To what might be his home for the next three years without Suzanne ever in his arms again. A Quaker. He'd had no idea they called themselves priests.

All the way back to his quarters, Johan argued with himself. He couldn't accept that the man who married them was a Quaker and not a priest. It didn't make sense to him. He sought out his master, seated behind his scarred desk, adding figures.

"Vann, your children, they were taught at the Quaker school, ja?"

"That's right." Vann placed a thick finger at the bottom of a column of numbers.

"What did they think of the Frenchman who is a minister?"

"None is French." Vann's jaw jutted, suggesting a challenge.

Johan frowned. "But I met one."

Vann sighed, his heavy lids sinking over his large eyes as if he planned to give Johan a set down. "I'd have expected a French priest at St. Joseph's, but they've got an Englishman at the Catholic church—he keeps very busy. Imagine he could use more assistance, but I haven't heard anything. But there's *no* French Quaker minister."

"Where is this Catholic church?" Johan's pulse quickened. But the priest was an Englisher. "Why does no one speak of it?"

Vann clucked his tongue "They want to keep it

quiet. Some people here are scared of the Catholics."

He'd take Suzanne to the priest. And he'd try to talk with him before then. And get his opinion. Were they married or not? First, he'd better find that minister. He should have talked to the Quakers instead of running away—wouldn't do that again. When next they met, he would shake the information out of the man. With the way Johan was feeling lately, it might do him some good. He was itching for a good fight, and Nicholas was thousands of miles away.

27

"Working all the time"—that was Johan's excuse, but Suzanne decided to take matters into her own hands.

The coachman assisted her and Sarah from the carriage.

"Merci."

Several young women crowded near the forge.

Suzanne frowned at their elaborate attire.

"Look." Sarah tugged at her arm. "They're all watching Uncle Johan work."

Suzanne's fists balled, matching the tightening in her chest. No wonder he couldn't visit. She took Sarah's hand and pulled her toward the bevy, all unaccompanied. Where were their fathers or their brothers? Her cheeks heated as she realized she had no male companion, either. But this was her...husband? She certainly felt like a jealous wife.

Johan's golden queue bobbed against his broad back as he called out to another man, hammering the hot metal. "I'll grab the fuller and mandrel for when we shape that iron, next." He turned, revealing dark circles under his eyes.

And he didn't even notice her. Her eyes began to water. *Must be from the smoke.*

~*~

Johan wiped the sweat from his brow, sensing

movement in the small gathering of women. He'd never imagined them to be so interested in blacksmith work. Perhaps it was because of the fancy pot rack he and Friederich were making.

How he wished he could sleep better. If he wasn't completely exhausted at night, he lay uncomfortably in his hammock and imagined what married life might be like. Papa warned him about intimacy without the sanction of marriage. But he *was* married. Was it wrong to desire to be with her, to touch her soft skin and hold her close against him?

As he turned with the hot metal, he could have sworn he'd heard Sarah's voice but he daren't look away from his work. When he paused, he spied only a trio of young women, each waving brightly colored fans.

Perhaps Suzanne hid behind her claim of memory loss. She acted as though their vows had never been said. But if she didn't accept a Quaker's pronouncements as valid, then perhaps they could be married by the English priest at St. Joseph's. He needed to talk with her about it.

As he removed the horn-like mandrel from its peg, his gut twisted. Suzanne had been so ill that theirs was not a real wedding. He'd been wrong to think she was in her right mind. But she'd answered every question so plainly. Even the priest believed she understood. The physician said she might not have. Perhaps he should act as though their marriage never occurred. Free her to marry whom she wanted.

The onlookers pursed their lips and gasped in surprise, looking over their shoulders.

What now? Irritation prickled his scalp. He was too tired to get involved with the customer's problems.

He'd prayed for some sign from Suzanne. Had made himself prone before the throne of God, but there had been no answer. Unless "wait" was an answer.

He sighed. God no longer cared to hear from him. He lifted the fuller, this one especially good at pounding fine grooves into metal, from its spot on the wall near the forge. This Etienne, her old beau, he imagined the fuller driving him away from them.

Johan lifted the molten iron from the fire. Not hot enough yet for the next piece. Glancing toward the onlookers, he almost dropped the rod as he placed it back in the fire.

Suzanne's eyes burned with anger, and her full lips were pulled into a tight, censuring line.

He nodded at her but she continued to glare.

Johan removed the iron rod. Blazing orange—just right. From the corner of his eye, it seemed as though the other women were dispersing quickly.

Sarah waved her hands at the ladies for them to go, like she had with the chickens back home.

He laughed. Johan hit the piece with one precise blow before setting the flattened segment aside to cool. His frau, what did she need to cool off from?

~*~

Suzanne hoped her tone was a cold as she felt despite the heat from the forge. "I see you're very busy, but I need to talk with you."

Friederich nodded at him. "Go on."

Stepping out of the forge area, Johan lifted Sarah up to give her a kiss and then set her back down. He turned to Suzanne.

She crossed her arms. With narrowed eyes, she

dared him to touch her.

Johan dared.

He took her elbow, sending a shiver through her, and firmly guided her away from the wood smoke and acrid metal fumes.

She made her voice formal. "Wyatt wants to know if his carriage is ready."

"He could have come himself to ask. Why are you here?" He didn't have to sound so irritated. Should be glad they'd come.

"I…"

Sarah grabbed his arm. "We wanted to see you. We missed you!"

Johan snorted. "You have a funny way of showing it."

"She's jealous of all those ladies watching you." Sarah raised her eyebrows in smug superiority of this knowledge.

"Sarah!" If Suzanne had a fan in her hands like all those twittering girls who'd run off, she'd have been tempted to use it to swat the impertinent child.

Johan's cheeks reddened as he stooped to whisper to Suzanne. "I miss you, too, and I'm also jealous." He squeezed her hand and released it. Johan pulled Sarah over and kissed her tawny head. "We need to test Wyatt Scott's new carriage. But Vann wants a rider or two."

Sarah bounced on her toes in expectation.

"Vann doesn't want Mister Scott being the one to say if the coach handles well. He rides like the demons of hell chase after him." Johan's brows knit together as he shifted one hip to the side and appraised the two of them.

Suzanne laughed. "Vann is *très intelligent*. And

Johan, I feel sure the colonel's coachman would be happy to take it for a ride." It warmed Suzanne inside to see the smile of affection that passed between the two cousins. "Sarah and I could go along."

The little girl jumped. "Yes, I love riding. Please say yes, Uncle Johan."

Johan pinched her nose. "Ja. Go play with the hoops over there." He pointed to a clearing near the well.

Two dimples creased the child's cheeks as she ran off.

Johan wrapped his hand around Suzanne's and led her to the privacy of the small garden behind the buildings.

No wonder those young women flocked around him when he worked. Johan had become a very appealing man. Even more than she'd imagined in her artist's mind when she labored over painting the enthralling youth he'd been, often setting aside other work her art instructor had assigned. "You begin to look more like Nicholas." Suzanne's words caught in her throat. They sounded like an accusation.

Johan rubbed his jaw. "Ja, but I'm more handsome, don't you think?" His crooked grin told her that he was jesting. But it was true.

Suzanne jabbed a finger at his chest. "You have circles under your eyes. Aren't you sleeping well? Do you walk in your sleep here?"

He laughed. "They tie me in the hammock." Johan drew her toward him, his warm arms enfolding her.

Memories came over her in waves. This big man had sat her on his lap like a little girl and let her cry into his shirt night after night when she awoke from her nightmares, his beard brushing the top of her head.

She'd fallen in love with him. With his kindness. She trembled as intense gratitude flowed through her. God had provided for her. Surely, Johan *was* her helpmeet.

This search to replace what she'd lost was absurd. God had already given her what she needed. And somehow, on that ship, even in her darkest hour, somehow her soul had known. She reveled in the feel of his steady arms around her.

"Suzie?" Johan's shaky voice jarred her senses. "Would you accept a marriage blessed by a Quaker?"

She stiffened. "What do you mean?"

There certainly were plenty of Quaker ministers in Pennsylvania. She tried to tug free, but he held her there like a vise. She recalled other arms wrapped tight around her. Another promise. Etienne implied they would marry. Johan claimed they already had. And was now changing his story. Etienne had known her all her life. And this man only a few months. Had some woman in Philadelphia caught his eye?

She yanked away from Johan. The guilty look on his face confirmed her suspicions. He hadn't been telling her the truth about something.

"Please, I need to know if you'd accept only a wedding conducted by a Catholic priest."

This seemed the most ridiculous question to her. She'd met her Maker on that ship. First and foremost, He required a relationship with her, whether she professed to be a Huguenot, a Roman Catholic, a Lutheran, or even a Quaker. Grand-mère had her own faith, as did Papa. She'd attended church with Johan and now with Wyatt at the Anglican church. Suzanne wasn't sure she could claim any particular denomination as her own. Did Johan not understand what had happened inside of her, in her soul?

"Johan, Master Vann needs you!" Anton popped his head above the bushes. "Pardon me! Those men are back again. He wants you to keep an eye on them. And he asked if the ladies would like a ride home in Scott's carriage."

28

As the coachman assisted Suzanne and Sarah up, he mumbled, "Don't know how Master Scott thinks this light coach will get him all the way to Virginie."

"Oui, I agree." Sarah and Suzanne settled into the padded leather seats and they set off. The carriage lurched.

Suzanne clutched Sarah. "I think the horses are excited about the new carriage."

Sarah squeezed her arm. "I'm excited, too. Mister Scott told me he might race it when he gets it."

Suzanne kept an arm wrapped around Sarah. "Don't you dare go with him."

Sunbeams flickered off the metal trimwork as they road down city streets bordered by hardwoods whose foliage was awash with red and yellow.

The pink of her gown seemed to clash with nature. She fingered the hand-me-down clothing, a pretty day dress belonging to Christy's wife.

In another lifetime, mother-of-pearl buttons would line her under blouse, and two large cabochon rings would adorn her fingers. Chains of gold with glittering crystal beads would circle her neck, reflecting light as she moved. Her hair would be woven into hundreds of small braids and decorated with pearls.

She touched Sarah's golden hair. Johan had seen her own completely unbound, had brushed it for Suzanne when she was ill. A rush of pleasure went through her at the thought of his warm hands touching her face, of him pulling her into what he would call a hug and she would term an embrace. How she missed being with him. She sighed.

The carriage driver slowed the bays as they turned onto their street, horseshoes clanking against the cobblestones. As they pulled into the long drive, a silver-haired stranger emerged from the stables, dressed only in buff breeches and a shirt covered by a vest. No jacket. Dirty riding boots immediately brought Guy to mind. This man had ridden long and hard.

The man's aristocratic face rose in their direction and he froze. The slim man ran with a speed that challenged Suzanne's senses, and without a sound, like an animal. He exuded sheer physical power as he approached the carriage, staring at her. His solemn, almost statue-like visage transformed into disappointment as he neared, then stopped. The man glanced away, a quizzical look washing his classical features.

"Father!" a dark-haired boy called as he darted from the carriage house. He was half-naked, wearing a breech cloth, leggings, and a loose tunic.

She tried not to gape but couldn't prevent it.

This must be Colonel Christy and his son. But was the child an Indian? The boy let out a whoop and his father hoisted him overhead and spun him around several times.

Once the carriage was halted, the driver helped her and Sarah out.

"I miss my Papa." Sarah pressed a tear-streaked face into Suzanne's skirt.

She stroked the child's hair. Noel was a good man. Like Johan.

Carrie Fancett Pagels

"You must be Suzanne and Sarah." The striking man drew near, his son close at his side.

Up close, Suzanne could see his hair was un-powdered. His complexion was that of someone in his early middle years—it didn't match his white hair.

"He looks like a ghost," Sarah whispered in German. "But a nice one."

"I'm William." The boy tapped his chest. He narrowed his almost black eyes at Sarah as though challenging her.

"I'm Sarah and I hope you like to play chase."

With that, the boy ran off and Sarah followed.

"Forgive my lack of manners. I'm Colonel Lee Christy and you gave me a bit of a start."

She curtseyed. "Suzanne Richelieu." If Johan continued to obfuscate she'd not use his name.

"My wife was also French. *Métis* actually." He gestured toward where the children ran. "As I'm sure you could discern, my son is, as well." His tight smile asked a question.

"He's a handsome boy."

"Gets those good looks from his mother." Sadness tugged his features downward. "You wear my wife's dress."

Suzanne blushed. She smoothed out the pink linen-and-silk gown. "Oui."

Cool gray eyes appraised her. "It suits you."

~*~

Now that he knew who to watch for at the forge, Johan and the other new men would be better prepared if something happened on their watch. If only it was easy to look at his beloved's face and know how she felt. From what he'd seen there, a Quaker minister wasn't acceptable for a wedding. Johan would woo her, win her.

He'd received Suzanne's request to come to Christy's house. Was it true that the boy had come home? Was God answering his prayers again?

Skies full of billowing white clouds covered and then released the sun's rays as he walked. Soon it would be autumn. Back at home, the hay would need to be brought in. But his family had no harvest this year. How would Mama and Papa make do? How much of the funds Suzanne had left were used by Noel to bring his family across?

Wyatt Scott threw the front door open. "What fortune you sent the ladies. Providential. Come in and I'll get your beautiful wife for you." He offered one of his contagious smiles over his shoulder. "And your little cousin, too, or niece, or whatever you wish to call her. Sarah."

Johan followed Scott, and when the other man ran off up the wide, curving staircase, closed the door, and found his way to the parlor to the right. He lowered into the settee and waited. Dust motes floated, and the room didn't hold its usual spicy scent.

He rose as Suzanne entered and resisted the urge to pull his sweetheart into his arms. Sarah launched herself at him, and he lifted her up and kissed her on her cheek before setting her back down.

Colonel Christy followed them, his arm slung around the shoulder of a boy dressed in buckskins, a feather dangling from the side of his black hair. Eyes as black as crow's dominated the child's somber little face.

Wyatt Scott beamed in contentment as he joined

them. He motioned to Johan. "Colonel Christy, this is Suzanne's husband, Johan Roush."

Suzanne chewed her lip but didn't correct him.

Christy was busy holding the squirming boy to his side. "Pleasure to meet you."

William demanded something in an unintelligible language. He broke free from his father and poked Sarah in the chest. "This Johan is of your tribe, your blood. You belong with him."

Johan tensed. Surely, the child's father would intervene. If Johan were free, he'd take Sarah with him.

Sarah shoved him away from her, taking the boy off guard.

William fell backward to the floor at Suzanne's feet.

She reached down to help him up.

But he was crouching, growling, his teeth bared. And he held a knife in his hand.

Christy placed two fingers at the juncture of the boy's arm and shoulder, effectively knocking him to his knees. "Put it down, William."

Suzanne fanned herself vigorously and peered up at Johan, her eyes wide.

"He's funny!" Sarah covered her mouth and laughed.

Christy led the boy away, telling William in a matter-of-fact voice, "We are not Iroquois, Shawnee, nor any other tribe in this household. Kindly desist from pulling a knife on our guests in the future."

Suzanne took Johan's hand. "Perhaps you should come back another day. I'm sorry."

How could he leave them there with a child such as this? Yet he couldn't stay. "Ja, I'll be back tomorrow." He draped an arm over each of "his girls," as he was beginning to think of them. His dream of buying property near where this child had just come from—was this a crazy plan?

Suzanne tilted her head at him, her cheeks pink, her face longing for something. A kiss? "Tomorrow, then."

~*~

After reaching Christy's property the next day, Johan followed the sound of children's laughter to the back of the house.

Sarah and the dark-haired boy were throwing a leather-covered ball at each other and shrieking. They paid him no attention.

He hesitated, wondering if he should stay and watch them. He wouldn't interrupt. No one was being scalped, and they both needed some time for fun, for play. They seemed happy.

Spying Suzanne walking through the rose garden, he went to her. She bestowed a pretty smile upon him, as though he were the finest gentlemen in the world. Her pink gown flounced around her. She reminded him of a rose that unexpectedly bloomed in early autumn, like the opening bud she now touched. "Johan?" That one word was like a caress.

He closed the span between them. The undisguised longing in her eyes warmed him. But her chin was set in stubbornness, causing his head to swim in confusion. She took his hands and rotated him so that his back was to the mansion. Then she carefully stepped up onto his boots and pressed both of his hands together between her own. She held them fast near her embroidered stomacher as she slowly leaned in toward him, tendrils of dark hair tossed by the light breeze. He could scarcely breathe. She looked so lovely, so delicate. But part of him wanted to crush her in his arms and never let her go. When he tried to move his hands, she resisted.

He swallowed. "What are you doing, Suzie?"

She was trying to balance herself atop his feet, avoiding the shoe buckles while straining toward him.

"I desire that you kiss me, and I don't wish you to hug me." Her eyes turned dark as she moistened her full lips and tipped her head back.

His legs tensed. He lowered his head and covered her warm lips with his own. She tasted of honeyed tea. He tried to tug his hands free to pull her closer, but the pinch she gave his hands reminded him to stop. When she didn't pull away, he moved his mouth more forcefully against her parted lips, his entire body gripped by a passion he wasn't sure he could contain if they didn't stop this instant.

She jumped back from him, more tendrils falling around her ivory neck. Tears began to stream down her face. "I want you to remember that kiss!" She lifted her quivering chin.

How could he ever forget it? He might just have scorched the earth beneath his feet.

~*~

Such a kiss as that, Suzanne would have remembered. Turning her back to Johan, she clutched her arms and trembled. If he had some other story this time about their exchange of wedding vows, she'd scream. Why didn't he just offer to marry her again? If he thought he could run off with some girl from

Philadelphia, he was wrong. After that kiss, *she* might propose to *him*. Could she keep her thoughts pure? Would it be she who considered their kiss while they were apart?

Warm, firm hands squeezed her shoulders, massaging the tension from them. It felt so good, but she knew she should make him stop. Her body didn't listen, and she leaned back against him. Every day spent in the company of the irresponsible Wyatt Scott made her long for the security of her Johan. And Christy—he reminded her so much of her father and brother that it was like a wound being reopened. Johan was a balm to that injury.

Two wild banshees came running toward them.

Johan's hands fell away and he stepped back.

William and Sarah stopped in front of them. They were panting as hard as Johan seemed to be. Good. Let him think about what he was doing.

~*~

Johan kissed the back of her warm neck, her upswept hair soft against his cheek. She shivered and he released her before he acted on his own strong impulses. He waited for his heart to slow.

She did want to be his frau.

Did his grin look as goofy as it felt on his face? But he couldn't stop smiling. Not through the entire afternoon of playing with the children.

The three other adults watched him, drinking tea and laughing at him as he swooped William and Sarah around the stables, through the rose garden, and around the perimeter of the maze.

Johan hoisted William overhead like a bird,

holding him there with one hand under the boy's firm belly.

Colonel Christy finally came to him. "I apologize for my son's behavior yesterday." His lips compressed as though he refrained from saying more. He seemed to force a smile. "I might take up blacksmith work myself or make my soldiers do so if it would give me that kind of energy."

"Let me down." William began to twist and Johan set him down.

Scott joined them, looking from a beaming Suzanne, who raised her fan to cover her blushing face. "Too much chocolate at the coffeehouse, Johan?" He glanced between Johan and his beloved. "Or something else?"

The colonel watched Sarah roll her hoop with a rod. "They'll be good company for each other."

Johan nodded. "Ja."

Sarah threw her hoop aside and came to his side. He mussed her hair. "Sarah, I must go now."

She squeezed his hand and turned her face up for a quick kiss. Then she chased William into the evergreen maze.

Johan had to talk to Suzanne before he left.

Scott and Christy were both grinning at him.

"Excuse me. I must go. I say my good-byes now."

Suzanne looked like the mistress of this grand estate. But after that heated kiss—perhaps he could keep her happy as his wife. He sat next to her at the small tea table, its ironwork so suggestive of France. He brought her hand to his mouth, her fingers scented with roses and tea. "Don't worry, love. I'll make everything all right between us."

Her face hardened, but her lips trembled as

though begging for another kiss. He could hardly wait for the next one. But he would have to. And he'd have to talk to the priest at the church as soon as he could.

29

Vann pulled Johan aside at the beginning of the workday. "Trouble brewing. I have a bad feeling. Keep watch after dinner."

"Ja, Master Vann." *But then I can't go to St. Joseph's tonight.* Johan sought out Anton, who was repairing an undercarriage, and Phillip, who was preparing spokes for a wheel. "We need to keep an eye out for mischief makers."

The day proceeded in a typical fashion, with their usual customers, including the young lady observers, but no newcomers. Street traffic slowed as twilight approached.

Shielding his eyes from the setting sun, Phillip pointed to a cluster of shabbily dressed strangers.

One, with dark darting eyes, looked back at them and a finger of fear jabbed Johan's chest. "A good breeze and their clothes will blow away."

Phillip moved closer. "Riffraff from the docks." His eyes narrowed as the gang gathered around the entrance, near where their employer sat at his desk.

"I don't like this." Johan slapped Phillip's shoulder and jerked his thumb toward the newcomers.

The top of Vann's grizzled head disappeared.

Behind them, Anton set aside the file he was sharpening.

Three more men appeared from behind a quince bush and joined the huddle.

Johan closed his eyes and prayed. *Oh, Lord, what*

now? What good would he be to Suzanne and Sarah if these men attacked him? He clenched his fists, ready.

Phillip grabbed a poker, red-hot from the fire.

Johan shook his head at him.

Phillip ignored him.

Johan knew he was responsible for his own conscience and his actions only. His legs seemed weighted with slag as he forced himself forward, prepared for battle, trying to gain eye contact. "Get away from Master Vann!" Johan yelled. "Now!"

A thin man, shirt peppered with stains, jumped back. When his eyes lighted upon Phillip behind Johan, he scurried away like a rat over the cobblestones.

Johan heard movement behind him.

Anton called out, "What's your business here?"

Tension eased a little from Johan's shoulders when he turned and spotted Frances, fists raised.

"I'm leaving—come on!" one of the intruders told another, a beefy man with jowls.

The two departed in haste.

Johan squared his shoulders and spread his legs. There were ten left against five if he counted Vann. Was his son there?

"Just go on out of here unless you have business with me." Vann's tone was firm, but Johan heard the fear. "Don't..."

A thump and a thud followed, and a squat man with massive upper arms separated from the group. He brandished a thick club in his paws.

Vann lay slumped across his counter, his head red with blood.

Behind him, Johan heard rustling. He hoped the others were picking up hammers or punches— something to defend themselves and Vann.

One of the wharf rats called out, "We don't want any trouble with you men. We just don't like this African thinking he can be master." The thick accents announced their recent arrival in the colonies. Scottish perhaps? Vann, himself of three or four nationalities, was the sixth generation of his family here. Not African. These were the worst sort of ignorant men, those bullies ganging together to assault an innocent man.

"Let me at that fool so I can poke his eyes out," Phillip croaked, the wrinkles on his brow gathering sweat.

They weren't yet ready. They needed to take them on as a team. He held up one finger to Phillip behind his back, their sign to wait.

Johan cleared his throat. "You don't work at the tannery, do you?" All that time he had worked extra to redeem Suzanne—it would do him no good if a club struck him down.

Another man laughed, his bloodshot eyes visible even from ten paces. "What does it matter to ye? We're white men, aren't we? We should stand up for each other."

A few of the group cawed out their agreement, but Johan ignored them. "We didn't seek your help—this is a good man, a kind master. Leave now so we can tend to him."

One intruder tapped his foot and placed his wiry arms on his hips. He resembled a scarecrow, with his hair sticking out under his hat and his arms and legs too short for his clothes.

Johan would imagine him as such when he fought him. When he drew his blood.

"Not until we're done helping *Mister* Vann know

his place and that his type isn't needed in Philadelphia."

Tannery workers' arms were as big around as their legs, while most of these men looked as if they'd never seen an honest day's labor.

As Johan took two steps toward them, the stench of cheap ale struck him like a slap. He called over his shoulder, "Phillip, you know what to do for Suzanne, ja? If I fall from one of these *drecksack*—dirt bags."

The scarecrow raised his small club as Johan heard himself roaring.

Behind him, the others echoed him, picking up the sound and charging toward the men.

Suzanne's stories of the wild Franks, woodsman warriors resisting the invading Romans, flew through his mind, the pictures vivid. He and the men in animal skins, their faces painted, blended into the thick forest and then launched upon the intruders. Yes, he was running through the Black Forest, chasing off those who dared invade his territory.

As swinging arms whirled, some of the cowards ran, taking their stink with them.

Then the fighting was a blur as he pounded his fists into one man after another, taking three stinging jabs to his face before he grabbed a cudgel and smashed it against the column that supported the entryway, the wood splintering.

The scarecrow, his face white, seemed to blow away with the gust of wind from the river.

Anton lifted one man up by his collar and tossed him onto the rubbish pile.

The big man with the larger club backed away from them, escaping down the street, but not before Johan memorized his face. Anger squeezed Johan's heart like tongs holding a burning lump of metal.

Then, in stepped another man—Wyatt Scott, fists flying, pounding one of the men before bringing another to his knees and giving Johan a reprieve.

His breaths coming in short bursts, Johan bent over. Like a bellows, he forced himself to slow the opening and closing of his lungs as he curled forward, placing his hands on his thighs to steady himself. Blood mingled with sweat and dripped in dark pools onto the ground.

Now Vann would surely leave this place. His home for generations. Like Johan had departed the Palatinate. This good man would likely flee to those mountains that were said to look so much like those in Johan's homeland.

Scott wiped blood from his mouth and motioned to Johan. "Come on—those cowards are all gone."

Johan moved toward the master, a friend even, who'd been so good to him. "We have to help Vann."

Anton tapped Johan's back as he eased behind him in the tight space and then lifted Vann's right arm up over his own shoulder. Johan did the same with the left arm, sharing the load.

"Vann, we move you now." His head dipped toward Johan's, smearing blood on his chin as they turned him in a semicircle.

When the carriage shop owner groaned, Phillip laughed nervously. "Such a good sound."

"Ja."

"Father!" Vann's son, Abram, appeared in the doorway.

Johan didn't want to judge the boy, but where had he been? They lowered Vann to a cot.

Reaching into his pocket, he located his

handkerchief, embroidered with a small *fleur de lis* in the corner, one of his mother's. *Dear Lord, where are they and are they safe?* He resisted the urge to wipe sweat from his own brow as blood dripped from a cut near his eye. Vann's injuries were far worse and he pressed the cloth into a gash, to staunch the blood flow.

"Better get him a physician," Scott urged.

"Ja, get Dr. Gill."

Phillip wiped his hands on his linen breeches, turned, and jogged off toward the physician's home.

Soon, the Welshman arrived and examined the patient. "Willbeallrightinaweekorso." With his thick melodic accent, the words were strung together.

"All well in a week or so?" Johan scrunched his eyebrows together.

Phillip lightly touched the physician's arm. *"Bitte*, please say more slowly."

"Willow bark for tea." Gill poured out several packets worth of powder. "For pain and swelling."

Johan took them. "Ja."

The physician held out a vial of pungent, greasy ointment. "Rub this salve into his wounds."

Phillip turned his away and Johan coughed at the odor.

Dr. Gill laughed, and closed and latched his leather medical case. "Strong smell but good results."

Johan wasn't sure how to make payment, and Vann was sleeping. He searched for the words, clenched his fists at the embarrassment that tongue-tied him.

Dr. Gill wiped his glasses and looked up at Johan, his brown eyes gentle. "Someone must run Vann's businesses for him until he heals."

Abram Vann was too young to run the shop for his

father by himself.

Johan's chest squeezed. "I'll do what I can to help." *More work, longer hours, and precious little time for Sarah or Suzanne.*

~*~

Two days and Vann still barely stirred.

All the men chipped in to get the orders done, under Johan's direction.

He left the forge to check with each one to see how they fared.

Phillip stopped him before he could get to the wheelwright shop. "Johan, that surveyor is here. The one we saw sailing to the Jerseys. Come see."

My peace I give to you.

Those words, spoken to his heart, quenched the gnawing anxiety he'd had in his gut since meeting the Quaker preacher, whom he hadn't seen again. Johan followed Phillip to Vann's office.

The man's navy, dusty frock coat announced he'd ridden long to get there.

Vann's son peered down at a substantial black leather case, set atop the counter.

"Monsieur, I can afford only a small repair to my case, but it must be sturdy." He cleared his throat and adjusted his white neck cloth. "My tools are necessary for my occupation, and I cannot risk losing them if they should fall out."

Abram assessed the man through half-closed eyes. "My father charges a fair price, and you've given me no reason as to why I should reduce it."

The Frenchman turned in Johan's direction, as though sensing onlookers. His cheeks reddened. "The

Quaker teachers sent me here."

All the steam went out of the master's son, who'd been schooled by the Quakers. "I see. Why didn't you say?"

The surveyor eyed Johan nervously as he came within an arm's length away. This man was the one who'd married them. And he was a surveyor. Not a priest. And not a Quaker minister. *But he is a very good liar and actor.* Johan's hands clenched. No marriage ceremony had been conducted. Only a drama meant to give comfort to a dying woman and her beloved.

Suzanne was free to do whatever she wished. But that kiss—surely he hadn't misunderstood its meaning?

The master's son turned to him. "Johan, I want you to work on these clasps."

He glared at the surveyor, wishing his eyes could pierce the trickster's black heart. "Ja, I'll do that, all right." Johan heard the irritation in his voice.

Abram Vann seemed about to say something to him—probably a caution about his insolent manner.

The surveyor moved closer and gently touched Johan's arm. "I wanted to ask you the other day when I saw you, but you ran off. Did she live?"

Yanking his arm free, Johan glared at him. "She lived." What if they had acted as man and wife? Fierce anger raged through him, his arms and hands shaking. "How could you?" He turned and walked away, trying to calm himself.

"Monsieur Rousch!"

He ignored the fake priest. He needed to go hammer something. When he returned a few moments later, the surveyor had disappeared.

Abram tapped his quill against his ink bottle,

releasing a little of the black substance back inside. "How does that man know you and your wife?"

"We...were on the same ship over."

The young man's features twitched. "He wishes to speak with you when he returns."

"Ja. Fine." He was tempted to visit the ale house after the last several days' events, but he'd not do so.

"My sister sent for you. Father wants to see you."

"Now?"

"Yes, go ahead. I'm tallying our receipts and I can manage."

Johan dipped his chin in farewell and strode off toward the Vanns' home, a two story white clapboard located nearby, facing the street. Dark green shutters shone in the sun. He mounted the three broad steps and raised the door knocker just as Vann's pretty daughter opened the door.

"I saw you coming, Mr. Roush." She motioned for him to come inside. "My father is weak, but he wishes to speak with you."

Johan followed her into a spacious foyer, the scent of clove-studded oranges wafting from a chinaware bowl set upon a half-circle table abutting the paneled walls.

She led him to an eight panel mahogany door and opened it.

He entered the elegant room, outfitted in blue-and-white bedding, with matching curtains. Delft tile surrounded the fireplace. Vann squinted up at Johan from his massive bed, where he lay buoyed by plump pillows.

The young woman closed the door as she departed.

Purplish blotches still marred Vann's face, as they

did Johan's own, but his master's cuts appeared better healed.

With his continuing work, Johan's abrasions had difficulty healing.

"Come here, Mr. Roush."

He raised his eyebrows at this salutation. "Ja?" Johan went to his side.

"Johan, when I recover I'm heading out for those blue mountains in Virginia. I'll start all over. Get myself some land."

Hair on Johan's arms stood up. That was his dream—to go to where the low, rolling mountains were swathed in blue mist. To settle in a valley like his home in the Palatinate. But he had his own contract, Suzanne's, and now Sarah's care. And if Vann sold his businesses, then might they not be sold to another master, perhaps one who was cruel?

Vann coughed and removed his sleeping cap. "I want to talk with you about something."

Johan helped Vann sit up and offered him water.

His master raised his bushy eyebrows. "Are you afraid of living in the wilderness?"

30

Finally he'd been able to go see Suzanne and Sarah. He'd failed to visit with the priest yet. Perhaps she'd forgive him. Scott would have shared about the attack on his master. Twisting his hat, like his gut was doing, Johan waited at the mansion's side door, birdsong echoing from the nearby trees.

Sarah rushed out and hugged him. "You're here!"

"Ja." Johan patted his cousin's soft cheek. "Can you come play in the garden while I talk with Suzanne?"

His beloved, wearing a light floral gown, stepped through the doorway and stopped. "Oh, Johan, you are covered in bruises. And cuts. Wyatt said you could have been killed."

"I'll be fine." He pressed a kiss to her cheek and she ran a finger along his swollen jawline.

"You two are like lovebirds." Practically flying from them, Sarah ran to the maze of gardens

Suzanne shrugged. "Sorry, we'll have to work on her manners."

"Ja, we..."

Her dark lashes lowered. "I want to talk about us."

Her flashing golden eyes and her lips so close to his put indecent thoughts into his head. Another kiss, this one longer, with his arms wrapped around her so tight that...they needed to be properly wed. "I have to tell you something difficult. Suzie, the man who married us is definitely a fraud."

She pulled away. "How do you mean?"

"I've seen him dressed as a Quaker minister, and he also travels the Jerseys as a surveyor."

All the ardor in her face disappeared. "I'm not your wife?"

He hung his head, shame heating his cheeks. "It doesn't seem so."

Her pretty features bunched together as confusion and fear washed over her face. Pressing one finger to her lip she said, "I see." She opened her mouth as though about to ask him something.

"Mademoiselle Richelieu!" Wyatt Scott appeared in the doorway. "What good fortune!"

Suzanne blushed prettily at the attention. "Why thank you, Monsieur Scott. I'm glad you're so happy to see me." She opened and waved her fan, turning her eyes to briefly give Johan a look of irritation before smiling back at the other man.

"A gentleman by the name of Etienne LeFort has arrived in port looking for you, and I'd remembered how you'd been introduced by Johan."

Johan's mouth seemed stuffed with linen. *The one she called her fiancé.*

Suzanne's face suddenly drained of color, and then her eyes widened. "Oh!"

"Perhaps you two aren't man and wife?" Wyatt's crooked smile vanished. "But that's none of my concern."

Both he and Suzanne said nothing.

Bees buzzed as they feasted on rose nectar in the nearby bushes.

"LeFort said he was overjoyed to receive your letter. And he brought the most beautiful creature in the world along with him." His high cheekbones flushed.

How could Johan have imagined Scott had feelings for Suzanne? His entire body seemed charged with his affection for this new woman.

"Who is she?" Suzanne's voice cracked.

"Daughter of French plantation owners in Martinique. Descendant of some island ancestors, too, by the looks of her luxuriant mane of hair and tawny skin."

If Johan hadn't been so distracted by Scott's intense demeanor he'd have asked something about Etienne.

"I am to rendezvous with her tonight." Wyatt winked as he ducked out the door. "Wish me well!"

~*~

The hurt on Johan's face broke Suzanne's heart. She'd been prepared to tell him that it made no difference to her which man of God had married them as long as they both looked to the same Savior for guidance in their life together. But with an imposter having performed the ceremony onboard, where did that leave them? "Johan, I..." She wanted to tell him that she loved him. That she wanted to marry him.

Wyatt crooked a finger at Johan. "Come on, I'll give you a ride in the carriage back to Vann's."

"Ja. Danke." Johan stood before her, his hands knotted.

Wyatt clapped him on his shoulder. "Don't worry about her."

She stood in the doorway watching them go, wanting to throw herself into his arms and tell him she wanted him and not Etienne. Certainly not with what she remembered about him. Suddenly chilled, she rubbed her arms and went in search of Colonel Christy.

Now in his paneled office, Christy fixed his silvery eyes upon her. "How can I help you?"

Suzanne's chest, neck, and face burned in embarrassment. Her mouth seemed to work of its own volition, and Suzanne heard herself spilling out her story to this stranger.

Colonel Christy pulled his chair closer to her, listening to her intently. When she was done, he nodded, then rose and went to a tall bookcase.

He reminded her of her father in many ways. Tears rolled down her cheeks with the remembrance of that wonderful man's love. She hadn't allowed herself to mourn these months since she had lost Papa.

Christy gave her a gentle smile, a deep crease forming on one side of his face. "Don't worry, God has a plan for you."

Just what Papa would have said.

Christy returned with a leather-bound Bible and opened it. "I often find comfort in this book."

Oui, just like Papa. Only she'd never listened before. Not like she should have. *Forgive me, Papa. Forgive me, Father.*

31

The surveyor's large leather case had been saved for last in Johan's week's work. He was so angry with the imposter, he hadn't been able to focus on the job until several days had passed. Catching his friend Phillip's eye, he gestured to the lawn beyond the shop. "I'm going to move this over to the shade to test the new fittings."

After lifting the surprisingly heavy trunk up and down several times to determine that the new handle held, he hauled it over to the grass and set it down. Then he tested the top to ensure that it closed correctly with the new clasp and hinge. When he reached in to adjust the edge of the top surface, a mechanism released.

A false bottom. Johan lifted the wooden tray with one finger. What was the Frenchman hiding?

Rays of sunshine broke through the long branches of the leafy oak trees overhead and illuminated a battered chalice, a cut-crystal decanter, and a silver container for wafers—items that a Catholic priest would need for the sacraments.

Johan sank to one knee. Could it be the Frenchman hid his activities and identity as a Catholic priest? Was that why he'd demanded Johan say nothing about him being a priest, before the Frenchman performed the ceremony on board ship?

Had Johan not been Lutheran, he'd have crossed himself, so great was his relief. A booklet under the box for the consecrated host caught his eye. He opened the pamphlet to the middle. Row after row of German surnames were listed with baptisms notated by name and date, some only weeks earlier. Might his and Suzanne's names be recorded in this book? Or another like it?

"*Pardonez moi*, but please close my case." The young Frenchman's dark eyebrows rose in alarm.

"Father?" The same dark eyes that had sympathized with Johan on the ship now pierced his own. Intense happiness battled with anger. "Isn't that what I should call you?"

"You don't wish me harm, do you?" The young man's gaze darted around to look at two nearby customers.

Johan bent forward and whispered, "Are you a Catholic priest?"

He gave only the slightest of nods. "I cannot talk with you here. But come to St. Joseph's tonight."

~*~

Suzanne's morning passed in a blur of breakfast and squabbling children.

William and Sarah chased each other around the house before she sent them out to the gardens and then for quiet reading time ordered by Colonel Christy. Now the two little troublemakers were napping, and she and Christy retreated to the parlor for their daily chess match.

The maid slipped in behind them, setting up their afternoon tea service. Bohea or gunpowder tea today, by the faint aroma.

"Let's battle there by the window, we've got such

good light."

"Oui. And I have a concern I wish to share." Colonel Christy flipped up the end of the cherrywood table, holding the edge as he swiveled the support out from beneath to hold it up. "What is it?"

"My…Johan says he wishes to buy land someday in the mountains of Virginia. Do you think that is safe?"

He arched his eyebrows. "I would think not, but I'm a military man…"

"My brother, also." She'd sent word to the Huguenot parish in New York explaining where she was and her circumstances.

The colonel's eyes widened. "Your brother serves in the French army?"

"Oui." Behind him, she glimpsed the portrait Sarah had mentioned of a woman who resembled herself. Madam Christy was reported to be part Indian, but her picture recalled one put away in an unused guest room at Grand-mère's chateau—Tante Isabelle's when she was young.

Christy secured the opposite side of the table and pulled up two heavy Queen Anne chairs. "Your brother taught you to play?"

"Oui. Shall we use this set?" Suzanne procured the hand-carved wooden chess pieces and board from the rectangular dining table.

William and his father had played long into the evening the previous night. Candle nubs sat squat in puddles of wax atop the candelabra, and had dripped more than a few hard lumps onto the damask tablecloth.

She'd need to speak with the maids.

When she struggled with the heavy set, Christy's

gray eyes lit with amusement as he realized her quandary. Effortlessly, he secured the chess set and brought it to the gaming table by the window.

"Merci. Let me at least pour us tea." Her heels sank into the thick woolen carpet as she went to the sideboard. Drawing closer, steam redolent of bergamot and orange emanated from the delicate, and expensive, teapot. She poured each of them a cup. A silver bowl of sugar cubes with tongs tempted her to sneak just one and pop it into her mouth, but she resisted. She placed two in her teacup and three in Christy's and stirred with the silver teaspoon left there.

Johan would have tossed a half dozen sugar cubes back and thought nothing of it. Would have smiled at her and said, "Ja, they're good." She held back a laugh. And Etienne, he'd have put only one or two in his coffee and then pilfered another five for his pocket for later. She frowned at his deceptive nature.

Tonight, he'd visit them here.

Fear forced her heartbeat to quicken. Trying to dispel her anxiety, she inhaled deeply, drawing in the sweet scent of the fresh lemon pastries as she plated the dessert, and brought the tray to the table.

"You don't have to see LeFort, you know," Christy intoned, as he removed his cup and saucer. "He'd have no claim over you here."

If only Guy could advise her. In truth, she knew what he'd say. She set her tea and their dessert plates on the table, and then returned the tray to the sideboard.

Christy cleared his throat. "Wyatt has taken some strange notions about the woman who accompanies LeFort." The slight change his voice's timbre notified her of his serious concern.

Having experienced a quick growing-up period during the past year, she'd learned to better read facial expression, tone of voice, and body position. Otherwise, Colonel Christy would be completely undecipherable. She had changed. Six months earlier, she'd have dismissed any alarm. "I'm not so naïve as I once was, Colonel Christy."

His pale face colored. He must have misunderstood her meaning.

She settled in the chair across from him. Suzanne clarified. "It's not that I condone a man taking a mistress, nor flaunting that woman before his intended wife."

He cleared his throat. "I fear not only for you but for Wyatt and his newest infatuation."

They exhaled at the same time.

Chewing her lower lip, she watched as he placed the last of the chess pieces in the perfect center of its space. Christy lifted his teacup, his eyelids lowered as he drank. "Yours must be a good brother to teach you this challenging game."

She ran one finger around the smooth edge of the fine china. "Yes, he loved the battle of wits." Suzanne frowned, pictured Guy as a soldier, saw him in her mind with Rochambeau. How could he have burned Johan's family out?

"Mine, also." Christy's voice was low, his brow furrowed.

She looked at him, hunkered down over the board. Would he think her impolite if she asked? "Your older brother, what kind of man is he?"

Christy sat back and his chair scraped the floor. He exhaled as though sorrow and disappointment resisted showing their presence. "Everything a gentleman is and everything he should not be. Including that of philandering. In line to become a duke."

Suzanne sat up at the edge of her chair. "What do you think a gentleman should be?"

"What I think and what comes to fruition are two different things."

"What about for all men?"

Christy's lids closed halfway over his almost transparent eyes. "Hmm, well, we should all try to be kind and thoughtful of others, generous with our time and resources, and willing to fight for what we believe is right. That would be a start."

Etienne LeFort, a supposed gentleman, possessed none of those qualities. But she knew someone who did. Could they somehow make a life together? Would Johan marry her? Last night he'd shown no inclination to fight for her.

Suzanne stared at Christy, blinking back the moisture in her eyes. "Please excuse me...I...there is something I must do." She pushed away from the table.

"I think I understand."

She headed down the hall and quickly exited the house, then fled down the walkway to the street and onto the pathway adjacent it.

People cast curious gazes as she stepped by, alone, dressed in her fine clothes. She should have asked Lee Christy to accompany her. But she needed time to think, to rehearse what she'd say to Johan. How she would ask him to marry her.

Before long, she arrived outside Vann's building, the scent of burning metal almost comforting. But Johan wasn't among the wheelwrights, nor the blacksmiths, so she returned to where she'd spied his friend.

Phillip sat in Vann's office, a small room in the front, away from the heat of the forge. Bread crumbs clung to his upper lip and he set his sandwich aside.

Suzanne motioned her fingers up by her lip, and he scrunched his mouth and then brushed them off.

"Is Johan here? I didn't see him."

The edges of his eyes tipped downward. Phillip's mouth opened but no words came out.

"What is it?" Fear began to gnaw at her.

"Hasn't he told you?" Phillip cocked his head, eyebrows furrowed. "He doesn't work here. Vann gave him his freedom."

Her gut clenched. "He is released?"

Phillip grabbed her arm before she sank. "I thought he was with you, Suzanne."

What a fool she was. They weren't married—at least he'd confessed that. Unable to find her voice and struggling to keep her dignity, she tortured her handkerchief much as she would have liked to strangle Johan. She took her time returning to Christy's home, stopping at the inn—just in case.

"Good day, mistress." The inn keeper rose from his seat. "Good to see you appearing so well."

"Merci." She glanced around the room, praying Johan would appear.

"Your husband retrieved your letters for you. Sorry I didn't send them on sooner, but my missus is ill."

Letters? "I'm sorry to hear she's sick."

"She'll be fine as a fiddle in no time."

The buns set at a nearby table reminded her of Johan. Surely, he'd not have left without saying goodbye to her and to Sarah. Had he received word from someone? "Monsieur, do you recall anything about the letters?"

He scratched his bristly cheek. "One looked French. Maybe that fancy Frenchman who came looking for you sent that one."

"Came here?"

The innkeeper puffed out his chest. "Had the nerve to ask to check my rooms. I booted him out. Sorry, if he was a friend of yours."

"Not my brother?"

"No, miss, the crazy fellow claimed you were his bride-to-be."

Etienne. "I'm so sorry."

"Not your fault. A madman that one. Said he sought some marquise's granddaughter."

She affected a laugh and pressed a hand to the modesty piece covering her chest. "Most unusual."

Someone entered and she startled, hoping it wasn't Etienne. Turning, she exhaled in relief as an older woman toted a basket of hard rolls to the counter.

"Merci, monsieur, I must get back." Suzanne hurried out and then wandered through side streets. How would her encounter with her former beau go, if he was so impertinent with the innkeeper? Fear settled over her. She had no desire to reach for her grandmother's rosary, nor her grandfather's coins. Instead, when she finally arrived at the house, she went up to her room to read Christy's Bible.

~*~

Pleasant Quaker folk surrounded Johan and Sarah as they walked. Strange that when he'd gone to get her,

Christy's son and she were hiding in the garden maze rather than napping. After telling William that they'd return before dinner, he took her hand and told her all about his good news. Now they sought out answers for his dilemma.

Only a few more blocks to Chestnut Street. Saint Joseph's was right around the corner from the Quaker Alms House, straight ahead.

His little cousin tugged at Johan's hand. "How can Aunt Suzanne have a fiancé?"

Johan frowned. "She can't. We're going to set things right." His contract was redeemed, and he had the possibility of funds to release Suzanne if he'd manage Vann's businesses for him. Now if only she'd reject her old fiancé.

"I like this church. It's pretty."

The rectangular Roman Catholic church possessed a small but lovely courtyard in front. Nothing clearly distinguished it as a church, however. No statuary in sight.

Johan pointed to the entrance door. "Let's go inside."

Sarah peered up at him with those clear blue eyes so much like her father's. "Come sing for me, Uncle Johan, in here." Sarah pulled him into the small sanctuary.

Rustic, nothing like Aachen Cathedral. But he wondered how the sound would be in the space. He looked around the empty building and when satisfied there was no one listening, he began his vocal exercises, the sounds vibrating in his throat and sending a warm feeling through his entire body. As he offered up his first song of praise, he closed his eyes. The words resonated in the cozy nave and came back to his ears.

The door to the sanctuary creaked open, revealing the Frenchman surveyor. "Are you ready to hear the truth?"

~*~

After an unusually quiet evening meal, each in their own thoughts, Sarah and William had gone upstairs to prepare for bed while Suzanne awaited her visitor.

Soon, Christy's ancient servant found her in the parlor. "Etienne LeFort here to see you, miss."

"Merci."

"Colonel Christy got him in his office."

After following him out into the hallway, and walking the first few steps to the office, Suzanne paused and sent up a short prayer. *Fear not.* But she did fear this moment.

Inside the room, Etienne stood with his back to her in front of the fireplace, his attire perfection in French tailoring, the fabric extravagant. When he turned, what would his face reveal? For an instant, she recalled him in such array, for their imagined wedding, and for just a moment, she was hopeful that he'd be her wonderful childhood friend. He swiveled, and her heart squeezed in her chest. Onboard ship, during the marriage ceremony, she'd thought the groom had been Etienne, attired as he was now, but then he'd been erased, replaced by a taller, more virile man—one with golden-brown hair and sea-blue eyes.

Palms damp, she took another step toward him, glad she'd worn a modest gown, recalling a crushing kiss that she hadn't been able to break free from.

His face revealed none of the joy she'd hoped to see there. A frown formed between his dark eyebrows, and his lips twisted in distaste.

No matter whether she was adorned in fine silk or covered in pig slop, Johan's eyes had always caressed her with love—unlike Etienne's judging eyes.

Johan would never abandon me—he's here somewhere. He must think she wished this meeting with Etienne. How hurt he must have been to realize she'd sent her old fiancé a letter.

Etienne's handsome face no longer stirred her. She pulled herself up, almost rising upon her toes. "We need to talk, my old friend."

"Indeed we do, if you think my fiancée will be attired in inferior clothing such as this." Reaching into the inner pocket of his blue wool coat, he retrieved a narrow box. He unsnapped it and removed the contents. Crooking a finger at her, he motioned her forward. "Your grandmother's necklace. At least let's put these jewels upon that fair neck of yours."

A cold pudding could have been dumped into her stomach. The topaz necklace had been left at the DeMints' chateau. She sank into an upholstered chair and brought her hand up to touch the cool stones as he draped them around her. Maman had done so the last time she had worn them. Tears trickled down her face.

"Where did you locate the necklace?"

"Paul DeMint gave it to me before I was sent packing to Martinique. Days after you'd abandoned me. Said it was all I'd ever have of you." His fingertips brushed against the back of her neck, and he lifted up a tendril of hair, twisting it between his fingers. "Said you were to belong to my brother, not me. That was why you ran, wasn't it?"

She allowed this to sink in. Why hadn't Etienne come after her, tried to help her? She knew why. He was a coward, always had been.

He laid a sheet of paper on the table. "Your mother left a letter saying you were to stay with Madame DeMint and that she consented to our marriage. I have it here."

Maman's handwriting...

Tears streamed down her face. She missed her mother so much. But Maman had told her to come on to the colonies, not to return to Etienne.

Etienne's hard as diamond eyes averted. "But when I went to find you, no one could tell me where you were." His was the face of an actor. "I tried to shake it out of Jeanne, but she refused to tell me, that little..."

"She didn't know," Suzanne whispered.

It sounded as if Etienne expected to enforce Maman's permission to marry, as though it was an order. And if he believed that, then to what lengths would he go to accomplish his aims?

"I expect you to pack your belongings and be ready to sail home within two days."

What if she didn't want to? They spent an hour talking stiffly but politely, as though she'd never known him.

Etienne dismissed most of her questions about the plantation in the Caribbean, not that she wished to go there anymore. Tomorrow, she'd take action.

32

A sundial in a courtyard she passed revealed that Suzanne made good time on her walk. The din and hum of building so prevalent in this New World city dissipated the further she journeyed up Third Street. The echo of work activities at the busy Quaker Almshouse replaced the construction noise. In the shadow of its tallest brick building, the rectangular structure of St. Joseph's Church hid. She pushed the heavy entry door open.

Holy incense surrounded her, bathing her in its spicy aroma. Adjusting to the dim light, Suzanne moved forward into the sanctuary. About eighteen feet wide, the interior resembled the Huguenot church in the countryside near Grand-mère's. She moved forward and settled herself on the plain wooden bench and bent her head over her hands. *Lord, what do I do now?*

A new church, beautiful in its rustic simplicity, yet nothing like the cathedrals of France. Was her life in these colonies to be the same way? *Lord, could I have a simple but lovely life with Johan?* She pressed her eyes closed and waited.

You chose. Tears welled in her eyes as God gently spoke to her heart. As though painting a canvas in her mind, God showed her that onboard that ship as she lay dying, He'd allowed the vision of the sea waiting to swallow her up. *You chose life.* A new beginning. One where she lived with her own faith and relationship with God. *You chose your life partner.*

A man's soft English voice carried to her ears. He approached, arrayed in Jesuit raiment, from the back of the sanctuary. The young priest held sacraments. "Might I help you?"

"I have questions." She swallowed back her nervousness.

"Let me set these down. We have a couple renewing their wedding vows this evening." His voice was soothing but his words sent a tremor through her.

How she wished she and Johan were doing the same. "I've come to ask about marriage between a Catholic and a Protestant." She tensed, anticipating the scathing look Grand-mère's priest would have given her.

Instead, only concern lit his kind face. "What's your opinion? If a man and woman both have Christ as Savior and ask a fellow believer to witness their vows—is it a valid union?"

She shrugged. "I don't know."

"Search your heart. I think you know." His eyes seemed to pierce hers and to look to her very soul. "But if you ask whether a Protestant and Catholic may marry, we have many such marriages here. If a man and a woman both have Christ as their Savior, then this can be granted...at least from the Jesuits' perspective."

Smoothing the folds of her skirt, Suzanne took a deep breath. Her father would have agreed and welcomed Johan as son. More than anything, she wished for him to be her husband.

The priest raised his eyebrows. "I caution you that those marriage vows might not be recognized should you return to France."

She planned never to cross that ocean again.

~*~

Suzanne turned to the cherry sideboard in the Christy's dining room and touched the bouquet. Oversized late roses and early fall camellias clustered in the tall Chinese porcelain vase and lent their fragrance to the beeswax candles. Servants had pressed the finest linen tablecloth and laid it out earlier in the afternoon. Two sterling candelabras flanked the flowers, their candlelight glistening on the shiny cherry surface of the table.

Now if only William would stop the dreadful scraping on his violin for Christy's friend, Colonel McCready, who sat watching in rapt attention.

Suzanne's nerves were strung tighter than William's violin strings. This dinner and what she hoped was her final meeting with Etienne need to be over with—done.

"Bravo!" The auburn-haired man clapped as William ceased his racket.

Suzanne caught the boy's arm before he left the wood-paneled room. She whispered, "Why do you pretend to be so bad a musician?"

The boy's dark eyes seared her as he shrugged away her touch and disappeared from the room.

She'd stifled her gift of art because she hadn't been able to bring to life the young man from the woods near Grand-mère's—Johan. In actuality, he was a much better man than she could have imagined or painted. Yet she'd driven him from her by her own idiocy. Where was he? Must she endure the evening ahead alone?

When would Etienne and that woman arrive? She no longer cared if the islander was his mistress. But poor Wyatt—he'd chattered incessantly the night before about the woman's incomparable beauty. He couldn't answer a single question about his impression of Etienne other than commenting that he was "not worthy of Evangeline." There was heartbreak ahead for Monsieur Scott.

~*~

Johan returned, as he'd been instructed to do and watched as the Frenchman lit the candles on the altar of St. Joseph's. "You're a Jesuit priest?"

"Oui, Father Francois. That's why I asked you to promise me onboard ship. That you would keep secret that I was a priest."

Circumstances were as Vann had suggested. "So although there's acceptance of many faiths in Pennsylvania, there's fear of Catholicism?"

"Oui, and a little fear of the French, also." He gave a wry smile. "Some fear we'll force conversion. But here in this parish, we minister to all God's children, German Lutherans or French Catholics. I've been very busy since I arrived, even though I must do much of my work in secret for Catholics are barely tolerated in this area, although some would say otherwise. And your wife's needs, monsieur, were my first official act. I wasn't supposed to risk anything onboard but…God spoke to my heart. And I obeyed Him. Fortunately my superior is a tolerant man."

Johan pulled at his high neck cloth, unaccustomed to its snug fit. "Is our marriage recorded in your book?"

"Oui."

The church door burst open, bringing cool air and Phillip, who bent over panting as though he had run the whole way from the shop.

"What is it?" Johan went to his friend's side. "Is it Vann?"

"No."

The priest came forward and touched Phillip's arm. "Calm yourself and tell us what's wrong."

Phillip shook his head twice then sucked in a long steady intake of air. "Yesterday, Suzanne came looking for you. I told her Vann released you."

"Ja?"

His friend looked up at him. "Why didn't you tell her, Johan? About Vann and his offer?"

Johan shrugged. "Was going to tell her later. *Überraschung.*"

Phillip's mouth dropped open. "A surprise all right. Like it will be when that snake, LeFort, abducts her and sails off tonight!"

The news hit like a punch to his gut. "Nein!"

Phillip huffed, "LeFort's carriage driver came to the shop for a repair. Said it had to be done tonight. But the man was scared. Etienne was in a hurry to get his mistress to the ship but couldn't find her. Planned to locate her and lock her in their room if need be. And was going to be bringing another woman on board with him, too. Suzanne Richelieu, he said."

Johan was halfway out the church door before he turned to the priest. "Thank you."

As they dodged carriages and horses, crossing several streets, Johan balled his fists. "You go to LeFort's driver and tell him not to come until very late, and I'll get ready and go on to Christy's."

~*~

A beautiful woman with dark eyes and elaborately coiffed hair slipped from behind Etienne. Her powdered face contrasted sharply against darkly rouged lips and cheeks. Ivory satin set off her dark hair, as did the sheer netting floating around her shoulders.

Suzanne blinked and tried not to stare at the woman who held her former beau's interest...if not his heart.

One corner of Etienne's lips moved upward in a half-smile. "May I introduce Evangeline Favret. She's the widow of my plantation's former owner."

As she sank into a curtsy, the island woman's heavy scent overpowered even the roses.

Suzanne blinked and then whispered to Christy, "Should we open the windows?"

Christy's silver head ascended slightly, his lips barely tipping up in a smile that she recognized—one of amusement and disgust covered with a veneer of civility.

Colonel McCready lifted the window at the far end of the room, almost as though he had heard her words.

Christy grinned at her.

The fabulous mistress was being presented on Etienne's outstretched arms. This close, the woman's eyes didn't seem to focus. What was wrong with her?

"*Enchanté*, Evangeline." Suzanne prayed her voice didn't sound like a croak.

As the woman kissed her cheek, Suzanne held her breath. The cut of Evangeline's bodice dipped low to the point of vulgarity. Suzanne touched her own modest topaz-filled neckline, her ecru lace ruffles dropping back against her three-quarter sleeves.

Etienne's eyes grew cold as he appraised Evangeline. "I brought her away so that she might begin to overcome her grief."

A pang of guilt squeezed Suzanne's chest. She'd been judging this woman who had lost her husband.

Christy bent and kissed her hand. "Please accept my condolences, Madame Favret. We hope you enjoy your dinner with us this evening."

Evangeline's head lifted and her eyes became more alert, then her gaze darted about the room.

Wyatt emerged from the shadows near the hall stairs, startling Suzanne.

She drew in a sharp breath.

Evangeline merely lowered her dark eyelashes and raised one hand languidly for the young man.

Suzanne exhaled as Wyatt drew her away from them and pulled a chair out for Evangeline at the far end of the long table, near McCready.

"Offer you some strong libation, LeFort?" McCready's deep voice carried across the room. He removed the stopper from a crystal decanter of sherry. "Think you might need it."

Christy chuckled and shook his head. "Colonel McCready, one would think you resided here."

Etienne ignored the two English officers and kissed Suzanne's cheeks before quickly releasing her. Nothing in his brief touch indicated he'd ever been her intended.

Her heartbeat slowed to a dull, hard thumping. How could she ever have been so naive?

A servant brought in a tray, accompanied by the

delicate aroma of seafood mingled with more seasoned fare.

Christy motioned toward the long table. "Suzanne and Etienne, would you mind taking your places at the table?"

Wyatt's sensuous grin indicated that he was already seated exactly where he wanted to be—close to Evangeline.

McCready brought the sherry to the table and pulled the Chippendale chair out next to Evangeline, where Etienne's gaze had settled.

A dark head popped up from underneath the dining table.

"William!" Suzanne jumped, but then began to laugh as the boy, dressed in buckskins, ducked back under the table, apparently scrambling further down.

Christy sighed. "My pardons."

"No need," McCready jovially insisted. "Got five girls at home myself, and they all enjoy a good prank on their father."

Her old beau stared at the back of McCready's ginger head.

Christy stepped forward and held her chair for her.

A servant placed shrimp and crab pâté on Wyatt's, and then Evangeline's creamy china plates. Butter and herbs wafted up, mingling with the enticing scent of fresh seafood.

Christy celebrated evensong earlier.

Suzanne was surprised when, after he was settled, he didn't ask a blessing upon the meal. Two giggling children may have distracted him, she surmised, as their small bodies brushed past her legs en route to him. She closed her eyes. *Lord, bless this meal and bring peace to me and this household.*

Another servant placed small rounds of toasted bread upon their plates. Taking a bite of the crackers and the seafood, each pair seemed perfectly suited.

Suzanne's stomach hurt. She pushed the wonderful food around her plate as Christy and Etienne discussed the market for sugar.

Etienne cleared his throat. "Monsieur, Suzanne has a long-standing betrothal to me."

Colonel Christy's thin lips tipped up only slightly and his silver eyes narrowed. "I'm afraid her contract was redeemed, and she's desperately needed in her current situation."

His dark eyebrows raised, Etienne sputtered, "Surely you cannot be serious?"

"Indeed, I am."

Why was the colonel telling this falsehood? Suzanne's fingers closed around the topaz necklace, a choking sensation building in her throat.

Two small forms flew from beneath the table.

Sarah, dressed in a short deerskin dress, chased William, who brandished a small hatchet. "Drop it, William!"

"Monsieur, I can see why you'd need help with that little savage, but…"

Christy stood as the children fled the room in a blur. Other than the rapid rise and fall of Christy's chest, Suzanne could discern no emotion in him. "He's my son, Monsieur LeFort, and he is no more savage than you."

"Here! Here!" McCready agreed from the other end of the table, pouring himself another glass of sherry. "Boy looks no more Indian than his father nor…me." He cleared his throat.

Etienne's eyes were wide as he stared at the weapon left carelessly on the floor by William. A muscle in his jaw twitched. "We sail for France very soon."

Wyatt laughed at something Evangeline had whispered in his ear. He pushed away from the table and pulled her chair out. He gestured to the hallway, and Christy nodded at him.

Suzanne's head was pounding. If Christy *did* release her from her contract, where would she go? Johan had obtained his freedom. He wouldn't have abandoned her.

The doorman appeared at the entrance and slid the pocket doors back.

She caught a glimpse of a couple beyond him.

The woman's abdomen, round with child, bulged behind the servant's narrow form, as well as a man's long leg in cream-colored breeches.

Suzanne's heart nearly bounded from her chest.

"Monsieur and Madame Guillame Richelieu!" The ebony-skinned servant teetered aside as Christy took Suzanne's elbow and guided her to the doorway.

"Guy?" She shook so hard and her tears blurred her vision so much that she couldn't have walked without the colonel's guidance. "Jeanne!"

Guy crushed her in an embrace before kissing her cheeks. He glared at Etienne. "Please tell me that swine, LeFort, is not my brother-in-law! I was told by the innkeeper that my sister's husband had received my missives."

"No. He's not." She should have listened to her brother long ago. Turning to Jeanne, Suzanne embraced her friend gently, aware of the prominent swell of her abdomen. The child—Guy's? Surely not.

He never would have compromised her like that. Her brother implied Pierre LeFort was the father. As she held her old playmate, Suzanne felt tension grow in Jeanne's arms and looked up.

Both Guy's and Jeanne's gazes fixed upon Etienne.

Turning, she saw that her old beau's face had drained of color. His mouth agape, he pushed at his wig. She looked from him to Jeanne.

Something passed between the pair.

Jeanne clutched Suzanne's hand, her fingers trembling.

"I heard you'd died, Guillame." Etienne threw back some sherry and then wiped his mouth. "I'm glad this wasn't true."

"*Moi aussi*," Jeanne asserted, her head rising higher and lips narrowing as she linked her arm through Guillame's. "How *tragique* for my baby to not have his father. And for me to have lost my husband."

Guy patted her hand and gazed down in adoration. "All I've lost is my good looks, *mon amour*." He kissed Jeanne, bringing a smile to the beautiful lips of Evangeline.

Wyatt looked as though he might plant a kiss on that woman's cheek at any moment.

Etienne's voice tightened. "My brother wasn't so fortunate."

"I'm sorry for your loss." Guy's voice held true remorse. "I can only hope that he repented of his sins before he died."

Etienne placed an index finger on his cheek and narrowed his eyes.

Guy seemed to be talking of Etienne as well.

Her stomach clenched. In her soul, Suzanne understood—Etienne was the father of her friend's baby. Sadness and disgust flowed through her, but were quickly chased by the fresh wave of a pure thought—what a marvel that Guillame could be so good. That he could take on this child as his own. That he would love Jeanne and protect her from the LeForts.

She was filled with love for Guy, and a deep admiration that brought more tears streaming down her face...and an even deeper disgust for Etienne. Thank God, she'd been protected from him, or she could have ended up in Jeanne's predicament. And what would have happened to her? She'd have never met the one she loved.

"Ja, I heard that." a loud voice echoed in the hallway beyond the dining room. "We should all repent before we die and it's too late." Johan's laughter softened the harsh tone of his words.

Doves seemed to beat in her chest. "Johan!" His elegant attire shocked her but he opened his arms to her and she went to him.

After a too-brief embrace, he released her and took a step back.

"Vann bought me this wedding suit." Johan raised one arm, displaying a fine white shirt beneath a blue linen coat. His velvet breeches were spotless, and ornate silver buckles shone on his polished shoes.

She smiled. He'd be her handsome husband even if he wore his farm clothes and was covered in manure. *Thankfully, though, he's not.* Stepping into his arms, again, she let him rest his head atop hers, felt his big hands rest on her back, pulling her close. Never letting her go. She drank in the scent of him.

"Suzie, we have an appointment tonight at St. Joseph's. Are you ready?"

Etienne rose. "For what? Who is this man,

Suzanne?"

Etienne and Guy stared at one another for a long moment before Etienne broke eye contact.

Carriage wheels sounded from the drive near the house.

Christy pulled the curtain aside. "Looks as if your coach awaits you."

Suzanne squeezed Johan's hand and got up on tiptoes to kiss the cleft in his chin. He moved his mouth down to cover hers and pulled away too quickly to suit her.

"We have a wedding at St. Joseph's tonight for those who care to attend." Johan kissed her forehead. "May I escort you?"

"Oui," she laughed.

He reached out and touched her hair, pulling something from it.

Mortified, she pulled away.

"Just a little lint." His eyes danced in mischief. "No insect this time!"

Guy stifled a grin. "Jeanne, shall we join them?"

"Of course."

"I'm coming, too," Christy called out.

Scott's and Evangeline's seats stood empty.

"I'll keep your guest company, if you wish," McCready offered, getting up to pour himself another glass of sherry. "We'll call your boy downstairs to play a game of cards with us after I'm done guarding him." He pulled open his jacket, revealing a brace of pistols.

Johan squeezed Suzanne's hand. "Christy will bring Sarah," he whispered in her ear.

Guy pivoted in Etienne's direction and made a mock display of slapping his palm to his forehead. "Oh, I forgot. Rochambeau wanted me to advise you that if you don't return to Versailles to manage your family's affairs, your mother is coming to retrieve you. She fears you've too much time on your hands and have run amuck of the local gentry there. Something about a lynching party, I believe, if you return to the West Indies. The islanders say the lady you brought here didn't voluntarily accompany you. Can you imagine that, Etienne? Whatever could people be thinking, telling tales like that about a gentleman such as yourself?"

33

The carriage lurched and Suzanne tumbled against Johan in the seat.

Wyatt drove at a breakneck speed as though someone chased them.

Mon Dieu, let me live to make it to the church.

Johan clutched her close to him. As his warm lips caressed her forehead, a thrill pulsed through her.

They rounded the corner and Wyatt's coach rocked over the cobblestones in a steady rhythm as its progress slowed.

Her husband kissed her again. "You don't have to do this. Our marriage is already recorded at St. Joseph's. The man on the ship wasn't a surveyor..."

Lost in the sensation of Johan's snug embrace, Suzanne wasn't sure she heard him correctly. "No?"

He released her and she yearned to feel that closeness again. His gaze trailed from her upswept hair to her satin pumps.

Her heartbeat quickened as his hand settled on her shoulder. "Nor was he a Quaker."

"He was a priest?" So her dream had been true.

"Father Francois is a Jesuit priest, *ja.*"

Relief and gratitude flowed through her. A wave of mounting excitement washed away those calming emotions. She considered kissing him. "We're already married."

"Ja." He pushed aside a curl, his rough finger grazing her forehead. "That wouldn't have stopped

Etienne from taking you with him, though."

A shiver traveled her spine. She stroked his arm, reveling in his strength. "No. Whether I wanted to go or not."

He pulled her closer. "I've got you now."

Suzanne relaxed into his warmth, but his chest tensed beneath her cheek. When she tried to lean back, he held her close. "What's wrong, Johan?"

"You're sure you want me, ja?" His fingers worked into the base of her hair.

"Johan, this ceremony is a vow renewal. We're already wed."

"I've felt so guilty. I thought you agreed to marry me on the ship only because you were dying. You were leaving me. I wanted you to have family there—I wanted to be that family for you."

"Oui, I understand. But you and Sarah are my family now." Her breath caught in her throat and tears welled up in her eyes. "And I chose you then as my husband. I choose you now. Forever." A sharp turn of the carriage almost bounced her onto Johan's lap.

His strong arms drew her the rest of the way up. He kissed her until she couldn't breathe and then leaned his head against hers. "I choose you, too, forever. Ja, I like the sound of that."

So did she. And the feel of his kiss.

~*~

Reflections of flickering candlelight from the nave's many votives danced in Suzanne's wide eyes.

Guillame and Jeanne came into sight, and Johan resisted the temptation to kiss his Suzie's parted lips. There would be kisses soon to last a lifetime.

"Johan and Suzanne, did you read of our news?" Guillame grinned.

Johan groaned. "So sorry, I failed to deliver your letters to Suzanne."

She poked him with her sharp elbow.

Her brother arched an eyebrow. "While Jeanne and I were in Montreal, we ran into your uncle from Aachen."

"Literally!" Jeanne giggled. "I bumped into him on the street, when I wasn't looking and I hurt my ankle."

"The poor man took us to the nearby convent where'd he'd been staying." Guillame smiled at his wife. "And Father Vincent introduced us to his old friend—a lady he said he'd accompanied to the New World decades earlier and whom he'd never ceased praying for after she disappeared in the back country."

"But your Tante Isabelle is found now." Jeanne's girlish voice bubbled over with enthusiasm. "And Johan's uncle can stop worrying about her. So he's staying on in Montreal and will make a journey here later to see you."

"She's alive?" Suzanne's eyes widened, but then crinkled shut before she opened them again.

"Ja. Good news."

"Oui. Then she'd be next in line to inherit."

Guillame leaned in. "No, I don't believe so."

"Why not? How could Louis object?"

"Our aunt is Mother Superior of the very convent where we sought aid for Jeanne."

"She's a nun?"

"Oui. With no plans to return home."

"Nor I." Johan's bride gazed up at him, her eyes full of love.

His new brother pointed to the sanctuary's

entrance. "I need to get Jeanne seated."

Christy hadn't yet arrived.

Johan's neck cloth seemed to tighten, and he ran a finger underneath it. Sweat dripped from his hairline.

Clucking her tongue, Suzanne released his fingers from his cravat. "Leave it alone, Husband. You're ruining it."

Husband—the very word sent tremors through him. In the shadows at the back of the church, he pulled her into a tight embrace and kissed the hollow at the base of her throat. Her pulse beat strong against his lips. He inhaled deeply of her sweet perfume. Forever she'd be his frau.

Releasing her, he pulled away to appraise her in the dim candlelight. Her amber eyes were filled with a longing that caused thoughts of the evening ahead to run through his mind. He bent to smooth the wrinkles he'd put in her dress. "There, now I make your dress match my clothing. Both are rumpled."

Her heavy sigh could have blown powder from his hair, had he worn any. She looked almost as aggravated at him as she used to look back home.

Ja, *she is herself again.*

Fresh air blew in as the door opened, causing the unshielded candles to flicker. The large pillar lamp beneath the hurricane glass never wavered.

"Here we are!" Colonel Christy accompanied Sarah toward them, the scent of cinnamon mingling with the incense of the church.

The child threw her arms around Suzanne.

His new family was here. One day, maybe soon, Papa, Mama, Nicholas and Greta might be, too.

~*~

Evangeline gently touched Suzanne's sleeve. The island woman's countenance had transformed to one younger and sweeter than evidenced earlier in the evening. "Wyatt and I wish you bon chance. We depart for Virginia as soon as..." She glanced to where Scott stood, beaming back at her. Crimson flooded Evangeline's cheeks. "As soon as the vows are said, we are off. I'm so grateful that God has spared you from a life with that wretched man."

Wyatt joined them, his handsome features awash with love. He took Evangeline's hand and then turned to Suzanne. "They're ready for you, *Madame* Rousch."

"Oui, we're coming."

This ceremony would help Johan realize she wanted him. Always.

Colonel Christy stepped through the entryway and strode to the front of rectangular room.

Evangeline and an animated Wyatt conversed with the English pastor of St. Joseph's, off to the side.

Father Francois waited there, also.

Incense and lemon oil imparted their mellow scents as Johan steered her forward. The witnesses were from the earthly realm, unlike in her dream wedding. Suzanne wondered if she glowed with the radiance she saw on Johan's face. *My husband.* The recollection of Maman, Grand-mère, and the many other relatives, those who now resided in heaven, ran through her mind.

Johan bent down and whispered, "I'm not sleepwalking, am I?"

She laughed. "No. And this is no dream, is it?"

"No." His large hand enfolded hers.

She watched as Guy protectively placed an arm

around Jeanne's shoulders. Her brother was alive and with her. Inhaling, suddenly doubting this decision to renew what had already transpired, she squeezed her husband's hand. "Johan, this is real. I know it was before, too. But I thought you might…"

Sea-blue eyes answered for him. Ja.

~*~

God was answering all Johan's prayers. After the many months of waiting, of being sure that He no longer cared to hear from him. When he'd given up hope, God had blessed him abundantly, humbling Johan to his core. His freedom from the indenture contract. Work as Vann's manager. Acquiring the skills he needed to join Vann in the Shenandoah Valley later—his fondest dream. His parents safely joining them and making it possible for Sarah to be cared for by her family. And now…

Suzanne was giving herself to him. Freely. Under no compulsion or fear. Anticipation coursed through him. In front of all these loved ones, she said that she chose him. A peasant who loved her. And she loved him. That was the best gift she could give him. And he'd give her his gift, too. Those gifts, they came from God. He'd never forget that again.

~*~

The priest stared into her husband's eyes. "Johan, do you still wish to…"

"Ja." His gruff voice echoed in the sanctuary.

Johan released her hands and left her at the altar. Where was he going?

Father Francois whispered, "It's all right, Madame Rousch. Wait." He smiled and gestured to the narrow balcony where Johan now stood.

Her husband's beautiful tenor voice resonated through to her very soul. He'd been the heavenly being singing to her during the ship ceremony. Tears of joy flowed down her cheeks.

The rest of the mass was a blur.

Wyatt and Evangeline waved good-bye.

Johan brought her a shawl and wrapped it around her shoulders. "We'll be at the inn."

The same inn where she'd awoken to the strange young man in her bed. Only he hadn't been a stranger. He'd been her own dear Johan. Her husband. She thrilled at the thought of his title. But this night would be different. And even though the thought excited her, a thread of fear wove through her.

Christy joined them, regret tugging at his features.

He must miss his wife.

"Danke, Colonel Christy, for keeping Sarah for us tonight. My wife and I now have our first child, a daughter, little Sarah."

Suzanne's cheeks grew warm. Tonight they might even make another child together.

"I'm sorry. I shouldn't have put it like that." Johan ducked his head. He must have realized what she was thinking.

Guy kissed her cheeks and then Jeanne. "My friend, my sister now, don't be afraid. You've married a good man. This is right."

"Oui."

~*~

Someone had laid out the light blue nightgown

she'd worn when last she stayed here. In this same room. But tonight the chamber grew more confined somehow. Suzanne hadn't commenced disrobing.

Across the room, Johan's fingers ceased their struggle to unfasten his fancy clothes. "I need help, Suzie. I can't get these buttons—they're too small and slippery."

She exhaled, staring at the nightgown laid out on the bed as though it would rise up and clothe her later. The wood floor creaked as she crossed it and stood in front of Johan. Why should her knees shake? Her husband had never given her any reason to fear him. Raising trembling fingers to the bottom of the vest and avoiding his eyes, she began to slip the tiny silver buttons through the tight openings. "This is an unusual waistcoat." There were no frogs or toggles to easily unfasten.

"Ja, they don't usually have buttons on them." There was a waver in his voice, and he let out his breath as though he'd been holding it.

His flesh warmed the material beneath her hands as she released each petite closure, one at a time, until she was near the top.

Johan's hand wrapped around hers. "Stop."

"What's wrong?" She was suddenly lost in his passion-glazed eyes and leaned in against his firm chest.

Johan lowered his mouth to cover hers.

She grasped the front of his vest as he embraced her, but she wasn't close enough. Her heart hammered like the tools Johan struck against the anvil at Vann's shop. When he released her, she swayed and he caught her elbow.

A frown of concern fought with desire and

excitement on his handsome face. "Don't you need help, too, Suzie?"

When she didn't reply, he began to assist her as one piece of clothing at a time was removed and hung on pegs on the wall. By the time she was in her chemise, she was trembling so violently, she was afraid she might fall down.

Johan lifted her, his powerful arms wonderful and warm beneath as he carried her to the bed. He gently pulled the coverlet up over her.

"Can you get the last two buttons for me?" He kissed her forehead and then each of her fingertips.

The only thing she was afraid of now was that she might stop breathing altogether before he joined her in bed.

Johan bent down and nuzzled her neck as he had at the church. "I love you so much."

"I love you, too." She unfastened the last two buttons, and he removed his vest.

Johan smiled down at her as he finished undressing. His hands were shaking, too. "We need to get started on those twelve children I want."

How could I have thought him angelic? She reached over for his pillow and threw it at him. "Eleven! You forgot about Sarah."

The pillow hit her softly in the face on its return.

Johan pushed it aside and settled himself beside her on the bed. His bare shoulders obscured the candlelight behind him on the nightstand. "My *frau*, eleven would be fine."

How serious he sounded! "Husband, I thought you'd learned..."

He kissed her full on the mouth, lingering there. "Ja. God's will, not mine," Johan murmured as he turned toward the light. He leaned over and blew out the candle. "But we can try, can't we?"

Author Note

Johannes Adam and Susanna (Sehler) Rousch had twelve children. Nine of their ten sons fought in the American Revolution. While this novel is inspired by their lives, it is a piece of fiction. The Palatinate, indeed, was invaded by the French during this time frame and many people immigrated to America, as did my ancestors. Temporary amnesia, such as Suzanne's, can be caused by extreme illness or injury. Some people never fully recall portions of their life before the event.

Thank you

We appreciate you reading this White Rose Publishing title. For other inspirational stories, please visit our on-line bookstore at www.pelicanbookgroup.com.

For questions or more information, contact us at customer@pelicanbookgroup.com.

White Rose Publishing
Where Faith is the Cornerstone of Love™
an imprint of Pelican Ventures Book Group
www.PelicanBookGroup.com

Connect with Us
www.facebook.com/Pelicanbookgroup
www.twitter.com/pelicanbookgrp

To receive news and specials, subscribe to our bulletin
http://pelink.us/bulletin

May God's glory shine through
this inspirational work of fiction.

AMDG

Free Book Offer

We're looking for booklovers like you to partner with us! Join our team of influencers today and receive at least one free eBook per month. Maybe more!

For more information
Visit http://pelicanbookgroup.com/booklovers
or e-mail
booklovers@pelicanbookgroup.com